Well, hello there!

I'm so excited to finally share with you my new novel, *Elites of Eden*. I had so much fun creating the first installment in this series with *Children of Eden*, but there was so much more to the story living in my imagination that I needed to share with you all. *Elites of Eden* continues where *Children of Eden* left off, but focuses on a new main character, Yarrow, who may have more in common with Rowan than they both believe. This book drives you further into the adventure of the world of Eden and gives you a more in-depth look of what life is like for the Elite people that make up its inner circle, which you will quickly see is far different from the life Rowan had before. Thank you for all your support in this journey. It means the world to me and I am forever grateful to you, my readers. Without you, this would be just another idea in my mind.

    See you in Eden . . .

Always,

Joey G

ALSO BY JOEY GRACEFFA

Children of Eden
In Real Life: My Journey to a Pixelated World

ELITES OF

EDEN

A NOVEL

JOEY GRACEFFA

New York Times Bestselling Author

WITH LAURA L. SULLIVAN

PRESS

—

ATRIA

New York London Toronto Sydney New Delhi

First published in Great Britain in 2017 by Keywords Press,
an imprint of Simon & Schuster UK Ltd
A CBS COMPANY

First published in the USA in 2017 by Keywords Press,
an imprint of Simon & Schuster, Inc.

1 3 5 7 9 10 8 6 4 2

Simon & Schuster UK Ltd
1st Floor, 222 Gray's Inn Road
London
WC1X 8HB

www.simonandschuster.co.uk

Simon & Schuster Australia, Sydney
Simon & Schuster India, New Delhi

A CIP catalogue record for this book is available from the British Library.

HB ISBN 978-1-4711-6731-7
eBook ISBN 978-1-4711-6732-4

This book is a work of fiction. Names, characters, places and
incidents are either the product of the author's imagination or are
used fictitiously. Any resemblance to actual people living or
dead, events or locales is entirely coincidental.

Printed and bound by CPI Group (UK) Ltd, Croydon, CR0 4YY

Simon & Schuster UK Ltd are committed to sourcing paper
that is made from wood grown in sustainable forests and support the Forest
Stewardship Council, the leading international forest certification organisation.
Our books displaying the FSC logo are printed on FSC certified paper.

This book is dedicated to those who seek change in making this planet a better place. To those who understand the importance of how each action we commit directly affects the footprint we leave behind on our environment. I hope this story never becomes our reality.

1

WE MOVE THROUGH the world like a pack of wolves, striding on long legs, bright-eyed, ravenous. We are beautiful, and a casual observer might think us soft because of that beauty. But we have teeth no one can imagine.

We move like soldiers, from the pre-fail days when humans fought wars. The lesser creatures step aside. Most openly stare. Only the boldest look away from us. To not admire us is a grave insult. They will be remembered. Punished.

Our uniform skirts swish around our legs. The daughters of lawyers and politicians, we know how to bend the rules to our own whims. The Oaks Code states only that all students wear the green leaf-and-tendril motif of our school. The oak stands strong, supporting the tender vine. Most of the students conform exactly, looking like the identical, mindless clones they are, fitting in seamlessly with everyone around them. Not us.

My skirt is long, made not of printed fabric but individual cutouts in the shape of oak leaves in all the red, gold, and orange colors of fall. The leaves overlap and flow in a cascade to my mid-calf, though there are several strategic slits that reveal my leg to the thigh with the slightest twitch. I've seen vids of an oak forest in autumn, the trees looking almost like a wildfire as those dying flame colors toss in the late-season wind. When I move, my skirt rustles like the forests none of us have seen, or will ever see. My top is the pale yellow-green of a new-sprouted spring leaf, skintight, with embroidered tendrils snaking up my ribs.

<center>~~~~~~~~~~</center>

PEARL LOOKS LIKE a butterfly flitting through a forest. There's a suggestion of the traditional leaf-and-tendril pattern, but most of her dress is made of iridescent nanoparticles that change from green to blue to silver whenever the light hits them. Her tights are shimmering silver. She'd be a hit at light-night at the Rain Forest Club.

(I bite my tongue, glad I've only thought that, not spoken it out loud. The Rain Forest Club hasn't been popular for several months, once the Kalahari kids started going. Losers. If Pearl had heard the comparison . . .)

Our outfits have upset the school administration many times, but there's nothing they can really do about it as long as our parents are paying the exorbitant yearly school fee. Sometimes they try to appeal to our better natures. Ha! Good luck with that. But come on, how can we really respect anyone who calls themselves "sister" and "brother"? No one on the entire planet has a sister or brother. I don't understand why the Temple servants use those words. Are they trying to make us nostalgic for the good old pre-fail days? The time when people had so many children—so many brothers and sisters—that humans overran the world like vermin and destroyed it? Can you imagine living back then? The world must have been positively squirming with humanity. Ugh.

Today, there are only like a million people. That's a nice, manageable number, I think. Enough to keep the population going without inbreeding. Enough so that I'll never run out of hot new guys to meet. (I figure, given that there are only like six truly gorgeous and semi-worthwhile boys in this school of 200, there must be, what, 30,000 potential hotties out there? That's 7,500 for each of us, even if we don't share. And we usually share.)

More important, a few million people should be easy to dominate. Back before the Ecofail, queens and presidents ruled far more than that. Pearl figures that she shouldn't have any trouble at all taking control of only a million people. She rules the Oaks boarding school easily enough.

She's school chancellor. It's an official position, voted on by all the other students. But even if she hadn't been elected, she'd still be in charge of everything.

I'm her vice chancellor. That's not an elected position. I serve at her whim. And Pearl has been pretty whimsical lately.

"Yarrow," she hisses, in the voice that pretends to be a whisper but projects embarrassingly to Lynx and Copper, walking at our flanks. "What the bikking hell do you have in your hair?"

I touch the staggered layers of my blond hair self-consciously, and feel my jaw clench, though a second later I force a smile. "Do you like it?" I ask. This morning I was playing around with one of the hair painters and put a streak of aqua in one of the strands. I forgot that streaks were so last year. I'd meant to take it out again, but I must have been in a kind of daze and never got around to it. I haven't been sleeping very well lately. Weird dreams.

"No," Pearl says flatly, and I hope that's the end of it. I'll strip it out and go back to my natural color at the first break. But Pearl smiles, and her dimples do absolutely nothing to make it look less like a snarl.

And the insults begin.

"If Brother Birch and a jellyfish Bestial had a baby—and

then never hugged it—it would look like your hair." Pearl gives a self-satisfied smirk at that, and I have to admit it is one of her better ones. Still, Brother Birch is always telling us to respect the Bestials. They're different, but they feel a calling and follow it, almost like a Temple servant. Should we mock that?

Copper and Lynx aren't as clever, but just as mean. "You look like an outer circle tramp high on synthmesc who fell into a tub of blue-green algae soup," Copper says with a snicker.

"Yeah, and you're so poor you sucked all the algae out of the rest of your hair, and saved that last bit for your boyfriend," Lynx riffs gleefully.

"Your boyfriend who has pox."

"Your boyfriend who can't read an autoloop timetable."

I smile. Now they're just being silly, and the sting melts out of their insults. We tease each other like this all the time. And yeah, sure, sometimes it hurts. But none of us means anything by it. I start to laugh along with them.

Until Pearl says, "Your boyfriend who's a second child."

I stop cold. It's a bad insult. It means someone who is an outcast, unloved. Someone who shouldn't exist. But it's just one of those words we four toss around, like "tramp." It doesn't mean anything, really. It's just another playfully cruel insult. I even called Pearl that once, in the second week after I transferred to Oaks. She was so impressed at my nerve that I became her second in command, much to the disgust of Copper and Lynx. They tried calling her second child afterward, but it didn't have the same effect. I'd been the first one brave or stupid enough to do it. Pearl likes innovators.

So it's nothing. Nothing at all. Why, then, does something knot up painfully in the pit of my stomach? Why do I feel like my throat is squeezing shut?

"What's wrong with you today?" Pearl asks. She walks off before I can answer, and I scramble to keep up. Already, the other girls are trying to move into my place, literally and metaphorically. I have to squeeze back into my position at Pearl's side.

Though I've only been here at Oaks for a short time, my life at my last school feels like a distant blur. I was at the Caverns, another one of the three or four top schools that the elite scions of Eden attend. From the moment I shed the glossy black uniform of the Caverns and donned Oaks' leaf and vine–pattern green plaid, I felt like my life was really starting. As if the time before had been meaningless.

That first night Pearl stuck her head into the doorway of my private room, her pale silvery hair swinging almost to her waist, and said, "Who the hell are you? No, scratch that. Who the hell are your parents?" Then she winked at me, because of course all the students had been briefed to not ask me. My mom does spy things in the government that no one is allowed to talk about. It's the worst-kept secret. Instead of going home to visit her, I have to go to the Center. She's *that* top-secret. I go there once a week, right after classes on Friday, and stay until Saturday morning. It takes away prime wilding time, but that's family, right?

The night I arrived, Pearl invited me into her room and she, Lynx, Copper, and I got tipsy on spiced *akavit* cocktails. I like to think that she adored my winning personality, but I know that first night she welcomed me just because of who my mom is. That's okay. If I'd been boring she might have paid attention to me out of self-interest, but I wouldn't be her friend. Being Pearl's friend is the most exciting thing that ever happened to me. She makes me feel alive, free, fierce.

Most of the time.

We might have every intention of ruling Eden within a

few years, but for now we're obedient students. Our wolfish stride automatically slows, becomes less glaringly aggressive, when we spy the tall, gaunt form of headmaster Brother Birch in his leaf-green robes. We want to appear like regular students. We know how to play the game.

"Good morning, Brother Birch," Pearl says, flashing him a smile bright as the sun. We mumble the same.

"Good morning, girls, and may the blessings of the Earth be with you." He nods benevolently. Although he's the head of the Temple of Eden—the most powerful cleric in the world—as well as headmaster of our school, he wears the unassuming robes of the lowest member of his order, and calls himself brother as if he were just ordained last week. He's not very old, considering his rank; in his forties. But then, he was raised in the Temple, an orphan. His dark hair is a little too long, feral, as if he just ran his hands through it, but his goatee is neatly trimmed and lightly oiled. It smells like . . . I frown. It's sharp and cool, almost medicinal. Tormentingly familiar, but I can't quite place it. It makes me want to lean in closer to Brother Birch every time I see him. Of course, I don't.

He seems like such a simple, kind man. Yet I know he has been initiated into the deepest Mysteries. He makes me feel off balance, though I can never tell why.

"How are you adapting to our school, Yarrow?" he asks me.

My nerves flee, because the answer is so obvious, so genuine. "I love it here!" I gush. "The students are amazing, and I've made so many friends." Well, three friends, two of which want my place. Lots of other students are nice to me, though. That's the same as having friends, right? Who has time for more than a few close people?

"And your studies?" Brother Birch asks, raising his eyebrows slightly.

"Ah, well . . ." I flush.

"Sister Margarita says you cover your Eco-history notes in drawings. Horrid doodlings, she calls them." He smiles and presses his fingertips together. "We must pay a bit better attention, mustn't we?"

I nod, speechless, and he makes the Sign of the Seed between his chest and mine—a closed fist that rises and sprouts as if the fingers are a growing seedling. I bow my head as I am expected to do, and he touches the crown of my head with two fingertips in blessing. "I am watching you with particular interest, Yarrow," he says.

The girls manage not to giggle until we get into the classroom, out of earshot. "What the *hell*, Yarrow?" Copper asks. "*Particular interest?*"

"Ooohhh," Lynx purrs, "does Yarrow have a *thing* for Brother Birch?"

A thing? Ew. Like I'd have a thing for a guy three times my age, and a clergyman, at that. I mean, he isn't bad-looking, and there's something about his eyes, a peculiar brightness shining even through the flat lens implants every citizen of Eden wears. But he's definitely not my type. My type is more . . .

Come to think of it, I don't know what my type is. I try to picture my ideal mate, and I can't see anything except shadowy images. First, a tall, slim form that seems very far away, and then a larger shadowy figure, broad-chested, looming closer . . .

I shake my head, and make myself laugh along with them. Again. It seems like I've been the butt of all the jokes today. My face aches with so much smiling at their jokes at my expense.

So to make myself feel better I find someone to hurt.

Ah, there's the perfect target—Hawk. He's one of the most popular boys in Oaks, and the richest. He's a real power here, the male equivalent of Pearl. He shouldn't be so easy to hurt . . . if it weren't for one little thing.

The poor idiot thinks he loves me.

I start out sweet. If you're cruel all the time, then your cruelty loses power. You have to temper it with kindness, affection, empathy. Empathy is especially important. How can you truly hurt someone if you don't understand them deeply and truly? I can read other people pretty well. Pearl says I study them, stare at them, like each person is a new species I'm discovering each time I see them.

Sometimes I feel like I understand other people better than I do myself.

Hawk is already in his Egg, ready for class to begin. The Egg is a virtual reality pod that encases each student individually, giving us a fully immersive learning experience. I watch his hand caress the controls of his datablock interface, toying with the many sensory options he has at his disposal. The movement is so sensual I can't help but picture that dark-skinned hand caressing something alive. My skin. *No, Yarrow, don't start getting sentimental and attached.* Those are Pearl's words I hear in my head. *Love makes people weak,* she says, and probably believes. *Love is for* other *people, to feel for you. If you indulge in it, you'll lose your power. You'll be a slave, no better than some outer circle peasant prole reporting to his factory every day for the rest of his life.*

So I don't think of Hawk touching my bare flesh. Instead, I envision him caressing something far more exotic and unlikely: a cat. No one has seen a cat for more than two hundred years. No one has seen any animal other than humans. We have vids of them, though. I've seen wildebeest by the thousands stampeding across a plain, hurling themselves into rivers, only to be snatched by crocodiles. I've seen elegant hummingbirds flirt with flowers, and sinuous snakes twine around trees. All stored in the cold, dead bytes of a datablock.

Now all those things are gone. It will be centuries before the Earth is healed enough for humans to survive outside of Eden. Here we only have people and technology, and a few hardy species of algae, fungus, and bacteria that provide our food.

"Meow," I say, and narrow my eyes as I slide into the Egg beside Hawk. They're made for one person, and it is a tight squeeze. He doesn't seem to mind. The autumn leaves that make up my long skirt part, exposing a long swath of bare leg. He looks . . . then looks back at my face. His mother raised him right.

"Hi, Yarrow," he says, scooting over to give me a little more room. "Did you like the flowers I sent to your room?" They weren't real flowers, of course, but lovely clusters of lilacs spun in synthetic silk.

"Flowers?" I ask, widening my eyes and tilting my head slightly. How bad should I be? Should I simply deny receiving them, or . . .

"Oh!" I say after a long moment of pretending to remember. "I did find some kind of weeds outside my door. I assumed the cleaning staff forgot to remove the trash." I giggle and tilt my head fetchingly to one side. "I'm afraid I suggested to Brother Birch that Jessamine should be fired immediately."

Bikk, I slipped up again. I shouldn't know the cleaning lady's name. She's so far beneath us. Pearl would never let me live that down, if she knew. I'm always doing embarrassing stuff like that. I'd say it's because of my mother's work: I tend to notice trivial details. Then Pearl would give me a look of near disgust, as if knowing a cleaning lady's name is like knowing the name of a piece of garbage. Unthinkable, laughable.

Hawk doesn't even notice that part. I can see his face tighten when I bad-mouth his gift, but he's too well bred to react. *The upper classes don't get mad*, Pearl says. *We get even.*

I've made the first cut, now I have to sweeten it. Stab . . . stop . . . kiss . . . then twist. That's how you make it really hurt. Swiftly, I lean in and kiss his cheek. Or, I try to kiss his cheek. His reflexes are good, and he turns his head so fast my lips land on the edge of his. I fight the urge to recoil in confusion. I don't want to kiss him, not really. I just want him to love me. I want everyone to love me. I want to own them. I want to have loyal people around me who will never leave me.

Still, the quick kiss has the desired effect. His face relaxes, and he smiles. I'm forgiven.

"Never mind," he says. "I'll send you more. Better flowers."

I was almost telling him the truth. I did get the flowers, but as soon as I saw them I gave them to Jessamine to throw away, or put in her no doubt squalid little apartment, or anything she liked. I couldn't stand the sight of them.

He leans against me in the tight confines of the Egg. "Are you looking forward to the Snow Festival tonight?"

I shrug. "It's an excuse for a new dress." I've seen sixteen snow days in my life, and they must have been pretty boring because I have hardly any memory of any of them. Only the barest abstract recollection of the dances, the feasts, the merriment. The only image that is truly clear is a memory of staring up to a small patch of sky, seeing the stars seem to multiply as snowflakes formed, then filled the heavens in a blizzard that lasted exactly one night. Where was I for that Snow Festival?

"It always seems weird to me, too," Hawk says, catching my jaded tone and interpreting it as he likes. When someone has a crush on you, they'll put the best spin on whatever you say. "I mean, there's no natural precipitation here, and we have to conserve water, so why does the EcoPan program one night of snow every year?"

"And one day of rain six months later," I add. The snow is always at night, but the rain falls in the daytime. I remember being somewhere high for one Rain Festival, feeling exposed, with a sense of nervous excitement, tilting my head back to catch fat raindrops on my tongue as the noonday sky grew black with artificial thunderclouds.

"I think the EcoPan does it to make us feel a little more normal," Hawk muses. "I mean, look at this." He fiddles with the controls of his Egg and suddenly we are surrounded in a panorama of a Snow Festival from many years back. It must have been before I was born. The clothes all look out of date, the sort of flowing, casual, free garments in muted colors I imagine our grandparents wore.

The Egg is designed to give students a full immersive experience. I don't even know why we have teachers, really. They could just program our lessons into the Egg and take the rest of the day off. Inside the Egg, the temperature drops, and despite the singing and cheers of the crowd that seems alive around me, there is a hushed feeling. I'm right there, in the crowd, the darkness kept at bay by lamplight. My senses are sure of it, even if my mind knows it is all an illusion. I can't help but smile when an elderly woman next to me raises a wide-eyed baby up into the air, holds out its chubby little hand to catch a snowflake. Hawk hits another button, and the scene shifts jarringly to a frozen artificial pond, solid for one night only. Couples glide awkwardly on its surface, and the Egg drops a VR hood over my head and makes me feel like I'm skating alongside of them.

When Hawk turns it off, I'm breathless. The Egg has returned to ambient temperature and is just a machine again, its delusions hidden. But my cheeks feel raw and rosy from the recent cold.

I shake my head against the unexpected sensation of exhilaration. I'd meant to make myself feel better by making someone else feel worse. Instead, the person I'd meant to hurt for entertainment, for power, for practice, has made me feel alive. Happy, I'd almost say.

Why does that feel like a novelty? Aren't I always happy? What reason do I have to not be happy? I have everything.

I feel a strange uncertainty, and it makes me angry. So when Hawk leans close and asks me for the first dance at the school Snow Festival tonight, I lift my chin haughtily and snap, "I'm not going to that stupid kids' party. My friends and I have other plans."

We don't, and I know we'll be there because we've been planning our outfits forever. But at the end of class Pearl slides up to me.

"Did you hear, the outer circles are having a contest for king and queen of the Snow Festival. The winner gets money, and a night in the innermost entertainment circle."

I'd heard something about it. "An effort to boost morale among the lower classes, right?" I ask, not really interested.

"Exactly," she says. "And what do you think they're going to do with all that morale, huh? Start making decisions? Wanting things above their station?" She laughs derisively. "No good can come of letting outer circle proles get their hopes up about . . . anything. Why let them into our circles, even for a night? Next thing you now they'll be wanting their kids to go to Oaks!"

"I'm sure you're right, Pearl," I say uncertainly. Pearl cares far more about these things than I do. But she probably has a point. "But what can anyone do about it, if the powers that be have authorized . . ."

She silences me with a look. "Oh, you sweet little thing! I *am* the powers that be."

<hr />

THE LAST CLASS of the day is a tedious hour of Earth Stewardship, where one of the Brothers dozes while our Eggs instruct us on the finer points of geology. It is just starting on something called fracking, where people, not satisfied with destroying the Earth's crust, began bikking up the inside of the planet, too. We haven't gotten very far, though, when the bell tower chimes the end of the school day, and we jet out of our Eggs faster than the Brother can jolt awake and shout, "To be continued tomorrow!"

I love our bell tower, the Oaks carillon, the arrogance of those giant chimes looming over the campus. They boom our schedule out to half the inner circles, screaming to the world that we are the ones who matter. It is *our* waking and studying, playing and sleeping that count, not yours. So what if you want to sleep late? If carillon rings to wake Oaks students at 6 a.m., you have to get up, too.

The last bells peals still echo over the elite heart of Eden as we run to our dorms. They are set up with two or three bedrooms around a common leisure room. Before I came to Oaks, Pearl was the only student with a private room, arranged through some scheming of her own, and no doubt her parents' money. When I arrived mid-term, though, there were no spare dorm rooms, so an extra teacher's room was converted for my use. I'm on the opposite side of campus and closer to their supervision, but my big bedroom, private bath, and little parlor for entertaining are the envy of all the other students. Particularly Pearl. She keeps mentioning to the staff how isolated I feel away from the student body, so I'm sure as soon as a shared dorm opens up I'll be out.

For now, though, it gives me a little something to lord over Pearl.

Pearl grabs my hand and hurries me along with an uncharacteristic enthusiasm. We're supposed to be above actually getting excited about anything.

Usually we meet in her room, but today she drags us into mine. It makes me uneasy. Pearl likes to be in charge, at the pinnacle of everything, the cynosure of every eye. If she's putting the attention on me, she must have a reason for it.

"We're going out tonight!" she says to the others, and explains her idea to steal the Snow Queen title from some undeserving outer circle girl.

2

IT MIGHT NOT sound revolutionary, but it is. Oaks has very strict rules about leaving campus. It's a boarding school, which in a way is kind of silly because every student is from one of the inner circles, nearly all from the innermost, nearest the emerald eye of the Center. We could walk to our family homes every night in a quarter hour, or hop an autoloop and be there in minutes. But the Oaks philosophy is that living together builds a community of leaders who will be able to work as a team to lead Eden in the future. Our fellow students are our families, more than our biological parents. We live, study, eat, and sleep together. No one in Eden has a brother or sister, of course, thanks to the strict one-child policy, but the student body of Oaks comes close.

We can only leave the campus on a pass. The pass has to be authorized both by a parent and the school. Most of the students go home for a night or two every other weekend. I go every Friday night to visit my mom at the Center, where she works and pretty much lives. Families can also give permission for students to go out into Eden at night, to parties and clubs. The school isn't crazy about this—they'd rather we stay in, studying or something else dismally dull—but they usually let us. We go out a couple of nights a week at least, to whatever club is most popular.

However, it is a cardinal sin, and grounds for dismissal, to sneak off campus without permission.

Usually it wouldn't be a problem to get our parents to give us last minute permission and then hustle it through the school bureaucracy. Tonight, though, everyone is expected to be at the Snow Festival. It is a mandatory gala, an obligatory bonding moment we absolutely cannot miss.

So when Pearl tells us that we're sneaking out, even my jaw drops a little bit.

"What's wrong, Yarrow?" she asks, tilting her head to the side with that kittenish expression she uses right before her claws come out. "Don't you like my idea?"

I can feel the tension in the air. Lynx looks like she's dying to say something that might push me in the wrong direction, in opposition to Pearl. She wants me to scoff at the idea, create a breach that she can slip into. But she doesn't quite dare speak in case the balance shifts the wrong way. Copper is positively quivering, waiting to see what will happen. After an eternity, I say musingly, as if it is my own idea I've just come up with, "The school Snow Festival is so boring. I think we should look for something better to do."

Pearl flashes her feline grin, and it makes me feel like I just passed a killer test. Her approval is so hard to win, but when it comes, it feels like a blessing.

"Thought you'd like it," she says. "I'm glad, because we couldn't do it without you."

She needs me! I feel proud, though a shiver of dread tickles my spine. We are known for getting up to some serious hijinks, but this is bigger than anything we've done before.

"Oh, don't look so worried, Yarrow," she says dismissively. "The school makes a big deal about sneaking out, but it's just for show. Come on, do you really think they'd expel us? The school's entire reputation for greatness is based on having people like us attend. We give them prestige. If we get caught, then our parents will write a retroactive permission note ... wrapped around a generous donation. We'll be fine."

She's probably right. I mean, that's what money and power are for—to shield you from the bad things in life. Nothing bad has *ever* happened to me. It never will. I smile at Pearl, feeling suddenly safe, and part of this very special sisterhood that I know will last my entire life. "I'm down for whatever you want," I assure her.

Lynx—looking a little disappointed that there wasn't more drama—is ready to get on board now. "Fantastic idea, Pearl!" she gushes. "But how are we going to get out?"

"Leave that to me. Or rather, leave that to Yarrow."

When Pearl explains her plan, I feel a sick twist in my stomach. I can do it. Of course I can do it. It's just . . .

I gulp, but force a smile through tightly clenched jaws. "No problem!"

While they talk about the details of the plan, I zone out, looking at the decorations around my room. I change décor every few weeks; I can't decide what suits me. Right now, it looks like the inside of a psychedelic cave or a swirling galaxy of stars, the walls adorned with winking crystalline lights in shades of topaz, purple, and pink. They're off now, but at night I can lie in my bed and pretend I'm floating in the middle of a nebula. Even when my eyes are closed I have visions of twinkling lights all around me, like they are imprinted on the insides of my eyelids. The multicolored crystal lights all around me feel familiar, safe.

Then Pearl reveals the crux of her plan, and it startles me out of my daze. "We're going to sneak out through the Temple."

The school campus connects directly to the Temple. It is

supposed to remind us that we, the elite, have a special duty to the Earth. And of course, being good little children, we can visit the Temple whenever we like, to pray for forgiveness for the sins of our forefathers. Like it's *our* fault the Earth was destroyed. The Temple is open to the outside world during the day. (When, let's face it, there's not much temptation to sneak out. Daytime is boring to the extreme. What, we're going to join the commuters? Tour a factory assembly line? No, the night is our time.) But at night it is locked.

When Pearl suggests sneaking out through the Temple, I can't quite help looking at her like she's crazy. Lynx gives a sly, secret smile. She foresees me getting caught, expelled, sees herself moving back into her old place as Pearl's right-hand girl.

"But there will be a Temple attendant at the entrance," I remind Pearl.

"Sure, but not at the other doors."

"But they're . . ."

"Past the Skyhall, in the priests' private quarters." Where anyone who isn't a priest or priestess of the Temple is strictly forbidden to venture. This could turn out *very* badly.

Despite my worry, I find myself looking forward to tonight. It will be a challenge, thrilling. Suddenly I feel oddly claustrophobic, like Oaks is closing in on me. That's crazy. The campus is huge. Sure, it is surrounded by a high wall. But there's nothing about it that should make me feel trapped.

But all I say is "I better wear sneakier shoes, then. I don't think stilettos are right for this job."

I can handle the risk in what Pearl proposes. It's the other part I'm not so sure about. But of course I'll do it. I'll do it with a smile.

THAT NIGHT WE dress and prepare for the party as usual. We have to put in an appearance or the headmaster might get suspicious. It's a small school, and if the most important, most popular people aren't there, people will notice, and talk. Anyway, the plan depends on being extravagantly seen.

I head to Pearl's room, but when my hand is on the door I hear her talking to someone inside. Probably Lynx, plotting something against me, so I pause and listen. The voices sound really intense, but they're talking too low for me to make out the words. One of them suddenly rises sharply, in a commanding tone, and I recognize the voice, but it's not Lynx.

It's my mom.

What on Earth is she doing on campus? Any why is she with Pearl? I press my ear closer to the door, but the door is unlatched and I accidentally shove it open an inch. The voices inside abruptly cease. A second later a scowling Pearl has flung the door open.

"What the . . . Oh, it's you. You're early."

I look past her. "Mom? What are you doing here?"

She'd been sitting comfortably on Pearl's bed. Now she uncrosses her legs and runs her fingers carelessly through her short blond hair. "I came to see you of course, darling," she says lightly.

"Yes, but why . . ."

"Though of course Pearl reminded me that the Snow Festival dance is tonight, so I'll come back another time." She rises, her usual brisk and efficient self.

"Okay," I say, wrapping my arms around her when she comes in for a quick hug, holding on just a little bit longer than she does, as always. I want to ask her more, but she's already out the door with a backward wave. Poor Mom. She hardly has time to see me. They work her to death at the Center. Well, she pushes herself hard. She has to, I guess. It's her job to prevent insurrection and rebellion in Eden. Since there's never been any, I guess she's good at what she does.

Still, I wish I could spend more time with her. More than once a week, every Friday night. My mom is the most important thing in the world to me. Mom is the one I love and trust, my touchstone.

"Pearl," I ask when Mom is gone, "what were you two talking about?"

"Oh, just girl stuff," she says. "Your mom has the best taste. I was going to wear those strappy sandals, but she told me that the silver pumps make my legs look longer." She models the shoes, stretching out her shapely legs for me to admire. "Oh, and she gave me these earrings. Your mom is so bikking cool."

I feel a surge of jealousy. I want Mom to give *me* advice about *my* shoes. I want her to give me shiny presents like the green-faceted gems that wink from Pearl's ears like tiny versions of the Center's Eye. That's the kind of stuff moms should do. I mean, she pays a lot of attention to me when I visit, asking about my dreams, my friends, what I do. Making sure I meditate and relax while I'm there. But I'd really like to do girly things with her occasionally. Get a mother-daughter manicure. Shop. We never seem to have time for all that.

Maybe Mom is planning something really special for me, and she decided she needed my best friend's help to plan it. Maybe she wants to do something over the next holiday, just her and me. Maybe she needs Pearl's help planning a surprise. I feel a little shiver of excitement. Yes, that must be it. My birthday is coming up soon, and Mom wants to do something special. Why else would she have gone straight to Pearl when she visited, instead of to her own daughter? When I help Pearl put the finishing touches on her hair, I find I'm in a much better mood.

PEARL PAID THE band to play our favorite song when we walk in, cued by one of our minions who hopes to join our inner circle, though she never will. The campus is decorated with silvery snow made of shimmering metallic nanobots that float and soar around at knee level with their micro engines. They're so glittering and pretty that they make the real snow look dull and dirty by comparison.

Pearl looks like an ice sculpture in white-and-silver lace that hugs her body. Her shining, nearly white hair is piled high, with a few tendrils curling over her cheeks. Every eye is on her, but she doesn't look at anyone in particular, or even seem proud. At most, she looks mildly amused, on the verge of boredom. I hear sighs of envy, a few low, catty remarks.

I was originally going to wear something fancy, but I modified my festival outfit to be more functional. After all, we might have to run, a thought that evidently doesn't bother Pearl. I decided on a flippy skirt the color of mercury and thigh-high black boots, with a glimpse of silver tights flashing between. My top is made up entirely of black artificial feathers, smooth and glossy as a raven's wing. I strut a half step behind Pearl. Any other time I'd be basking in the admiration, but tonight my eyes are on the door.

The song changes and Hawk is suddenly at my side, stroking the soft feathers on my shoulder. "Hello, beautiful." Just as I knew he would. Because he is in love, and people in love are so perfectly predictable. So easy to use.

Everyone is watching Pearl, who has grabbed her man of the week—or hour—and pulled him to a tabletop. She's gyrating on him, the ice queen showing heat, and even the disapproving Sisters and Brothers can't tear their eyes away, though they'll gently tell her to step down at any moment.

Just not quite yet. She's spectacular, and love her or hate her, no one can look away.

Except for Hawk. He hasn't even noticed her. Every drop of his attention is on me.

Perfect.

I pull him suddenly, almost violently, to me, pressing the length of my body against his. His eyes widen, but a second later he's kissing me back. I grab his hand, move it where I want it, and it feels so right and so wrong that I'm not really acting when I suddenly shove him away and make a loud sound, part indignant squeal, part frightened scream, that cuts through the music.

While Hawk looks at me in openmouthed bafflement, I back away, holding out my hands defensively. "How could you?" I wail loudly, and look around for someone, anyone, to help me in my pretend moment of terror. At once, Pearl is at my side.

"You monster," she says in a low voice that only those nearest can hear. That's okay, they'll spread the gossip lightning-fast. Pearl throws a protective arm around me. "How could you do that to her?"

One of the Sisters comes up to us, asking what happened, and Pearl murmurs something into her ear that makes her blush, then stares at Hawk as if he's a criminal. Hawk looks utterly flabbergasted. "I didn't . . . ," he begins, but of course he has no idea what he didn't do.

The Sister spreads her arms, the green folds of her robe opening like a macaw's wing, making a wall between us tender, innocent girls and the crude man who offended me.

"Please, Sister," I say weakly, "I'd like to go to the Temple if I may. He made me feel . . . unclean."

As we turn to go, I see Brother Birch lay a commanding hand on Hawk's shoulder and lead him away in the opposite direction. Lynx and Copper join us, and amid the sympathetic clucking of the Sister we are led to the Temple.

"I must return to the festival to chaperone the others," she says, and shakes her head sadly. "To think that this could happen in the Oaks, in the very shadow of the Temple! Young men are not what they used to be."

I stifle a mocking snort. What could that crabby old virgin know about young men?

"Will you young ladies be comfortable in the Temple alone? I'm afraid all of the Temple servants are at the festival tonight. Except for the door attendant, of course."

Which is exactly what we'd counted on. "I feel very safe here," I say piously. "As if I'm in the bosom of the Earth." How we all keep a straight face is beyond me.

She hems and haws for a bit, until I remind her that the snowfall will begin at any moment. Then, finally, she leaves us alone.

Pearl looks at me with unabashed admiration. "Worked like a charm!" she says, snapping her fingers. "Did you see the look on Hawk's face. Poor Hawk." She pulls a face of mock sympathy. "Do you think he'll be expelled?"

"Nah," Lynx says, watching me narrowly, "just labeled as a sex offender."

I laugh along with them, but when I remember the hurt confusion on Hawk's face I quickly say, "Let's find the door and get out of here. We want to go before the snow falls and we leave footprints."

The main section of the Temple, where worshipers congregate for the short daily masses and the long weekly one, is under a dome of opaque blue that in the sunlight looks like the arch of heaven, but now, just after dusk, resembles an ice cave. Everyday worshipers, those who haven't devoted themselves to honoring the Earth, like to have a roof over their heads.

The most sacred spaces in the Temple, though, are open to the sky, roofless courtyards and open starlit rooms. The priests say the Earth can only be properly honored outdoors. When a couple gets married, when a child is born, when an elder passes on to the infinity that awaits after death, they go to the Skyhall. We move there now. It is a room without a roof, open to the sky and the wind and, soon, the snow. Beyond that are several rooms the general public never sees: the inner sanctum of the high priest Brother Birch, and the Chambers of Mysteries, the labyrinth that holds the deepest secrets of our religion.

We creep into the Skyhall, clustered close, nervous despite our bold fronts. There are rows of benches, polished by the backsides of generations of worshipers. At the far end is the door to the outside. There's an alcove where a door attendant sits, unseen and silent. Probably asleep, I think. He won't notice when we sneak into the private chambers. If he happens to look out and see us gone, he'll think we just went back to the party.

"What will happen if they catch us?" Copper asks.

"We'll tell them Yarrow went mad after her violation and decided to forsake men forever and become a Sister," Pearl quips. I look at the door that leads to the forbidden rooms. My stomach seems to flip-flop. What on Earth ever made me think I could do this? I want to leave, go back to the Snow Festival and listen to Hawk call me beautiful, even though I don't care about him. I want everything to be easy and normal and safe.

Then Pearl asks, "Scared?" in that superior way of hers, and something strengthens inside me. I lift my chin, clench my jaw, and say, "Let's go." I surge forward, leading the way.

COPPER, LYNX, AND Pearl pour in after me stifling giggles. "I can't believe we're in here," Copper says as she looks around. "We could get in so much trouble." She makes the Sign of the Seed.

I don't see anything too mystically impressive yet. We're not in a room, but rather in a long, narrow, curving passageway lit by torches burning some chemical with a vague, strange smell. I've only seen an open flame a few times in my life. There's no wood or coal in Eden. Almost all of our materials are man-made, and not flammable. The torch fire dances hypnotically, casting long shadows down the walls.

We have no idea of the layout of this place—only Temple priests and priestesses are allowed in—so we split up to search for a door to the outside. Pearl heads in one direction, and Lynx immediately follows her. I turn to go the other way, and Copper hesitates, then follows Lynx.

I hate to be alone. Without people around I feel empty, flat. Sometimes frightened, though I'd never admit that. It's okay, I tell myself. They're close. I'm not really alone.

Above me, I can just see the first faint stars in the dimming sky. We need a door, and there are plenty of doors along the outer edge, but when I check them they turn out to be the simple cells of the Temple priests, holding nothing more than a bed, a table, a light.

Finally I come to a door on the inner wall. It has no handle, but when I touch it, it opens on well-oiled hinges. It is a hexagonal room, empty, with a door in each of its six walls. More doors! I choose one, and come to an identical room, also with six doors. I've gone through several of these before I realize with panic that I haven't been keeping track of my turns. I try to retrace my steps but I'm utterly disoriented. If it was daytime maybe I could guess my direction from the sun, but the faint stars of dusk shining through the open roof offer no clue. I'm lost in this honeycomb labyrinth. Every room is the same: empty, with six doors.

Until, finally, I come to a room that is different.

It is exactly like the others, except for one thing. In the middle, on a pedestal, is a glass bowl full of dirt.

I've found one of the Chambers of Mysteries.

No one except the few priests and priestesses initiated into the Mysteries is supposed to see this. Of course, like any unknown, people talk all the time about what the Chambers might hold. The mummified body of Aaron Al-Baz, the creator of Eden and savior of humanity. The coding for the EcoPanopticon, the vast computer program that keeps Eden running.

But what I find is at once more simple and more profound. No one on Eden has seen dirt—real, actual dirt—in more than two hundred years. After we destroyed the Earth and almost all living things, we had to retreat to this artificial sanctuary. The surface of the Earth is too poisoned to sustain life. The dirt is toxic. No seed would ever grow. Yet here, in this bare room, is a bowl of rich, black soil.

Is it real? I should leave. This isn't right. But I can't help it. I creep up slowly and bend my head, inhaling deeply. Oh, great Earth—the smell! It is deep and rich and unfathomable. It smells alive. I want to touch it, but I don't quite dare. Finally, I have to. I press one fingertip into the surface, leaving the faintest depression. Then I rub my fingers together, feeling the grit, watching it fall. I can't let one grain escape. It is, I'm sure, the only real dirt in Eden.

The smell lingers on my finger, and I rub it beneath my nose. It is remarkable, but . . . I don't feel as amazed as I should. Any other resident of Eden would have fallen to their knees to see such a sight. It would give them spiritual uplift, hope that one day our descendants might roam a wild and clean Earth again.

I feel none of those things. Instead, I feel disappointed. It's just so *small*. I feel a wild surge of irrational anger, an urge to smash the bowl to pieces, scatter the dirt on the floor. That can't be all that remains, I rage inwardly. The Earth is huge! There are forests, deer, grasses. This is a mockery of dirt. A travesty, a deception . . .

My hand reaches out, and I touch the lip of the bowl, pinch it between my fingers. I wouldn't, not ever. Whatever crazy thoughts are coming into my head, this relic is far too precious.

Then I hear a shriek from behind me, and someone grabs me by the shoulders, spinning me around. I can't let go of the bowl in time! In slow motion I see the bowl spin off the pillar. Pearl's ringlets tickle my neck as she giggles and squeals at having found me. "We found it!" she crows in my ear as the bowl sails through the air, smashes, the dirt scattering. She's so proud of herself that she doesn't realize what just happened. I shove her out the door.

"We have to go! Now!" I shout, giving her commands for the first time ever.

"What's that?" she asks, craning her neck over my shoulder.

"An art exhibit," I lie, and close the door behind us, panting. My eyes are wild, I know, and I try, and utterly fail, to look nonchalant. I'll be excommunicated. I'll be executed. "You've found the exit? Then let's go." Finally I force a grin that must look maniacal. "I'm ready for a snow party!"

Pearl leads us back to the corridor and out to the Skyhall, where we meet up with Lynx and Copper. A moment later we step out into Eden, just as the first snowflakes float down around us.

3

"YOU DID IT!" I cry as we run away from the outdoor stage where the outer circles had their Snow Queen contest. It has been snowing for hours now, and we're slipping and stumbling tipsily. The air is artificially chilled and the snow is rising in drifts, coating the world in white.

"Did you have any doubt?" Pearl asks, arching her perfect pale golden eyebrows.

Well, yeah. She was going up against every beauty in the outer circles. Some of the competition was as gorgeous as she is. Not that I'd ever tell Pearl that. What really clinched it for her was the story she told. She registered under a false name and gave a long monologue about her poverty-stricken family skipping breakfast for weeks so she could buy the material for the dress, which her mother painstakingly sewed between her three jobs. Her tale of smiling bravely through poverty was so exquisitely touching that even I had tears in my eyes as I watched from the sidelines. Her acting was amazing. (And of course, we have elocution classes at Oaks.)

Now we have our arms flung around each other, all rivalries forgotten (for the moment) as we giddily escape. Right now the photographers are looking for the lovely "Ruby" who just won everyone's heart, but they'll soon find out that not only has she vanished—she doesn't exist. Pearl is flushed with victory. As we swing into the nearest autoloop station she hands her entertainment circle pass to the nearest beggar.

"See," she says smugly, "the contest helped the poor after all." We laugh at the idea of the dirty, bedraggled man getting free admittance to some of the hottest clubs in Eden. Pearl decides to keep the other half of the prize—a credit-filled card—to fund our night of adventure. Because, of course, the night has only just begun.

I suggest we go to Arctica, a club whose theme matches this frigid night. It's popular with Oaks kids, and some of the other good schools, too. Which is apparently what makes it vastly unpopular with Pearl tonight.

"I have a better idea," she says. "Why go somewhere we always go and see the same old dull faces? Tonight, we're going to Tidal!"

I haven't even heard of it.

She rolls her eyes elaborately. "You'll see. And you'll thank me for it the rest of your life."

She takes us to one of the tallest buildings in the inner circles. I never paid much attention to it, though, because it is full of office buildings. Just more people scrabbling for money. Of course, these are already wealthy people scrabbling for a great deal of money, but still. Oaks students come from families with so much money that we never even really think about how people make it. Money is a given in our circle. Power and influence are what we and our families crave.

The tall building seems totally dark at ground level. "There's not a club here," I begin . . . then I see the line going down the street. A line full of people that somehow make me feel inadequate. They are beautiful. Well, so are we. But they have something else, a confidence even greater than ours. I'm not sure what it is. Maybe it is like we are all fearsome warriors, but my friends and I are still fighting a battle, whereas the people on line have already achieved victory.

They are all young, only a few years older than us. But they are adults. Those two or three years make a world of difference. I see that even Pearl has to take a moment to pull herself together. Once she does, though, she strides with every appearance of utter confidence past the waiting people to the front of the line. She gives the bouncer a slow smile and is about to glide past him. He stops her with a beefy arm.

"Over eighteen only."

Pearl gives a low laugh. "Don't we look over eighteen?" She narrows her eyes, flirting.

"No," he says shortly, and immediately turns to the glamorous women in line. They give us devastating looks and sweep past into the dark atrium.

Pearl is fuming, her face contorted in unfamiliar ugliness. I think it has been a long time since anyone thwarted her.

"No," she says suddenly as we walk slowly away. I can hear some of the fabulous women in line laughing at us. "We're going to Tidal tonight if it kills us. Come on." That's the Pearl I know and love! We walk along the imperceptible curve of the Circle until we come to the edge of the building. Then she ducks into the alleyway in between.

"There has to be a way in," she says as she breathlessly tries service doors, and finally finds an unlocked one. We sneak up a few flights, then find the elevators to the roof. But we're still not quite at the party. The elevator doors open on a high platform with a long ice-blue spiraling water slide that will take us to the wild party below us on the rooftop.

"No way!" Copper says, crossing her arms. "I'm not ruining this outfit in water this early in the night." Pearl looks like she agrees, though I think it might be fun. Without worrying about the delicate feathers on my outfit, I climb up onto the slide and launch myself down to the party.

It feels amazing, and somehow familiar—slithering down at breakneck speed. Inside the claustrophobic tube are bands of light that race past me as I fly, making me feel like I'm being sucked into a vortex. With each turn, more colors are added to the lights until I'm in a rainbow, sliding across the sky awash in a thousand colors. It's utterly thrilling! At the last moment everything goes black, and it's like I'm flying through outer space. I'm not sure where I'll land, but fortunately it's not in the big pool in the middle of the roof, but on a soft cushion. Staff members are waiting to help me to my feet. I'm hardly wet at all, which makes me wonder if they somehow managed to make synthetic water which, against the laws of physics, isn't as wet as other water.

Pearl follows, and the others, and we stand together in a world of blue and white. Tidal is ocean themed, and partiers dance and laugh and flirt all around a turquoise pool that heaves with realistic foam-capped waves. The snow makes it even more magical, drifting down in fluffy gusts.

Pearl catches my gaze and holds it. She's blazingly beautiful, triumphant. Falling snow settles on her long lashes, fluttering when she blinks, falling to melt on her flushed cheeks. She flashes me a grin of mischievous joy, grabs my hand, and pulls me into the melee.

We dance, our arms above our heads like trees tossing their branches in the breeze. We sing, our arms intertwined, latched around each other's waists like coiling vines. We drink until our eyes are glassy bright, until everything is hilarious. We crash into each other, almost hysterical with the sheer joy of being alive and young. I can't even remember that anyone else exists. The other people at the club are just a background for our happiness.

Someone gives Pearl a little golden pill, and she snaps it in half with her fingernail. One piece goes under her own tongue, and she holds the other half out to me on her fingertip. I hold her gaze as I take her finger in my mouth and slowly suck the pill down. For a second all of Eden seems to be still. Then she laughs and pulls me back onto the dance floor.

And then the pill kicks in, and things get a little crazy.

I don't know whose idea it is, but suddenly Pearl has her twinkling shoes off, peels her dress over her head, and is leaping into the crashing waves of the decorative pool wearing only her filmy slip. Her ridiculously expensive dress is crumpled on the floor, but she doesn't care. She's frolicking like a sea nymph, rising and falling effortlessly with the swell of the waves. Her long silver hair comes free from its pins and flows around her shoulders like molten metal. Around the pool, people stop and stare. I don't know if they admire her or think she's crazy. Probably both. All I know is that she dares to do things no one else would, and doesn't care a bit what the world thinks.

I'm always considering what people will think. Not that I let Pearl or anyone else know that.

"Come in!" she calls to me. The snow is swirling around her bobbing head, merging with the water the moment it hits the surface. "The water is warm!" She swims from one side of the pool to the other with languid, effortless strokes.

She draws me to her like a magnet. I want to be just like her. I need her approval.

I pull off my long boots, strip off my raven feather shirt, and leap into the waves. I have a vision of swimming to her side, dancing in the churning foam, diving under side by side with her like long-extinct dolphins.

Instead, I sink like a stone.

I can swim. I know I can swim! I remember going to

the pool at my parents' social club when I was a little girl. And the river in the Fifth Circle park with prop pebbles on the banks, and mechanical fish swimming lazily in the ever-circling current. Those memories are hazy and long ago, as if someone told me about them in detail but I wasn't paying very close attention. But I also remember being in water in other times, too, floating on my back in a weightless, peaceful world without sensation, a voice speaking soothingly from somewhere very close, telling me to relax, open up, everything is fine . . .

Now, though, the water is my enemy and it swallows me down. I flail, and even though I have enough sense in my panic to keep my mouth closed, the water gushes in through my nose and I'm sputtering, bubbling. Then my feet hit the bottom—it's deeper than I am tall, but only by a couple of feet—and I push off, launching to the surface, where I gasp a deep, grateful breath before a wave crashes over my face and I slip under again.

I'm thrashing my arms, but it doesn't seem to do any good. The water, which looked so cool and comfortable from dry land, is like a fist of fire reaching down my throat, choking me. I manage one more breath, and cry out, a raw guttural sound that I'm sure no one can hear over the music and laughter. Before I go under again, I think I can hear Lynx's shrill giggle. Is she watching me die?

Then I hear a huge splash and feel a hand grab my arm, dragging me, and I squirm in the grasp, grabbing whatever I can. Dimly, I see the face of the bouncer who wouldn't let us in. But he's not a person to me. He's breath, he's dry land, he's life, and I take hold of him with a strength that surprises me and do my best to climb on top of him, pushing him under. I don't care if I drown him, as long as I live. The snowy air is freezing on my face, but it is the sweetest thing I've ever felt.

He's twice my size, but in my unthinking terror I manage to hold him under the water just to keep myself aloft. When he finally shakes me, though, he puts a huge meaty hand on the top of my head and pushes me under. I struggle, but I'm at my end. Fuzzy blackness seems to creep in at the edges of my brain. My body grows heavy, unresisting. The world fades . . .

I wake up I don't know how long later, retching. I see faces, eyes, all around me, condemning, pitying, mocking. I don't know where I am. All I know is that it's not safe here. These people, this openness. I need to be somewhere small, safe, enclosed, out of sight. Behind a wall. Underground.

It all comes back to me when I see Pearl, shivering, the snow swirling around her disheveled beauty as she stands wrapped in some chivalrous or besotted man's coat. She winks at me as she rubs her goose-bumped arms, and the last swirls of that little pill she gave me a while ago numb the edges of what just happened, turning it from near tragedy to a bonding moment. Another shared experience, a story to tell.

The bouncer pulls me roughly to my feet, and Copper hands me my feathered shirt and high black boots.

"This," the bouncer says grimly, "is why we don't allow underage, overprivileged Center brats inside. You can wait in my office for the Greenshirts to come and make a report." He pushes me along before him, but adds, a little sympathetically I think, "It's heated."

As soon as we're in the tiny (but blessedly warm) office, Pearl draws herself up with dignity and says, "May we have privacy please?" in a tone that sounds much more like a command than a request. "We'd like to put ourselves together before the Greenshirts come."

The bouncer looks uncertain, but I give him my most pathetic, bedraggled look—which believe me isn't hard at the moment—and he says, "I'll be right outside."

As soon as he's gone, Pearl says, "There's no bikking way I'm waiting around for the Greenshirts to charge us and drag us back to Oaks."

"I thought you said we wouldn't get in much trouble if they caught us," I say, my voice hoarse. My throat hurts, feeling like it has been scraped raw.

Pearl rolls her eyes. "I didn't think we'd be caught. And we haven't. No one has scanned our eyes, no one has the slightest clue who we are. All we have to do is get out of here—"

"Past the huge guy guarding the door," I interrupt, but she ignores me.

"And slip back into Oaks, and no one will be any the wiser. We'll be in bed before anyone knows we're gone. The Oaks party is surely still raging. It's still a few hours until dawn, and you know it will last through breakfast." She yawns, covering her mouth with the back of her hand. "I know, I must be getting old! You girls can go back to the party if you like." As she's granting permission, I notice she's looking at the other two, not me.

"Yeah, but how are we going to get out of here?" Lynx asks.

Now Pearl is looking at me. "Come on, Yarrow. It's up to you."

Me? What am I supposed to do? Fight the guard? Feign a medical emergency? Wait a minute . . . emergency. There's a fire suppression system, and every room should have a switch to activate the alarm. If I can just . . . There it is! Without thinking, I pull the little lever and immediately a blaring alarm sounds throughout the whole building. I hear screams and pounding footsteps, and we burst out of the door into a frantic crowd. Over their heads I see the furious face of the bouncer—he knows full well we were the ones who pulled the alarm—but he can't reach us through the masses of screaming people.

The second we're sure we're safe we burst into giggles, and Pearl is hugging me. "Quick thinking, Yarrow!" I beam under her praise. Soon we're out of the building and home free.

Or so we think. Suddenly there are Greenshirts in the street. "The wet one with the feathers," the bouncer shouts to the officers, pointing to me. I guess my outfit was the easiest to describe.

"Come on," I say, grabbing Pearl and pulling her in the opposite direction. The Greenshirts are delayed by the crowd pouring out from the party, and the holdup gives us a chance to get around the corner.

"What are we going to do?" Copper pants as we run in our heels and wet, clinging clothes. "We can't outrun them."

Pearl pauses for breath. "One of us can. Yarrow, you run for the school team. You're the only one of us with a shot at getting away. Listen, we'll hide, and you lure them away."

I don't like that idea at all. "No! Let's go. If we hurry maybe we can . . ."

She silences me with a look. "I'm disappointed in you, Yarrow. I'd do it for you."

Some part of me is dying to believe that's true, so I let them hide in an alleyway . . . and charge at top speed directly toward the Greenshirts. This better be worth it.

When they round the corner, I come at them like a missile, so fast they stagger back and make futile grabs for me. In a second they're after me, their boots pounding. They seem to have forgotten there were four of us. I'm the closest target, and they probably figure that if they catch me, I'll give up the names of my friends. Ha! Not even if they tortured me.

I'm a little scared, and my feet hurt in these ridiculous

shoes. But at the same time, I feel strangely exhilarated. With my blood thrumming through my veins and my legs and arms pumping as fast as they can go, I feel completely alive.

We run through the streets of Eden, and though I'm faster than they are, my clothes and shoes keep hampering me. After a while they start gaining on me. I feel like it is only a matter of time before they close the distance.

I dash down a side street, thinking I can lose them. It's not until I'm all the way down the dim road that I realize it's a dead end. I'm trapped! Can I turn and get back to the open street before they realize where I've gone? No, there's no time. They're standing in the alley entrance. Not running now. They know there's nowhere I can go.

I can't let them catch me! This certainty envelops me, overwhelms me. I don't know why it means so much to me not to be caught. My mom will be mad, sure, but she's the chief of intelligence. She can sweep this under the rug and there won't be any record of the incident by tomorrow morning. But for some reason I feel like something truly terrible will befall me if the Greenshirts catch me.

The street level part of the nearest building is done in the popular style of faux stone that looks as rustic as an old farmhouse back in the pre-fail days. The dozens of higher stories are made of the same photovoltaic, energy-generating material that coats nearly all buildings in Eden. But the decorative lower parts are picturesque.

And climbable.

There's an open window about twenty feet up. My stomach seems to flip-flop. I want to be at school, safe. I want to go back to the Snow Festival and listen to Hawk call me beautiful, even though I don't care about him. I want everything to be easy and normal and safe.

But there's no other choice, besides surrender.

I begin to pull myself up the wall. It is simultaneously the hardest and the easiest thing I've ever done. My body, strong and flexible, seems to know exactly what to do, my fingertips digging effortlessly into the tiny cracks. Yet with every move something inside me screams *No! Go back!* I'm afraid I'm going to fall, but it's even more than that. It's like there is a special kind of mental gravity pulling me down, that I have to fight with every inch I rise.

Below me, the Greenshirts are shouting at me to come down. One suggests stunning me. Another points out that if I lose consciousness I'll fall, and that just means more paperwork for them. Post guards on the doors and wait me out, another logically says.

Finally I make it to the window. I'm sweating, and my heart is racing, even though my muscles aren't at all tired. I shove it open wider, so that I can fit through, and slither into a dark, empty room. My stomach lurches again. It seems so far down to the hard pavement. I could have fallen, broken a leg, died. Looking down, I give the Greenshirts a little wave.

I wonder if they waited for me all night down there. Apparently they didn't notice when I went to the roof and leaped to another rooftop. From there I just took an elevator down and slipped away into the night.

IT TAKES A lot to make Pearl look absolutely shocked. I manage to do it just by walking into class the next morning.

She's lounging in her Egg. All I can see of her are her long bare legs sticking out, elegantly crossed. Half the class flocks around her. They lean toward her like sunflowers yearn for the sun, all bowing toward her radiance. No one even sees me at first, so I get to hear what she's saying.

About me.

"I don't know what's going on in that poor girl's head," Pearl says. "First she makes that hysterical, unfounded accusation against Hawk." There are murmurs of sympathy around her.

What? I feel my face flush. *She's* the one who insisted that I lie about Hawk. The shame I felt when he gave me that look of hurt confusion still burns inside of me.

"And then when we were in the Temple, she starts raving about needing to escape, to be free. Next thing we know, she's gone. I figured she went back to her room, but this morning I heard that she actually snuck out of Oaks! Can you imagine? Now no one will tell me if my best friend is rotting in jail or sent home to her family or, I don't know, expelled from Oaks and sent to Kalahari School!"

They laugh, as if going to that good but second-tier school is a fate worse than jail.

"You know," Pearl says with a cloying kind of sympathy I recognize, the sweet act she can put on so well when it suits he purposes, "I really think Yarrow might be becoming a little bit unbalanced. Poor thing."

My jaw clenches until it hurts, my back teeth grinding. I can't believe she's saying these things about me, making me out to be crazy. Practically criminal. I understand that she's doing it to cover their tracks, so that no one will suspect that she and the others went out last night. But does she have to malign me like that?

And then it hits me. No one will tell her what happened to her best friend. *Best friend.*

I feel like a glacier melts within me, flooding me with warm emotion. Like I'm a synthmesc addict getting a fix. A button has been pushed somewhere deep within me. It is utterly surprising and completely soothing. Like love. Like food when you're starving.

Not that I've ever been starving. Or been in love, for that matter.

I forgive Pearl instantly. I would do anything for her, follow her anywhere. Because I'm her best friend. My face loses its flush and my jaw has unclenched by the time I saunter up and say, as if nothing in the world is amiss, "Good morning. Miss me?" I cast Pearl a slow, mysterious smile just as our professor tells us to enter our Eggs so our Eco-history lesson can begin.

The rest of the class goes to their Eggs, but Pearl just stands there, her mouth open, for an awkward few seconds after everyone else is seated. "How?" she mouths. She looks almost

annoyed, as if my returning apparently unscathed is a feat so
momentous only *she* should have been able to pull it off.

"After class," I whisper back, and slip into my own Egg.
Immediately, my pod lights up with our lesson for the day:
pollination. I'm in a field of virtual wildflowers, at the center
of a seemingly endless meadow. The Egg creates a perfect
environment, the toasty sun that warms my shoulders tem-
pered by a cool, gentle breeze. A butterfly in vibrant orange
and black stripes flutters around my head before landing
on my arm. I can feel the tickle of its tiny feet. Nearby, a
fat honeybee dusty with pollen lands on a golden flower, its
weight bending the stem. It sips at nectar, bobbing up and
down. Around me I hear the hum of a hundred other bees.
Bees that have been extinct from even before the Ecofail.

"By 2010," my professor says, "humans realized that
many of the pesticides they used were dangerous for bees."
His droning voice seems to meld with the buzzing bees in the
virtual world within my Egg. "Many were killed, and those
that survived were so weakened that the hives succumbed to
fungal invasions and colony collapse. By 2070, no species of
colonial bees survived. Although scientists engineered robotic
bees, they could not . . ."

He breaks off suddenly. "Yes? Can I help you?"

I lean my head out from the paradise of the sunny
meadow back into the chilly, bare reality of the classroom to
see what the interruption is. The artificial sun still beats on
my lower back, but when I see the cause of the disturbance I
feel a chill down my spine.

It's a girl. Just a girl, with an ordinary face and long, fine,
lilac-colored hair. I seem to hear Pearl's voice in the back of
my mind mocking her for her unfashionable color, the way
she did me yesterday. But Pearl's voice is only a distant whisper behind the sudden roaring in my ears. It sounds like the

ocean. I've been surrounded by simulated ocean noise in my Egg during lessons, but this time it is coming from inside my head. It grows louder as I look at her, vibrating like seismic shock waves.

And then it fades, and I feel calm. No, not calm. Empty.

I look at her objectively, sizing her up as if she were prey. Easy prey. Clothes that are well made but not exquisite. She comes from money—of course, if she's here—and can shop at the best stores. But she doesn't have the connections to buy custom creations from the best designers. The style is unusual, maybe even interesting, a dress with a handkerchief hem in spring-leaf yellow-green that has a gauzy overlay embroidered with the oak and tendril pattern. But it is nothing that Pearl would wear, so I dismiss it as substandard.

Her hair is long with a careless wave, the ends tumbling unevenly. The fashion at Oaks is for razor-cut hair with defined blunt lines. My blond hair is cut in asymmetrical stair steps. This girl's looks wild by comparison, like a meadow compared to a manicured landscape. Her mother probably cuts it for her.

Her face is . . .

I can't look at her face. That roaring sound threatens to return.

I shake my head hard to clear it. Maybe I'm getting a cold, and my head and ears are congested. Colds are rare in Eden. We've been vaccinated against almost everything, but the simple cold keeps mutating beyond our power to completely block it. Yes, that must be why I feel so strange. A cold.

I slip back into my Egg. Whoever this girl is, she clearly doesn't matter.

I let the virtual meadow fill my senses, waiting for class to resume. The professor is fluttering uncertainly. He wasn't expecting a new student. There's not a spare Egg.

"You can share for now," he says. "Pearl, will you . . ."

"No," she says loudly and clearly.

The professor makes a garbled sound of confusion. Only Pearl would be brazen enough to flatly refuse. I stifle a chuckle. I almost feel sorry for the professor. Not the new girl, though. Everything about her screams that she clearly doesn't belong here at Oaks.

"Yarrow," the professor asks a little helplessly. "Would you be so kind as to share your Egg with . . . what was your name again?"

"Lark," says a low, warm voice. I feel suddenly dizzy. So dizzy that I don't manage more than a croak, which the professor apparently takes for assent. I'm definitely coming down with something.

I don't even look as the girl slides in beside me. I move over as far as I can, but we're still almost touching. I can feel the warmth of her body along my thigh.

"Hi," she murmurs. Her breath tickles my hair. Bikking annoying! I stare straight ahead.

I can feel her looking at me. I'd like to tell her off, but I'll get in trouble if I interrupt class. I'm lucky enough to have escaped discipline last night. I can feel prickles of sweat start at the back of my neck, under my arms.

"My name is Lark," she whispers, and suddenly I can't take it anymore. My stomach heaves. If I don't leave now, I'm going to be embarrassingly sick.

"Move!" I cry, and before she can shift I shove her out so she sprawls on the floor, the zigzag hem of her skirt flying up over her knees. I don't care, I don't look back. I just have to get away. As I race out of the classroom, I hear Pearl say, "Well done." She thinks I'm putting on a show, telling the world that I won't be forced to sit next to some newly rich nobody. Humiliating this Lark girl. Pearl is proud of me. I feel a little warm glow beneath the feverish prickles, but I can't enjoy it. I race to my room, and as soon as I get there I'm violently sick.

Afterward, I lie on my bed with one arm flung over my forehead. My heart is racing. My friends come to check on me in the break between classes.

"How did you do it?" Pearl asks in naked admiration as she flops down on the edge of my bed. "Why aren't you expelled?" No *Are you okay?* No *How do you feel?* I scoot over to give her more room.

"Yeah," Lynx says. "I was sure we'd never see you again." She smirks, and I smile back with dangerous sweetness.

"You'd like that, wouldn't you, Lynx?" My nausea and dizziness have passed, and I feel better now. No, not just better. Different. Stronger.

"So . . . spill!" Copper insists.

I start to tell my story, but almost right away Pearl starts to look bored. She even yawns. The second I'm done she says, "Well, that's over now." I can tell the attention has been on me for far too long. "Come on, break's almost over. Ugh, Yarrow, you look horrible!" I run to the mirror, but I look the same as ever. Asymmetrically cut blond hair, strong jaw, high cheekbones, flat silvery eyes. I squint at my reflection. Do I look different? Maybe. I can't tell how, though. Nothing outward has changed.

"Yeah, Yarrow," Lynx sneers. "No more partying for you for a while. You look like a totally different person."

"Hurry up," Pearl says, going to the door. Expecting us to follow, as always. "We're going to be late."

I take one more look in the mirror, searching for any subtle difference, wrongness. No, I'm just me. Who else could I be? I smile confidently into the mirror. "I see you, Yarrow," I whisper to my reflection, then trot obediently after Pearl.

PEARL IS THE kind of girl who needs a project. When she is in charge of Eden—as I'm sure she will be—she'll be blissfully happy because there will always be huge, seemingly impossible projects for her to accomplish. In Oaks, though, she has to invent her own projects. Schoolwork is time-consuming but not exactly challenging. With a combination of intelligence and a network of people more than willing to help us on projects or even do our homework for us, the academic part of Oaks never really forces us to rise to the occasion.

So this beautiful bundle of energy and ambition is always searching for some new obstacle to overcome, some enemy to thwart. Sometimes her goals are risky, like when she talked us all into sneaking out last night. Other times they are frivolous, like when she lobbied to make high heels part of the mandatory dress code. But she is never happier than when she begins a campaign to make somebody's life miserable. Like a pre-fail cat toying with a mouse, she chooses her victims for her own amusement, usually more on a whim than through any fault of their own.

Now, for whatever reason, she has taken a violent dislike to the new girl Lark. It is hate at first sight.

I have to admit, Lark has certainly sparked some extreme feelings in me, too.

"I asked around," Pearl tells us at lunch, "and you're never going to believe where she comes from. She's an outer circle!"

"Everyone's from the outer circles compared to us," Copper says complacently as she picks at her noodles. Pearl gives her a lingering look of scorn, and I think that Copper isn't going to be a member of our group for much longer.

"I don't just mean the Third or Fourth Circle," Pearl says. "I mean the actual slums. Her mother is some supplies manager, and her father!" she chortles, and we all lean forward, desperate to know. She makes us wait for a long moment before she finally says gleefully, "He works in the sewers!"

As it turns out, Lark's father has actually risen through the ranks of wastewater management until becoming in charge of the entire water reclamation project for all of Eden. When you think about it, that's an important job. Eden is a closed system. We have all of the untainted water left on the planet, and it has to last us for hundreds of years more, until the world has healed enough for us to return to it. Without men like Lark's father getting filthy in underground pipes, Eden wouldn't survive. So, not glamorous, but vital nonetheless.

Of course I don't say this. I hardly even think it. All I can envision is a vast pool of sludge, and a deep feeling of revulsion at the thought of anyone having to dive into it. Ugh.

Lynx pounces on Pearl's indignation, taking her side right away. "That's disgusting!" she says, actually sliding closer to Pearl. The subtle dance of power. "Do you know, I thought she smelled weird. The stink of the family occupation must never wash off." She leans into Pearl as they laugh together. Copper chuckles obediently, her mind clearly elsewhere.

I say nothing at first.

I didn't smell anything bad when Lark was squeezed into

my Egg beside me. She smelled like a warm field of sweet clover.

Pearl snaps her fingers in front of my face. "Well? Don't you agree?"

Lost in my reverie, I've missed some important part of the conversation. "Of course," I say, wondering what I've just agreed to.

"Then it's settled," Pearl says. "We're getting that sewer rat out of Oaks and back into the outer circles where she belongs."

"How?" I ask.

"Time will tell," Pearl says. "Maybe we get her expelled. Maybe we make her so miserable she begs to leave." She chuckles. "Maybe we make her go the way of Cinnamon."

I suck in my breath. Cinnamon was before my time, but of course I've heard about her. She was a senior when Pearl first came to Oaks as a freshman. Cinnamon was the queen of the school, the Pearl of her generation. I don't know exactly what happened. Maybe she insulted Pearl. Maybe Pearl hated her just for existing, for being in a spot she coveted. Whatever the reason, Pearl wasn't there a month before Cinnamon hurled herself off the roof of the science lab. Sure, it was only two stories, but she smashed her legs and had to be in traction for a year. She never came back to Oaks. Never did much of anything after that, according to rumor. No one knows what Pearl did to her, but everyone knows she made it happen.

All because Pearl took a dislike to her.

Now it is Lark's turn.

"We need to find out more about her," Pearl says as she lays out her plans. "Get into her heart and soul, find out what her dreams are . . . so we can crush them!" She splays her fingers and then tightens them suddenly into a vicious fist. It looks like a parody of the holy Sign of the Seed. Instead of new life sprouting, she's destroying it.

"So I've decided," she declares in her imperial manner, "that one of us will have to befriend her. Not me, of course." She gives a disdainful laugh. "Now, who shall it be?"

She appraises us one at a time. "Not you, Copper. You're so soft you'd probably wind up actually liking that outer circle piece of trash." She turns to Lynx. "You have an uncanny knack for insinuating yourself into groups." Lynx beams . . . until she catches what Pearl really means. She stiffens as Pearl goes on. "You'll say absolutely anything to make the person in charge like you, won't you, little Lynxie?" She gives Lynx an I-see-right-through-you smile. Pearl likes having followers, but she wants them to know she's aware of their fawning tricks. I'm glad Lynx doesn't have her fooled.

Finally, Pearl turns to me. "Yarrow," she says, and lets my name hang there.

In my head I fill in everything she could say about me. I adore her, I would follow her on any of her adventures, do anything she asked. She knows this, and also knows that I analyze this trait in myself, question it, am always tempted to resist it, but can't. Lynx is easy to figure out. She sees a hierarchy and wants to be as high as possible on it. In me, though, Pearl doesn't see ambition. What, then? A minion she might not always be able to control? A tool that could at any moment become a weapon? I don't think she quite knows what she sees.

Sometimes, when I look at myself, neither do I.

"Lynx should definitely do it," I say. Lynx looks at me suspiciously, wondering why I'd lay something good in her lap. "Lark and I didn't exactly get off to a good start. I don't think she'll buy it if I'm suddenly nice to her."

I really don't want to do it, even for Pearl. I keep remembering the roaring in my ears, a sound from within that seemed to drown out all thought. Just picturing Lark's face makes me feel nauseous again.

But then I remember how I felt right after the sickness passed. Stronger, clearer, as if something unnecessary had been stripped away.

And that warm meadow smell of her . . .

"No, it should be you, Yarrow. Find her in the next class, apologize, and ask her to share your Egg. You'll see. A girl like that will be so desperate for friends and acceptance that she'll forget all about how you treated her and latch right on. You'll have her eating out of your hand."

What choice do I have but to agree?

I decide to be straightforward, and for the most part tell the truth. At the last class of the day I make a beeline for Lark and look her straight in the eyes with a big smile. "I'm sorry, you caught me on a bad day. I would have snapped at my best friend earlier, sick as I felt. But now I've gotten it all out of my system." I mime vomiting, deciding that being gross will make me more accessible. Lark gives a nervous laugh. "Anyway, please forgive me. I feel better now, and if you want to share my Egg for this class I promise I won't shove you out . . . or throw up on you!"

I hold out my hand, and though I see her own twitch toward it, she hesitates.

"Do you . . . remember me?" she whispers.

I search her eyes. Is she serious? While the primary qualification for Oaks is money and family, they also have reasonably high academic standards and they wouldn't let in someone who is absolutely feebleminded. "Uh, yeah? We met before lunch. I'm Yarrow."

She sighs gently, and finally holds out her hand. "Just checking," she says with a quirky little half smile that makes me think of a small, hopeful animal. I take her hand . . . and electricity jolts up my arm. At least, that's the way it seems. I let go quickly, gasping, and look down at my hand. For a terrible disjointed moment I don't recognize my own skin. I know it like the back of my hand, people say, but whose hand is this? My palm tingles where Lark touched it. I hear the roaring again, quietly this time, a distant background ocean noise. A hint of nausea returns, but it doesn't seem to originate in my stomach. It seems to be in my head. I feel a throbbing behind my eyes, pulsing painfully in time to my heartbeat.

"Are you okay?" Lark asks.

I shake my head, more to clear it than to say no, and try to force a smile. It must look ghastly, because Lark says, "Don't worry. I won't hold you to that promise not to throw up on me." She slides into the Egg, and though part of me wants to flee to my room again, I follow her.

"Where did we leave off yesterday, class?" our Earth Stewardship instructor says. "Ah yes, hydraulic fracturing, known as fracking. Humans used to think that earthquakes were caused by the gods wielding lightning bolts and magic hammers and whatnot." He gives a chuckle at mankind's ignorance. "Later, they learned that earthquakes were natural phenomena. Science prevailed. And then . . . science went too far. To extract the riches of the Earth they injected liquid deep underground. Not only did this result in contamination of the water supply, it also did what once only gods or nature could accomplish: it made earthquakes. Imagine—man-made earthquakes! Humans became so powerful they could change the Earth itself. He settles back for a snooze and lets our Eggs take over. We watch—experience—the equipment that sent pressurized liquid into the planet's very heart. We see streams turn black, plants die. And finally, we feel the Earth tremble up as if it were attempting to shrug humans off its very crust.

The Egg starts to vibrate, and projects loud cracking sounds like snapping bone. A foul sulfur smell fills my nostrils. I can hear students in other Eggs exclaiming in quick fear, followed by laughter when they remember this is just virtual reality. Suddenly Lark grabs my hand. "It's starting," she says under her breath. "I can feel it . . ."

"It's okay," I tell her, squeezing her fingers. "It's not real. A real earthquake doesn't feel at all like this."

"It's not that," she gasps, her eyes wild and desperate. "It's . . ." The juddering stops, the Egg is still. Lark exhales in a deep sigh. "I have a condition. Epilepsy. When the Egg started shaking I thought it was starting. We didn't have Eggs at my last school."

"Why did you change schools?" I ask, curious even beyond Pearl's assignment.

"I . . . My father got transferred to the Center, and I begged to be allowed to come here. My family didn't think it was worth the money, but I got them to agree to one semester, as a trial."

"But why?" I press.

"Well, doesn't everyone want to go to Oaks?" She shrugs as if it is obvious.

"I wouldn't think so," I say. "I'd think someone like you might have a hard time fitting in, making friends." I say it without malice, straightforwardly.

"Oh, don't worry about me," she says, I think with more confidence than she actually feels. "I can fit in anywhere. And I don't need friends, plural. If I get out of Oaks with just *one* friend, I'll be happy." Her gaze is so intense that I have to look away.

Our instructor is engaging us now that our Eggs have stopped their show. "Now that you've experienced an earthquake for yourself, can you imagine the magnitude of what our ancestors must have been doing, to induce such a dramatic . . ."

Without thinking, I interrupt him. "But that didn't feel at all like an earthquake," I say, leaning out of my Egg. "The last one didn't quiver like that. The whole ground lifted up, like the Earth was taking a giant breath. And it was quiet. Like all of Eden was waiting to see what would happen next. At least, it was quiet until things started falling."

I see almost every head lean out of its Egg and turn to look at me.

The professor looks confused. "The *last* earthquake? You mean, the last one you learned about in an Egg?"

"No," I say impatiently. "The last earthquake. The one that happened . . ." I break off. How long ago was it? For a moment I remembered it so clearly, the way the ground lurched up, knocking my legs out from under me. The way the very air seemed to cleave in two.

"My dear," he says. "There has never been an earthquake in your lifetime, or mine. Not in the whole history of Eden. The last earthquake felt by a human was before the Ecofail."

"But . . . ," I begin. I narrow my eyes, looking inward, searching memories that are dimmer than ever. I remember the way it felt. I remember the terror. I remember . . . trees falling. Trees? How can that be? There are no trees left on Earth.

Everyone is looking at me so strangely, like I've just lost my mind. Everyone except Pearl, who seems to be analyzing me, no doubt thinking this is some weird ploy to get into Lark's confidence.

If it was, I couldn't have planned it better. I duck back into my Egg, my cheeks flushed pink, my mind in confused turmoil. That's when Lark whispers ticklishly into my ear, "I remember the earthquake, too. You're not crazy."

I refuse to look at her. I'm breathing so hard I feel like my chest will explode. Then she adds something that makes me feel weak and strong all at once.

"You're not alone, Ro."

6

"WHY DID YOU call me that?" I'm trembling, and I think it must be with rage. What else could it be?

"It's your name," she says simply.

"My name is Yarrow," I insist. In the pre-fail days when there were billions of people, humans had last names. They had big families and worried about succession. Now, with only one child per couple and few family connections, we only have first names, which seems to make them more precious, more personal. I don't want someone corrupting the only name I have.

"Sure, and Ro is a pretty nickname. Can I call you that?"

"No," I snap, but I want to hear that name on her tongue again, a thousand times. It feels like a caress. "Stop talking to me. You're going to get us in trouble." I stare straight ahead for the rest of class, but when we rise I catch Pearl's eye and she gives a meaningful jut of her chin that means I better implement the rest of our plan: get Lark outside of Oaks tonight.

I don't want to do it. Without having any idea what Pearl's actual plan is, I know it is going to be something bad. Humiliating at the very least, and at the worst . . . I think of those rumors about Cinnamon.

But then it occurs to me, an inspiration. I can ask Lark out somewhere tonight, and then keep her to myself. I don't have to let Pearl do whatever she's planning.

It feels like a revelation. Ever since the first moment of meeting Pearl, when she almost instantly co-opted me, I've felt a visceral urge to please her. I feel twinges of that same sensation for the headmaster, Brother Birch, and also for the professors to a lesser extent. When I visit her, I feel it for my mom. It is a desire, a yearning, a hunger, to make these people happy. Perhaps for the first time, I question it. What did they do to deserve to be made happy by me? What is it about gratifying their whims that gives me pleasure?

Now, warring with that impulse, is a sudden mad desire to please myself. (But you have been happy, a little voice whispers in my head. You've had everything you've ever wanted, all your life. Why make waves?)

"Lark," I say suddenly, too loudly.

"Yes, Yarrow," she answers in her gentle voice.

"Come out with me tonight." I phrase it like a command, and hope she finds she can't refuse. "With us, I mean. We all have passes from our parents. Can you get one?"

Any other girl in Oaks would say yes instantly, shocked to be invited into our clique, eager not to let the chance slip away. But Lark looks hesitant. "It's my first day."

"Exactly. This is your chance to have a little fun, and make some new friends."

Lark glances outside the Egg. "Somehow I don't think a lot of people are competing to be my friend," she says, though it doesn't seem to bother her. Plenty of girls pretend they don't care, but you can feel their hunger to belong. Not Lark. She cares about something, though. I can feel it. Exactly what it is, I don't know.

"Thought you said you'd be happy with just one friend," I counter.

"Depends on the friend," she says, but slides me a sly little sidelong smile.

"So is that a yes?"

"Perhaps," she replies, and says nothing more for the rest of class.

I decide that "perhaps" is the worst word ever.

That night, though, I dress carefully. Perhaps might be a *no*, but I'm going to be prepared for a *yes*. I want to look beautiful, but not like I'm trying, or I care. I feel like one of those needy, desperate girls who will do anything to hide their desperation. This isn't me.

I look in the mirror at my carefully made-up face. I've darkened my eyebrows too much. They don't go with my blond hair. This isn't me.

Instead of wiping the makeup off of my eyebrows, I tear through a jumble of discarded accessories until I find that hair alteration wand that Pearl despises. I stare at my refection, at the blond hair in its chiseled stair-step cut. It doesn't look right, doesn't suit my dark complexion. I stare closer. Right at the hairline I see a hint of dark shadow. Frowning, I peer closer. It almost looks like my hair is growing in darker, like I have deep brown, almost black roots.

I laugh and pull away, blinking my eyes. They feel dry all the time these days. At my last checkup (I always have them at the Center, when I visit my Mom, with their on-site doctor) I asked if my lens implants could be causing the irritation. "Nonsense," he said. "You've had them since you were a few months old. They bonded with your neural network long ago. They're part of you now, and couldn't cause irritation." But even though I douse them with drops, they stay red and irritated. Sometimes my vision even goes blurry for a few seconds.

The weird illusion with my imaginary roots must just be a trick of light and shadow, I think. But it has given me an idea.

Why do an exotic color when I can do something more natural looking? The effect will be just as striking because it is so different. So even though I can almost hear Pearl's disapproval in my ear, I start running the color wand over my fair hair.

I like the result.

A few more touches—a matte rosy earth tone on my lips, a fine line of gold painted along my upper lashes—and I'm satisfied.

Yes, this is me. At last.

I should go straight to Pearl, but instead I go in search of Lark. I have to ask one of the servants where her dorm in. Turns out she got squeezed into a makeshift space that used to be the common room of three other girls who share a suite. They apparently aren't ready to give up their space without a fight. There's Lark's bed and desk shoved against the far wall, but the usual sofas, cushions, datablocks, strewed clothes, and food wrappers are still dominating the room. The other residents are sprawled around, taking up space deliberately so Lark can't have any.

She's sitting on her bed, ignored, perched on a corner with her chin resting on her tucked-up knees, curled as if she, too, wants to take up as little space as possible. At first she doesn't see me, and I watch the strange way she stares at nothing so intensely. I didn't think she was much when I first saw her, because she doesn't have Pearl's flashy beauty. No, Lark's beauty is more subtle, a beauty of line, of expression. Without any makeup or extravagant clothes, with only the curve of her lip, the shadow on her cheek, she achieves something that surpasses even Pearl. It is something simple and sublime.

Even those twin frown lines creased between her eyebrows look pretty. No one else at Oaks has them. No one ever worries about anything very important, for very long.

Finally she sees me, and her face lights up, instantly incandescent. "Your hair!" she gasps, clearly delighted, and I smile, hugely, unthinkingly, as if her approval was my only goal. "I love it, Ro! It's so exactly you."

She smiles at me, and I want to do things for her, help her, save her.

"You!" I snap, whirling around to face her roommates. "Get up and move those pillows out of here. And you, throw that junk away. This is Lark's room now." It is thrilling to use my power. I am an extension of Pearl, and even though they make surly faces they know better than to disobey me. Reluctantly, they get up and start clearing the room.

"Ro, you don't have to . . . ," Lark begins, but I shush her.

"I know I don't have to," I say loftily. "I never do anything I don't want to do." I wave my hands in a *hurry up* gesture to the girls, and they scurry.

"They're sheep," I say as they leave. "Have you read about sheep in Eco-history class? Passive herd animals that brainlessly follow their leader. I'm just making sure they remember I'm their leader." Well, vice leader, after Pearl.

Lark cocks her head at me in a piquantly birdlike movement. "But . . . wouldn't that make you just another sheep?" she asks. Pearl would take offense. Pearl would decide to destroy her then and there (if she hadn't already). I stop and think.

"We're all sheep," I say, at last admitting something to her I would never say to another person at Oaks. "We all want a path to follow. Oaks people just have a higher path. If we have to be shepherd, might as well be the lead sheep."

Lark bites her lip for a second. "But what if you could be the sheepdog?"

"The what?"

"The one outside the sheep, guiding them. The one who steers them away from dangers."

"The one who does their thinking for them?" I ask.

"Maybe. Until the sheep remember that they can think for themselves."

A moment of silence hangs between us. Finally, when it becomes awkward and uncomfortable, I force a laugh and say, "Come on, get dressed. Let's go out."

"I am dressed," she says. "This is what I'm wearing." She's wearing a simple yellow dress that leaves her arms bare, and woven tan sandals.

I shrug, feeling the old cruelty creep back. "Whatever. No one will be looking at you anyway." I hate myself as I walk away. She still follows.

Though as it turns out I'm right, because when I bring her to Pearl's bedroom Pearl ignores her like she doesn't exist and says, "Yarrow, great Earth, what have you done to your hair? It's so . . . so dark and dull!" She tosses her own hair as if some shade of silvery white is the only acceptable color.

"Yeah, Yarrow, what were you thinking?" Lynx begins, then her hand involuntarily goes to her own brown locks. She bleached her hair to match Pearl's once, but Pearl made her change it back.

"I don't know," I say, going to one of Pearl's many mirrors to check it out again. "I think it looks interesting. Different."

"Sure, if you call *boring* different," Pearl says. "Go change it back. This party we're going to tonight is special."

"Special how?" I ask, still looking at my hair. I push it away from my face, twine the blunt edges around my fingers to soften them. "You mean, security is actually going to let us into this one?"

I speak without thinking, and the look of sudden malice I catch over my shoulder in Pearl's reflected face feels like a slap. She has herself under control by the time I turn away from the mirror, but I can see the aggressive tension in her narrowed eyes. What I said was perilously close to criticism. Which is itself dangerously close to a challenge.

She decides to let it go, for now, though no doubt I'll pay in some way later. "Hello . . . what was your name again? Lake?"

"Lark," she tries to say, but Pearl talks right over her.

"I'm so glad you're not one of those girls who doesn't follow tradition. Do you know, there are actually some newcomers who refuse to hand over their credit chips? Can you imagine? When the tradition goes all the way back to the founding of Oaks." She holds out her hand, and for a baffled moment Lark extends hers as if to shake it. Pearl wiggles her fingers dismissively. "Your credit chip. Hand it over."

"Why?" I ask, for Lark.

Pearl manages to roll her eyes and flash me a warning look at the same time. "Duh, stupid. You know that new students always treat whoever takes them out on their first night. It's tradition." She stands up very straight, prim and proper. "And where would we be without tradition?"

So that's her scheme for the night, I think. She wants to fleece Lark of as much money as she can, knowing full well that her parents probably only just make enough money to afford Oaks. And Pearl really knows how to run up a tab. Private room, top shelf drinks, exotic entertainment—all charged to Lark. She'll run through her funds in minutes, charge the rest to her credit, and her parents will have to pay for it all. They'll probably be so mad they take her out of Oaks as soon as the bill comes.

It's a clever scheme, if Lark is weak enough to hand over her credit chip.

She does.

My hand twitches out to stop her, but then I think . . . no. Remember Cinnamon. Remember all the horrible things

Pearl has done to people, all the truly terrible torments she could dream up. Making Lark spend all of her money is relatively tame by comparison.

So with Pearl watching narrowly for my reaction, I decide to go along with it and pull my hand back. "Yeah, that's tradition. What can you do?" I shrug.

I'll pay for it all, I promise silently. My family has more than enough money to cover without flinching whatever damage Pearl can do tonight. It is nothing to a family like mine. Pearl will think she's won. Won't she be surprised when Lark is still here at Oaks.

Pearl grins like a satisfied cat, and says to me again, "Go change your hair so we can get out of here."

"No," I say.

"What?" It's like she genuinely doesn't understand me. I can tell the sudden disconnect between expectations and reality has jarred her. It's funny, really, though I keep a straight face.

"I like it this way," I say blandly. "I'm keeping it."

Pearl opens her mouth, then abruptly snaps it shut. It would be beneath her dignity to argue with me. But she'll remember.

"Let's go," she says brightly, pocketing Lark's credit chip. "This is going to be a night we'll never forget."

PEARL IS RIGHT, we have no trouble getting in. One look at her, and we're waved past scarlet ropes and escorted to the elevator by an adorable roller-skating girl dressed as a chipmunk. The host, it turns out, is a family friend, the fabulously wealthy playboy son of one of Pearl's family's closest associates. Who cares that they made their money in the last twenty years by shady deals and black marketeering? Their money has been made legitimate by its sheer size. Petty criminals go to jail. Gargantuan criminals move to the inner circles. Especially when they know how to spend all that money with style.

The elevator rises to the penthouse ballroom, and we step out into a giddy maelstrom of light and sound.

Pearl claps her hands. "A carnival!" she cries. If it had been for the populace, in the street, she would have turned her nose up at it. But since it has been assembled at fabulous expense for one night only for the privileged few, she is enchanted.

Frankly, so am I.

I've never been to a real carnival before, but this one has everything I could imagine. But bigger! Brighter! Louder!

My eyes are drawn immediately upward. The ceilings are arched and high, painted with frescoes that could stand alone in their beauty if they weren't overshadowed tonight by everything else going on. Drilled into these masterpieces are bolts and guy wires supporting a trapeze.

I feel Lark touch my arm. "Are they really wearing nothing but sequins?" she asks as the acrobatic pair swing and flip and grasp each other. It's not just a gymnastic performance, but a sensual one, too. When the muscular man catches his partner, she twines around him provocatively as they swing, clasping him around the waist with her legs, arching her back in simulated (or perhaps not) ecstasy. Across another part of the ceiling a man dressed as a fox, all in russet fur with pointed ears, steps his sprightly way across a high wire, his fuzzy paws mincing.

"What happens if they fall?" Lark asks.

There are no safety lines, no nets. The performers could die. So could whoever they land on. No one seems to think about this though. It's all part of the fun. Even I forget an instant later, my eye caught by a towering man on stilts. He wears horns, and his face is painted in a grotesque leer. He reaches up menacingly for the aerial performers, but they swing high above even his lofty grasp. Instead he reaches down for the little people below him, making them giggle and squeal as they knock each other down to evade him.

Pearl sails away from us toward the mirrored back of the huge ballroom, and her minions follow in her wake. Of course she doesn't care about Lark anymore, not directly. She has her credit chip and, as she believes, the key to her ruin. So she is going to enjoy herself.

Well then, so will I. With Lark.

With Lark beside me, my jaded eyes see all this luxury as if for the first time. The nature themes that are always so popular in Eden have been taken to expensive extremes here. I point out a girl in a fish motif. It is almost impossible to tell where her skin ends and her gown begins. Her flesh is covered in orange and gold crystals that mimic a koi's scales glittering in a sunlit pond. Somewhere around her midsection a luxurious silken material hugs her body and then swirls out in a trailing fishtail skirt.

"And there!" Lark says, drawing my attention to a man all in green, whose impeccably tailored suit suggests a slim, lithe frog. "He even brought his own lily pad!" And an underling, modestly dressed, to relocate it every time the wealthy young man wants to stand somewhere else.

Other people didn't bother with nature motifs. They just wanted to look as rich as possible. There is only a small supply of real jewels and gold in Eden, only what the initial survivors had with them, and by then of course most of them had nothing left at all. My practiced eye tells me that a good portion of those treasures are at this party tonight. Alongside them are artificial jewels, almost as expensive, even more beautiful. The entire room looks cut and faceted by a master jeweler to enhance its brilliance.

Without Pearl nearby, I feel suddenly free. No one to please. No one to judge me. No, that's not true. Lark is judging me, I can tell from the searching way she always looks at me. But I'm not afraid of her judgment. I feel like I want her to find out everything about me. Things even I don't know.

And I want to please her. I want Lark to have a fabulous night. I want her to see what money and friends and power can do. Taking her hand, I pull her into the swirl of people. "Let's dance!" I call out above the music and laughter. We become part of the carnival madness. In her simple yellow dress she looks like a meadow flower in the middle of strange orchids, but somehow this makes her seem all the more lovely.

I dance with a bare-chested boy in leather pants—but not too close because he has spikes sticking out of most parts of his body. "Is he supposed to be a cactus?" Lark asks with a giggle when I whirl away from him. Together, we dance with a young man in clown makeup, his huge painted-on frown weirdly twisted by the exuberant smile on his real lips.

All of a sudden, the music cuts off and the room goes black. Balloons start to drift down from the vaulted ceiling. No, not balloons—bubbles. Blown from some strange material, the perfect orbs glow with swirling mother-of-pearl light. I reach up to touch one, and the second my finger makes contact it explodes in an opalescent powder. I can't help breathing some in. I don't know what it is, but people around me are eagerly popping the orbs, opening their mouths greedily to eat or in-hale the glimmering dust. An easy sensation settles over me. Nothing too strong, just as if the weight of a few small woes has been lifted. It's a drug of some sort, but very mild. It makes the dark, the crowds, more comfortable.

Lark reaches her hand across the darkness to grasp mine just as a light appears at the far end of the room. A man dressed in deep violet steps up on a dais.

"Welcome to my humble abode," he begins, and is met with polite titters. He owns the top two floors of this build-ing, his home below and the ballroom above. They are easily among the most expensive properties in Eden.

"I have a few surprises for you tonight, my friends." On cue, the lights start to twinkle like rainbow stars, making the colors dance around us. They reflect off what I suddenly re-alize is a wall of mirrors. No, a mirror maze. I see the crowd reflected a hundredfold.

Colored spotlights wink on around the room, each lighting up a new treat that suddenly emerges from behind curtains or false walls. The stilt walkers and aerialists were just the beginning. The partyers *oohh* and *aahh* as he reveals a tunnel of love, a psychedelic bounce house, clear balls in which people can run and tumble and bounce into each other. I can see Pearl exclaim and clap her hands along with the rest. And yet I know for a fact that if she saw those things in a street carnival she'd mock them mercilessly, call them pathetic amusements of the masses. But because a rich man is putting it on for other rich people, she eats it up. They all do.

"But that's not all!" he says, as a row of purple lights along the wall makes an arrow shape to point to a gilded door. "Go through that door and you'll find Eden's very first roller coaster, designed from pre-fail blueprints. It starts on the roof and spirals all around the building. You can't imagine what a fuss my downstairs neighbors kicked up about that!" Those would be the slightly less rich millionaires. "But I smoothed it all over somehow." He throws back his head and laughs. "Now go and enjoy yourselves. And remember to vote for yours truly in the next election for circle governor!"

The lights come back on, and giddy people dash off to their favorite carnival activities and rides. They look like children, eager and almost innocent despite their priceless jewels and costly clothes. Maybe it is money well spent if it makes their jadedness vanish for an hour or two.

"What do you want to do first?" Lark asks. Her eyes are shining. This feels so right. I'm so grateful I've foiled Pearl's plan so we can just enjoy ourselves.

"Maybe the roller coaster?" I suggest. But when we head that way we see it is clearly the most popular, and way too crowded. "Later!" we agree in the same breath, and dash back across the room at random. We end up at the bounce house, hurling ourselves against the squishy walls with reckless abandon until we're panting and sweaty. We collapse on top of each other, laughing, and crawl out again into the party.

"Having fun?" a cool voice asks from behind us. It's Pearl, holding tall icy drinks. "Here you go," she says, thrusting the drinks at us. She leans close to me, and I notice her eyes are a little wild, her pupils dilated. She must have taken an extra deep inhale of that bubble powder. "Peace offering," she whispers into my ear.

I'm so hot from all that frenetic bouncing that I grab the glass and drink down half the red, fruity liquid right away. Lark takes hers, sips, and makes a face.

"Bottoms up!" Pearl says as she sails away again.

I gulp thirstily at the rest of my drink, and when I start cracking the ice cubes Lark laughs and hands me hers. "I don't like it much. You take it, and I'll find some water. Be right back."

I work on hers more slowly, scanning the crowd over the crystal sugared rim. (Sugar is one of the easiest things to synthesize here in Eden. No more sugarcane, but string a few carbon, hydrogen, and oxygen molecules together the right way and there you have it.) It's strange how even though I've been going to parties all my life, tonight I feel like an outsider. Like I shouldn't be in a huge, crushing crowd. Like I belong alone. It's not a feeling of inadequacy. It's just that all of a sudden I feel like my proper place is by myself. Or maybe with one special person.

Where did Lark go? Far across the huge room I think I see a flash of lilac, and I lurch in that direction. The drinks must have been stronger than I thought. All I could taste was cloying sweetness and the same artificial fruitiness that all "fruit" things have here. I dreamed of strawberries the other night. Small and plump, warm from the sun. I woke up just as I was biting into one. No one will ever know what a real strawberry tastes like.

I lose the lilac streak in the crowd, and whirl in the other direction. I'm so mad at the world all of a sudden. At stupid humans for bikking everything up. At the Earth itself for dying. Couldn't it have tried a little harder? We're just one species crawling on its surface! How did we win out over tigers and wild horses and germs and tidal waves, and all of the things so much more powerful than us?

How did we lose?

I think I see Lark, and shove past the partygoers toward the back of the ballroom. It's quieter here, but now I've lost sight of Lark, if that was even her in the first place. I turn again, and I'm looking at a strange dark-haired girl. A girl with a strong jaw, clenched tight. A girl with silvery eyes that look flat and wrong. A tall, strong girl who is being weak for some reason.

It's my own reflection. I'm in the mirror maze.

I don't want to look at that girl in the mirror. Something is off about her. So I turn back to the crowd I can see reflected behind me . . . only to find that they're *all* me. I'm surrounded by mirrors. They cast back a million images of infinity, with my face bouncing back and forth from mirror to mirror, smaller and smaller the closer I look, until I seem to shrink away to nothing at all.

I stagger backward, but the mirrors are all around me. Prickles of nervous sweat dot my neck and face. I start to run, but there's nowhere to go. Everywhere I turn, I'm heading toward myself. Like I'm dashing into the arms of a lover, I run to an image of my own outstretched arms, only to crash into cold glass. I turn, and turn again, and there's only me, me, me. My panicked face looks grotesque as I stumble, feeling with my hands against the mirrors, trying to determine what is real, what is lifeless image. My sweaty palms leave smears on the glass.

I try to force myself to calm down, but my heart goes at such a furious pace it feels more like a buzz than distinct beats. I keep thinking I see reflections of people behind me,

even though I'm sure I'm alone right now in this mirror maze.
The light, the mirrors, my addled brain are making me see
things that aren't there, molding horrific people out of tricks
of light. For a second I think I see a flash of lilac, then it's
gone. I whirl, and think I see a young man, tall and strong,
with chestnut hair and shadowed features. *You*, I see him
mouth as he points, steps closer. *You.*

"Leave me alone!" I scream.

Gasping, I whirl away, but I'm caught by another mirror.
I feel powerless to tear my gaze away.

I see people in masks. Not the exotic animal masks the
people at the party are wearing. These are people dressed
all in green, like temple priests almost, but these are more
like surgical scrubs. Their faces are covered in white masks
that cover everything except flat dark eyes. They bend over
someone strapped to a table, and I see the prone figure writhe.
Then they look back at me and point. This time with scalpels.

They break from their surgery and come closer behind
me. *I'm frozen.* I want to turn, to see that they aren't real.
They can't be. I want to run, but my legs are leaden.

When they get closer, they start to strip off their masks.
And oh, great Earth, what's beneath is hideous! Twisted,
misplaced features. Wounds and sores. They look like lumps
of clay trying to be people. Like figures created by someone
who has heard of but never seen a human.

With a startling moment of clarity I think: *I'm seeing our
souls. That's what we humans really look like, twisted and
ugly and horrible.*

And the worst part is that they're smiling with their
twisted mouths. I can see from their gestures as they creep
closer that they're trying to calm me. *There, there*, they seem
to say. *Don't worry. Everything is just as it should be.*

But it's not! I'm surrounded by monsters!

What is happening to me?

Finally, I can break away. I leave those horrifying visions far behind me. I can feel my heart racing frenetically. I get that same feeling I had when I first saw Lark, that dizzy nausea, that strange roaring that seems to surge through my body with the flow of my blood.

The drink, I realize. There was something in the drink Pearl gave me and Lark. Something strong. And I drank both of them.

I've got to get out of here. Out of this mirror maze, and out of this party. But there is no escape, and my thoughts mutate with each weird image of myself that I see. The trick mirrors expand me to enormous proportions, puffed out like a balloon, fat but empty. Another stretches me out long and thin, attenuated until my entire existence is no more than a narrow line bisecting the world into two halves. Which side do I choose? Do I have any choice?

I stumble desperately, calling Lark's name. Why doesn't anyone help me? I hear other people at the party, a distant rumble, but no one comes. I'm lost! I'm alone!

I scream, and run blindly though the maze. Suddenly I crash, and I go down with two mirrors on top of me. They splinter into a million fragments, and it feels like the Snow Festival, the cold pieces slithering down my skin. No, it feels like something else. Like sand, swallowing me up. Eating me alive.

I leap to my feet, shaking off the shards, and feel trickles of blood down my arms where some of them have pierced me. My blood is warm and alive, and it reassures me somehow to know that I have such vibrant, vital stuff inside me when the outside looks so false and dead. The wounds don't hurt, which is strange. In fact, my whole body feels numb, while my mind alternates between dull and sharp.

I have to get out of this maze! But everywhere I look now it is just me, me, me, endless me.

Wait, there's a mirror with only one image of me. None of that mirror-within-a-mirror infinity. I shuffle toward it, and the image stays true. No other mirrors are endlessly reflected in this one.

Feeling my way like a blind person, staggering under visual overload, I grope over to the next mirror and timidly peer in. Just one of me. I sigh. I'm out of the thick of the maze. Just a few more steps, and I'm home free.

But now the images shift from endless repetitions of myself to other people. Everything looks unnatural to me now, strange and otherworldly. Their faces look like animals that never existed, parodies of the life our planet lost. Paint and glitter, gilding and artifice—that's all that is left to us in Eden.

Instead of mirrors, I crash into people now. They seem to shatter, too, fragmenting into slivers of flesh. There are so many eyes on me! I can't stand it! I want to be alone, behind a high wall where no one can see me, where no one even knows I exist. No, I want to be with Lark.

I see a flash of pale bright hair across the room. Is it lilac? Colors are pulsing under shifting strobe lights and I can't tell. My eyes feel like they're pulsing, too. Like they're about to pop out of my head. Is the hair silver? The pale pink-purple of a flower? I follow the bright hair as it slips in and out of the crowd. The person always seems to be in shadow. They duck into an alcove and I think I've caught them at last. But I'm thwarted. There's a door, and when I open it, stairs heading up into increasing darkness.

I hear footsteps, heeled shoes clicking unseen above, and I start to run after them.

The darkness closes around me. The walls close around me. What have I done? I've run right into the dragon's mouth and it is swallowing me! The walls, the air itself presses on me, forcing me to my knees. I'm so small, so weak! I'm being crushed! No! I grab onto my head with both hands, pressing against my skull. I'm terrified my head will explode.

I hear a voice, soothing in tone but terrifying in meaning. *Die*, it coos gently at me. *Give up everything you have, even yourself.* The voice is like a caress, making me want to yield to the terrible things it is saying. *Forget, forget*, it whispers, enticing me closer to a void that seems to loom before me.

And then, the pain! Oh, great Earth, pain like I've never known. It's not from my wounds, not from my body at all. My body is still numb, hard and cold like a block of ice. The pain is from inside, from my brain, a memory of pain so exquisitely devastating that I start to weep, helplessly. Needles piercing my veins. Electrodes sending bolts of pain through my body until I scream. But worse than that are other kinds of pain. Pain of loss. Pain of powerlessness. Pain of the truth.

I see you, a voice says. The same voice? I don't know. I don't think so. This one is sharper, less soothing, more challenging. The other voice was a memory. This one is speaking now, another self within me. *What are you going to do now?* The voice sounds intrigued, studying me.

Stay here, die here, I moan. But no, whoever that is in my head, they're watching me cynically, expecting me to fail, but curious, attentive, in case I do not.

Whoever they are, I won't give them the satisfaction of seeing me give up.

I gather my numb legs beneath me and try to rise, but I can't quite manage it. I crawl instead, ever upward, clinging to the one thing I can think of to give me hope.

"Lark," I whisper. There are other names I want to call out, but they elude me now. So I call her again, louder. "Lark!"

Finally, I drag myself to the top, and use the doorknob to drag myself upright. If I can just find Lark, I'll be okay. I know, dimly, that whatever Pearl gave me is bikking up my brain. These things I'm feeling can't be real. Lark will help me. Like I helped her.

I'm on the rooftop. Faintly, a flash of reality comes back to me. The party. The roller coaster. But the roof is deserted. Why? Oh, I see now. There are yellow and black striped barricades around the ride station. It must have broken down. The roller coaster car sits lonely, a useless hunk of machinery now that some key element is awry. I feel like that roller coaster. A broken creation. But how can I fix myself if I don't know which part is broken?

"Lark?" I call, and the breeze takes the word away. I'm sure she came up here.

A figure emerges from the darkness. A girl, tall and elegant, with long hair reflecting faint light. I can't make out her face, but who else could it be? Smiling, relieved, I start toward her, my arms outstretched. It isn't until she is very close that the dim starlight reveals a face.

It's not Lark.

I don't know *what* it is.

It looks like Pearl, but her flesh writhes and pulses as if there were maggots crawling underneath her skin. I blink hard, and her face is normal again.

"There you are. Where's your new best friend?"

"I'm looking for her," I gasp. "I can't find her anywhere." *Please please please stay normal.*

"Well, it's time for Lark to get what she deserves. Did she finish her drink? I put enough synthmesc in there to have her hearing colors and seeing sounds. She's got to be pretty messed up by now." She chuckles and tosses back her silvery hair, and suddenly she is in slow motion. Her hair has become long strands of bloated worms. I shudder and back away. "I put a little in yours, too. Hope you don't mind. Just sit back and enjoy it. Let this weird world wash over you."

Her smile is just a little too broad. As I watch, it gets bigger and bigger until her face splits in two. Maggots stream out of the gash in the middle of her face. No matter how hard I blink, this time it won't go back to normal.

I pinch myself hard on the arm, bringing a moment of clarity. I remember now what this night was all about. "What do you mean? You're charging everything to her credit chip, right? Isn't that her punishment for . . ." For what? For being from the outer circles? For her family rising through skill and determination? It slips out before I can censor it. "For being a better human than you?"

Pearl recoils as if I struck her. She has fangs now, long and sharp like a tiger. She's drooling blood. "That's just the drug talking. But you better watch yourself, Yarrow. You're a little more interesting than those other predictable blanks, but don't push me too far." Her eyes glitter dangerously in that hideous face. "Now go and fetch Lark. Bring her to the roof. We'll see if that little birdie can fly."

I feel my stomach lurch. "What do you mean?"

Pearl winks at me. "It's amazing what you can achieve with enough synthmesc, and the power of suggestion. If you whisper the right words you can make anyone think they don't deserve to live." She throws back her head and laughs.

I say one word. "Cinnamon."

She nods, and with every bob of her head she grows in stature. She's a giant, a monster. I cower away. I want to run, I want to cry, to scream for help. But something makes me stay. Lark? Am I staying for Lark?

"Of course," the huge slippery horror that is Pearl says. "She thought she was queen of the school. Now, I ask you, what kind of queen can't take a little criticism? But after I told her a few choice things about herself, she found she just didn't have the will to go on. Poor Cinnamon." She tries, but can't keep a straight face. "That was only the second floor. How high up would you say we are?" She strolls to the edge and peers over, giving a long, low whistle. "It's a long way down."

Vertigo hits me, and I look up, away from the edge. Above me, the stars seem to pulse, then slowly start to swirl. There's something about the stars. Something about the stars and Lark . . .

My mind reels out of control, at the mercy of synthmesc. Lark flying through familiar constellations of stars. Lark falling, her arms wheeling, her eyes locked on mine.

"No!" I shout. I storm up to Pearl, actually grab that disgusting monster by the filmy front of her dress. Maggots pour out of her mouth, erupt from her skin, but I hold on to all that corruption for Lark's sake. It's not real, I tell myself. But I don't believe it. "You leave Lark alone, do you hear me? You're not going to hurt her!"

But the drug has made me weak. Pearl shrugs me off easily. I'm not even sure if my words have come out clear or garbled.

"Get your hands off me. That's the second time you've told me *no* today. It better be the last. Do you remember who I am? Who you are?"

No. That's the problem. I am in pieces, a shattered mirror.

"You can't hurt her," I insist. My voice sounds small.

"Can't?" Pearl's voice has risen to a hysterical pitch. "Can't! How dare you!" She takes me by the shoulders and shoves me backward. "I own you!" she shrieks. "You'd be nothing without me." She shoves me back again. "Without me, you'd be alone!"

Alone! That word tears at me. Alone! My comfort, my safety . . . my fear. Being alone.

"No, not alone," I mutter. "I have friends. I have brothers, sisters. A huge family. A family tree. They love me . . ." My voice rises. "They love me! You don't matter—they do!" My hands reach for her throat, and her eyes go wide. I don't squeeze, but I hold her there. She's plainly terrified. "Everyone hates you, Pearl! Do you really think you have any friends? They're afraid of you, so they pretend, but every single person in Oaks despises you. Even Copper and Lynx. Even me." I squeeze a little harder. "Especially me!"

"You idiot!" she shouts as she fights me. "You have no family. You have no one! You're a lab rat, a test subject!"

The shock of her words makes me loosen my grip. She looks shocked, too. Her mouth is open in a perfect O. Then she gives me one more shove, and I stumble backward. One foot lands on the edge of the rooftop. The other lands on nothing. My arms windmill as I try to catch my balance, and I see Pearl's mouth again become a perfect shocked O. Her hand reaches out for me. A clawed demon hand. I twist away . . . and I'm falling.

8

I CATCH THE ledge with my fingertips.

"Oh, bikking hell, take my hand!" Pearl shouts. But all I can see is her rotting, crumbling face, her gnarled hand reaching for me with sharp demonic talons. I can't touch her again. I won't take her hand. "Yarrow! Grab hold!"

One of my hands slips, and I turn away. I can't look at that monster Pearl anymore. Suddenly Lynx and Copper are there, too. "What's happening? Oh bikk, what did you do, Pearl? Help her! Move over!" More hands reach down.

But they look like monsters, too.

I look over my shoulder. So far down. But anything, even that, is better than letting those monsters get me in their clutches. They'll tear me apart. Then they'll put me together again so I become a twisted monster like them.

Pearl turns, running away on her clattering high heels. But all I can see are the stars whirling above me as my fingers start to slip . . .

———

SUDDENLY SOMEONE PUSHES between Copper and Lynx. Their hideous monster faces move aside, and oh, it's a real person! An actual beautiful human with real human features.

Lilac hair cascades over the edge of the building as Lark reaches her hand down to grasp my wrist. It tickles my face when she stretches down her other hand to grab the fabric at my shoulder. She doesn't look strong, but there is grim determination on her face as she strains to haul me up.

I don't need much. Her help is enough for me to get my other hand on the edge, to pull myself over the rim. My feet scramble for purchase, and then suddenly I'm over, falling on top of Lark, safe.

Safe.

In that strange mix of adrenaline and synthmesc, something washes over me. A new kind of vision. Like a rippling stream—crystal clear, but I still can't see quite to the bottom because of the disturbance at the surface. Still, for the first time in a long time, I feel close to something that has been eluding me for . . . I don't even know how long. Months? My lifetime? Those two things feel almost the same.

Sprawled beside her, I take her face in my hands.

"I know you," I say, looking in wonder at that sweet face I adore. How could I not have known my own dear Lark?

We get to our knees and stare through the night at each other. As the adrenaline leeches from my veins, I can feel the synthmesc taking hold again. My mind is becoming fuzzy, my skin numb. Just a second ago everything was so nearly clear! I saw . . . something. I can't explain it. I felt whole. For the first time in a long time, I felt like me.

"I can't hold on," I whisper desperately.

Lark misunderstands me. "You're safe now. I've got you. You won't fall."

I look at her face, at its sweet gentle lines, and think: there is truth. There is something I can hold on to. But it is slipping away by the second.

"I remember you," I tell her. "From . . . before." I frown.

Where did we meet? I know now that I've known her a long time, but how?

Lark's eyes light up. "You remember me? From before I came to Oaks?"

"Yes . . . no. I'm not sure. All I know is . . ." I break off with a gulp. "You're a part of me."

Then her arms are around me, and she's kissing me, and I feel the strangest mix of contentment and confusion . . . I break free and jump unsteadily to my feet. This is all too strange.

"I know you don't understand what's going on," Lark says soothingly. "But there's so much I need to tell you. So much you've forgotten. Yarrow, I have to tell you . . . you're not who you think you are."

I almost laugh. It sounds so melodramatic! At the same time it stirs a deep curiosity in me.

"What do you mean?" I ask.

"I don't know if I should tell you yet. We'd hoped you'd remember a little more by yourself."

"Who is 'we'?" I want to know.

She shakes her head. "I can't tell you. Not everything. Not yet. But you must feel it inside of you. The wrongness."

I close my eyes. That's it, exactly. A wrongness. Like every action, every word, every thought of mine is just a little bit off, in a way I can't begin to explain. "Please," I beg, "Tell me."

She looks at me sadly. "You have to give it time, Rowan."

"What did you call me?" I cry. That name hits me like electricity, coursing through my body from brain to fingertips and back again. It feels so right, and I don't know why. Who is Rowan? It doesn't make sense, and the confusion suddenly makes me furious.

What the bikking hell is she talking about? Her words make me tremble, but of course they are lies. Not even a lie that makes sense! "Get your filthy outer circle hands off me, you liar! You'd do anything to worm your way into our clique. You gave me your drink. You drugged me to try to confuse me! Well, it won't work. You'll never be anything but low-class trash. Get the bikk away from me!"

I have to leave. I have to get somewhere safe. But where?

My mom, of course. She might even be in her lab right now. She works odd hours, and even has a suite at the Center.

"Where are you going?" Lark calls after me as I run off. I don't stop.

———

UNDER THE EMERALD eye of the Center, I'm greeted by one of my mother's assistants, Buck. When I ask to see my mom, he tells me that she's there but busy, but I can wait and see if she'll be free later. He takes me to the sensory deprivation room to relax. I come here often. Here, I can sink into a bath of gel, lie in a quiet, darkened room, and shut out the outside until I'm completely calm. I must look a mess, but Buck doesn't react.

"My shift is almost over," he says as we walk down the corridor. "But I'll get you settled first before the next crew takes over. And I'll get a message to your mom that you're here."

"Thanks," I say. I'm almost grateful not to have to face my mom right away. I need to rehearse what I'm going to say about tonight.

I allow myself to be led to the dimly lit room. Black marbled walls, a deep obsidian pool sunk in the center of the room. The gel inside looks black, too, not the customary jade green. For a moment I balk at the change. But I've spent many happy, relaxing hours floating in that perfectly soothing body-temperature gel, letting my mind drift. It's like a trip to the spa, without all the annoying chatter of the masseuse and aesthetician. It's just floating freedom, peace and quiet. I let my clothes slither to the floor before I step in. The viscous gel is black and opaque, hiding my body modestly beneath.

While I wait for Mom, I think about Lark, and that feeling that I knew her before. But where? I scan my memories, but she's not there. What do I recall? Sitting as a splay-legged toddler on a white-carpeted floor, playing with a stuffed animal while my mom looks lovingly on.

Dancing at a Rain Festival when I was eight or nine, stomping gleefully in the puddles. Mom opens her mouth as if to chastise me, but then smiles instead, grabs my hand, and we jump in a puddle together.

My first kiss, with a boy named Zephyr, on the front porch of our house. I see the curtains part, catch a glimpse of Mom's understanding smile before she retreats, leaving me to my exciting new sensations.

So many lovely memories of growing up. A happy life.

But no Lark.

Relaxing, letting the dim light and soothing gel take me away from my worries, I settle into my memories. Some of them are crystal clear and diamond sharp, bright faceted moments in time.

But . . . what kind of beast was the stuffed animal? I stretch my mind back to my earliest childhood memories, and though I can clearly remember the room, the carpet, my mother . . . the soft floppy toy I hold in my chubby baby hands is a blur.

I think of the Rain Festival of my childhood, one of a handful of perfect memories of my mother that come back to me time after time in moments of distress. That is one of the memories that comforts me.

But it is incomplete. Parts of it are so vivid. The puddles beneath our boots explode in slow-motion droplets. But . . .

what color were my boots? What was I wearing? Where, exactly, were we that day? Is it strange that I can't remember these details?

No, I assure myself. A child isn't going to remember things with such clarity. I remember what is important—my mother's presence, my mother's love.

But what about my first kiss? I relax a bit more into the tub as I remember the feel of Zephyr's mouth on mine, the softness of his lower lip as I imagine a ripe fruit must feel, sun-warmed and sweet. That moment is perfectly etched in my mind. I even remember what I was wearing: a white summer dress with yellow-eyed daisies crocheted at the hem and sleeves. My mother, when she peeked through the curtain, had a dotted kerchief tied over her hair.

I sigh, reassured . . . and then it hits me. I have no idea how I met Zephyr. I don't remember his last name, or what his parents did, or where he lived. Nothing, before or after that perfect moment.

My eyes fly open and I sit up, making the gel slosh over the sides. I'm thinking so hard it *hurts*, and still, I find nothing.

I try, deliberately, to recall other days. Birthdays. I remember exactly two. And for those, only flashes, vignettes. Candles blown on a pink cake when I'm ten, Mom telling me in the pre-fail days little girls traditionally wished for a pony. Getting my first fully loaded credit chip when I was thirteen, so I could go on my first shopping spree. The moment of receiving that chip is complete, indelible. But what did I spend it on? What did I wish for at ten? What happened on every other birthday of my life?

I have no idea. I stretch my mind back and find dozens of crystal clear moments. But between them, nothing.

What is wrong with my memory? Why do I have these gaps? I'm so tired. Just the effort it takes to think makes me weary. I'm going to close my eyes, just for a minute before Mom gets here . . .

"HERE I AM, my dear," someone says. It's my mother. I relax immediately. It's automatic. When I'm with my mother, when I even think of my mother, I become calm, as though a switch has been flipped in me.

"Come now, you're late. We have a lot to do in this session." I open my arms to hug her, the gel slipping off my arms, but she slips to one side. "You know what to do."

I do. Of course, I've done this a hundred times. I smile. She smiles. Everyone in their green surgical scrubs smiles. We are all so happy to be here! Why is my heart beating a thousand miles an hour in my chest, then? Why does my jaw ache from smiling so much? Is it because I really want to scream?

No, of course not.

An orderly reaches into the tub and straps down first my left, then my right wrist. He smiles at me. I smile back.

He straps down my ankles.

Everybody smiles.

And then, I cease to exist.

"She's been showing signs of leadership," my mom says. Her voice is distant and clinical. "More evidence of dominant traits, less of a tendency to follow authority figures."

"It's a fine line," a surgeon replies. "Too much alteration, and you might as well lobotomize her. We can't take away her free will."

"Don't quote EcoPan directives to me!" my mother snaps. "I know the limits better than you do." She ticks off a list on her fingertips. "No unnecessary killing of any human. No robbing a human of its fundamental humanity. No complete removal of free will."

"What we're doing comes very close . . . ," the surgeon begins.

"EcoPan hasn't objected yet. People need to be guided. They still have free will. We just make sure they exercise it in the right direction. Children still have free will. They also have parents who help them make good choices. That's what we're doing here."

"We're going farther with this test subject than we ever have before."

Test subject? Is that me? They don't even look at me anymore. I'm just meat on a slab.

Mom! I scream. But though my mouth opens, no sound comes out. I pull at my bonds, but my body isn't moving. I'm paralyzed. The only things moving are my racing heart, my frantic mind. *Mom, please look at me! Let me go! Why are you saying these things?*

"It would be easier if we could just terminate them," Mom says, shaking her head as she checks my charts. "The troublesome ones, like her. But the EcoPan abhors waste, and every human must be preserved if at all possible."

"This one is special to the EcoPan for some reason," the surgeon muses.

My mom looks at her sharply. "She's not. We're all equal to the EcoPan." She walks across the room to get a rolling tray of instruments.

And then—oh, great Earth! Then the needles come.

"Tweak her dopamine levels to enhance her base-level contentment," my mother instructs.

Why aren't you saving me, Mom! You always said you would give your life for me. Why are you letting this happen?

"And then after you're done," Mom continues, "we'll begin another round of deep-hypnotic compliance suggestion therapy. Pearl told me there was some conflict about coloring her hair. Such a little thing, but it is best to nip resistance in the bud."

The surgeon comes at me slowly, precisely, and I can feel the needle tip meet a little resistance as it touches my eye, feel the stretch, the little pop as it pierces the jelly. No, no, no! Please make it stop. At least let me scream, and cry, and rage. Don't make me just lie here, taking it, as if this was all the most normal thing in the world!

Suddenly they're gone. My body is my own again. When I try to sit up, the restraints have vanished. I blink my eyes fast, shake out my limbs.

The room is completely empty. I'm dressed in a pale green hospital gown, and I feel a cold weight against my chest. It's a pink crystal on a braided cord. I clutch it in my hand. The people, the medical equipment, the tub—all gone. There's just me, perched on the metal slab.

And a door.

I slide off, and walk toward it. Just as I touch the handle, I hear someone behind me shout, "Don't touch it!" And I don't want to. Nearly every fiber of my being tells me to listen to that voice of authority, to obey it. Because conformity is comfort. Obedience is happiness.

But I remember the needles. The way everyone smiled at me, too big, too deliberate, before I suddenly became no more than a specimen. I have to get out of here!

I twist the handle, and I'm instantly in another room. It is huge, and far in the distance above me I see faint multicolored glittering, like stars in a disco universe, like the decorations in my bedroom. At first I think that's where I am. But I'm somewhere else. Somewhere much bigger. The air has a peculiar chill, noises have a certain resonance, that makes me think I'm underground. A cave? Oh, it is so lovely! The ceiling is covered with bright faceted crystals like the one I'm wearing.

They glitter in the low light in hues of pink and purple, ice-clear and burning topaz. Their light makes confusing shadows with something big at the far end of the cavern.

There's a smell, too. I don't think I've ever smelled any-thing in a dream before, but this is as clear as waking life. Clearer. Something sharp and fresh fills the air, high, almost minty notes. And beneath that, mysterious base notes that hint at darkness, moistness, decay. But not a scary kind of decay. The kind that comes with abundant life. The rich per-petuation of growing things.

Dirt, I realize. It smells like that glass bowl of dirt I discov-ered in the priests' inner sanctum. But that was small and ster-ile by comparison. This smells like a whole world of rich, wet, fertile earth. I feel the dirt beneath my feet, soft and nurturing.

I focus, and see that the shadows are cast by what first looks like a huge, many-armed giant. I look closer, and that's when I realize I'm in a dream. It's a tree. There hasn't been a tree on Earth for more than two hundred years.

Then I notice people, emerging wraithlike from the shad-ows under the boughs. Dozens of people. Maybe hundreds. I can't see their faces, but each has a glow at heart level, and I realize they each wear a piece of crystal, just like the shining stones on the ceiling. Small children dart all around me. Their voices are impossibly sweet.

The people suddenly stop. They are all facing me, though their faces are still in shadow. I start to walk toward them. They hold out their arms, welcoming, and I yearn to run eagerly to-ward them. They beckon me with their hands. Any moment, their faces will become clear. I can already tell that they are smiling, overjoyed to see me. *Sister*, they chant. *Little lost sister.*

The crowd parts, and I see one person sitting alone at the base of the tree. It is a young man, his hair a little long, his arms folded over his knees. He has a golden crystal hanging around his neck, resting over his heart. I feel an answering throb in my own heart. My hand reaches up to my chest, but my fingers grasp empty air.

The young man is looking at me. Not beckoning me like the others. Just waiting.

Waiting for me.

With my heart catching in my throat, I try to go to him. I have to. I *need* to. I need him like food, like breath. But my body is slow and sluggish. I move like I'm walking through water. Every step takes an eternity, and I don't seem to be making any progress. I want him to run to me, to help me, but he just waits.

Suddenly I hear screams behind me. I whirl around, and the people are all running around wildly. Old people are knocked down. A child stands alone, weeping. I turn back to the young man, and see that the tree is on fire. Flames lick up the trunk like living things. They sear the branches, and great fireballs erupt in the canopy.

"Run!" I scream to the boy. But he just sits there. I turn to flee, then turn back to him. I have to save him. But my legs are numb and powerless. I'm held trapped in a matrix of thick smoky air. He has to get away from there! Red hot cinders are falling all around, and above his head, I hear the ominous creaking of branches about to snap as the roaring fire consumes them.

There's yelling all around me, maddening movement, but all I can think about is the young man by the tree. I know him. I need him.

But the fire is growing. The entire tree in in flames. Black smoke closes around him.

The last thing I can see is the topaz glow of the crystal around his neck, and the burning glow of his amber eyes.

Second child eyes.

I WAKE UP in the black gel pool, with my mother looking down at me.

I yelp, biting it back just before it becomes a full-blown scream! The second I see her, images from the dream come back to me, tormenting me. For an instant I'm strapped down again while a woman who looks and talks just like my mother performs terrifying experiments on me. I cringe away from her.

"What's wrong?" she asks.

Everything! I want to jump up and run away. But I suddenly realize I have to play this very carefully. "Oh," I say breathlessly. "Sorry, you just startled me. And the bright light hurts my eyes."

She looks at me suspiciously, and I do my best to act normal, but inside I'm panicking. Part of my brain is telling me that it was just a dream, that I'm shaken by those bizarre—and surely false—images of my mother experimenting on me. But something deeper tells me to fight, to flee this monster who is staring down at me.

But she's my mother, my protector, my friend. The one who loves me more than anything. How can I tell my own mother that I'm terrified of her? She's the same small, serious blond woman. But she feels like a different person. I should be able to tell her about my dream, so we can both laugh about it. But somehow I can't.

Find out the truth, a voice seems to demand in a harsh whisper inside my head. There's something going on here I can't quite see. I need answers. But I know I'm not going to get them from my mom.

"Are you okay?" my mom asks.

No, no, no! I'm not okay at all. "Of course," I manage to say. "We had a late night, and . . . I might not have shown the best judgment. But my friends got me here." That's just a guess, but slowly the events of last night are beginning to filter back into my consciousness.

Wait, did Lark kiss me?

"Was Pearl one of those friends?" Mom asks.

"Yes, of course. We're always together. She's . . ." I gulp, but some instinct tells me I have to say it. "She's my best friend." The words almost make me choke. She drugged me, and then she almost killed me! Then she ran away. I want to punch her right in that perfect face.

"Did you do anything unwise?"

"I had a few drinks," I admitted. "And there were these bubbles filled with powder. They had something in them, some kind of drug, maybe. I'm fine, really. I just need some sleep. And maybe some under-eye concealer!" I try to laugh, but my throat is dry and it comes out as a cackle.

I have to get out of here—now! The Center has always been a sanctuary for me. Now it feels like a trap.

"You seem so upset," Mom says. "How about I give you a little something to help you sleep." Mom might be the chief of intelligence, but she has a background in neurosurgery. It's common for her to give me vitamins or sleeping pills or something to help me study. I've always taken whatever she offers without question. Now, remembering those needles coming straight for my eyes, I refuse to let her put anything into my body.

"No!" I say much too loudly. Her eyes widen, then narrow. She looks like she's getting angry. "No," I say again in what I hope is a more rational voice. She's still looking at me with suspicion. "I really don't need to take anything." Oh, great Earth, if she drugs me, there will be needles in my eyes as soon as I'm unconscious, I just know it.

She gets a syringe out of a cupboard and taps the tip to free any air bubbles.

"No!" I say, again. "I . . . I have class tomorrow. I need to get up early to study for a test. If you give me anything, I might sleep too late."

She kneels down and takes my hand where it rests on the edge of the black tub. For an instant her touch is gentle, soothing, and I think that I've been a fool to pay attention to my dreams. But then her grip tightens like a vise and she's trying to pin my arm down on the ledge.

I jerk my arm away and scoot to the far edge of the pool. I can't disguise the anger and fear in my voice. "I said no! I don't want that."

There's a heavy moment of uncertainty where I'd swear she's weighing the merits of grabbing me and holding me down. The tension hangs in the air. "You ungrateful little . . . ," she begins, in a malicious voice I've never heard before.

Then I have an idea. I put on my sweetest voice and interrupt. "I'm sorry, Mom. I know you're just trying to help. And you're totally right—I do need something to help me relax. Only, could I have something to eat first? I haven't eaten all day and I think it's making me snappy." I bow my head contritely. "I didn't mean to yell at you, Mom. It's just been a long night."

She studies me for a long time before finally saying, "Whatever you want, sweetheart. You wait here, and I'll get you some soup. Then you can have a nice rest. When you wake up, you'll feel like a different person." Her voice is sweet, but to me it is like an artificial, factory-made synthetic strawberry—*too* sweet, and unreal. We smile at each other, but it is more like animals baring teeth than an actual show of affection. We both know something isn't right, but I don't think either of us knows how much.

As soon as she's gone, my veneer of calm collapses and I'm gasping, my hand on my chest, tears trickling down my cheeks. If I'm here when she gets back, something terrible is going to happen to me. I know it.

I climb out of the pool, the black gel sliding slickly from my limbs to pool at my feet, leaving no residue on my skin. I run to the door and press my ear to it. It is thick, and I can't catch much, but I hear my mom talking to someone right outside the door. She says something like *flood the room with gas . . . easier.*

Without my will, my hand flies to my throat. Frantically, my fingers fumble for a cord that isn't there, trail down lower and find nothing. I look down at my empty hand, and remember the necklace in my dream. Wait, I own that necklace! Long ago I shoved it in some box or back drawer when Pearl mocked it. *A garish hunk of rock*, she'd called it. So I ignored the wrench I felt when taking it from around my neck, and put it away. I haven't thought about it since. Why was I dreaming about a magical cave covered with crystals like the one I own? It can't be a coincidence. I have to find that necklace!

As soon as I hear her steps go down the hall, I sneak out of the room, out of the lab, out of the Center. All the while I feel like a prey species must have felt back in the pre-fail days—as if something might pounce on me at any moment. Tackle me to the ground, tie me to a table, stick needles in my eyes . . .

Even when I'm safe back in my room at Oaks, I'm trembling. Something isn't right. But I don't know if it's with me, or the rest of Eden.

I start tearing my room apart. Those fancy clothes that used to matter to me so much now mean nothing. They're strewn around the floor, ripped and wrinkled as I search for the one thing that suddenly means more than anything else. I step on fine synthetic silks, the softest imitation doeskin, tear apart expensive necklaces to find that little hunk of rock.

When at last I find it, wedged in a crevice at the back of my closet, I clutch it to my chest and feel an almost palpable warmth emanating from it. A sensation of peace washes over me. Something strange is happening to me. A disjointed, separate sensation, as if there are parts of me I've been ignoring. It sounds crazy to say, but I almost don't know who I am.

But now that I hold this pale pink crystal in my hands, I know with absolute certainty that whatever happens, whoever I am, I am not alone.

I hear footsteps approaching again, another knock.

Automatically, I hide the necklace under my shirt, and cower in the corner of my room. Oh no, it's my mom, or Greenshirts come to drag me back to the Center. I try to hush my breathing, and hope whoever is out there goes away.

They knock again. Very quietly, I pick up a stiletto shoe and hold it like a weapon. Some fierce, irrational animal thing inside me growls that I won't let them take me.

"Ro, are you in there?"

I almost collapse with relief. It's Lark.

I open the door and pull her quickly inside, looking down the hall, paranoid, before slamming the door shut behind us.

"Look at this!" I say, pulling the necklace out and holding it in Lark's face at the length of the cord. "Where did I get this? Is there a place . . ." I break off, realizing I sound crazy.

But Lark takes my hands and says, "Go on."

And I do, brokenly and incoherently, ranting about my dreams and a tree that lives underground and a boy with golden eyes and a crystal cavern.

"It's just a dream," I say, with tears welling in my eyes. "But it means something. I know it does. And this necklace. It's important. I just don't know why!" I collapse on my bed, and Lark sits beside me, putting an arm around my shoulders. "Wait, was I horrible to you last night?" I sniffle. "I can't remember, but I think maybe I was."

She smiles forgivingly. "It was a hard night. Don't worry, I didn't take offense. But now, you're starting to remember," she says. "Last night . . . and more. Much more. In your dreams, at least. Maybe it's a good thing that Pearl drugged you. It opened your mind. Freed places that the Center locked up."

"I'm ready to hear what you know now, Lark. You have to tell me. Everything. Please, Lark!"

She presses her lips together, thinking. Then her face softens.

"You're right. I think I owe it to you to tell you the whole thing. Only, promise you won't run away, or scream, or hit me?"

I give a rueful little laugh. "That bad?"

"That bad," Lark confirms. And then . . . silence.

I clear my throat.

"I know," Lark says with a sigh. "It's just hard to tell someone something you think they won't believe. Do you promise you'll keep an open mind?"

And then, my world turns upside down. Inside out.

"I'd hoped once you saw me, spent some time around me, it would all come back to you. And I can tell it's getting closer all the time. But not nearly close enough. You just can't remember."

"Remember what?" I ask. That missing thing, it seems so near.

"Who you are."

I almost laugh. "I know who I am. I'm . . . Ro." I frown in confusion at that nickname Lark gave me, which feels so much more comfortable than my own name. "I'm . . . I'm me. That's all. Who else could I be?"

She takes my hands in hers. "Do you know why that name, Ro, feels so comfortable? So familiar? No one here ever called you that, did they?"

"No. Only you."

"But it feels like you, doesn't it? It's because that's your name. Or almost. Your real name."

She waits for my reaction. I feel a curious tingling along my arms, down my shins.

A prickling of premonition. Everything feels so close, as if there is a paper-thin barrier in my brain that could be burned away with the tiniest spark. "That name you called me last night," I say. "Rowan." I just barely breathe the name, a whisper of air, but it seems to fill the world around us.

"Your name is Rowan," Lark confirms at last. "You are a second child."

No, this is a trick, a lie Lark came up with to separate me from everything that is important to me. From Pearl, my mother, my school, my life. Those things call out to me, begging me to return to their easy predictability with a call I almost can't resist. But Lark is pulling me in the other direction, toward uncertainty, sadness, danger.

Truth.

I'm silent, my brain awhirl, and Lark goes on, thinking I'm paying close attention, but really there's a deafening litany of *no no no* shouting over and over again in my head. I want to scream at her, but I feel frozen, numb, and she talks on.

"You were—you *are*—a second child. You have a brother, a twin. Your mother hid you away for sixteen years, and then she arranged for you to have black market lens implants, so you could pass unnoticed. And she found you a family to live with. She was doing her best to make sure you had a normal life."

The word "mother" pierces my internal screams. I feel my tense face softening, my wild mind calming, just at the thought of my mother. But then it hits me, Lark isn't talking about my mother. My mom is at the Center. Who is this person she's talking about? Someone who loved me. Protected me. Gave me a future. But it's the wrong person. My mind reels . . .

"You met me just before your surgery," Lark continues. "I was best friends with your brother."

I feel like electricity is running through my body. A brother? I try to imagine his face, but all I can see is my own. I have a brother! I'm not alone in this world!

"You snuck out, and we became . . . friends." Her voice is tight with emotion. "Then a little while later, your mom was taking you for your surgery, and everything went horribly wrong."

The chorus of denial inside my head picks up again. I want to cover my ears, keep out whatever is coming next.

"Your mother was killed."

I'm like a statue.

"You escaped. You met Lachlan."

I gasp at that name. But why, I don't know. If I could

reach out my hand I could touch him, touch the knowledge, the memory of him, whoever he is. He's that close.

"He took you to the place where he and the other second children live. Where they hide away from the government. You got your lenses, and you were going to help the second children with an important mission. But your brother got arrested, and when we went to rescue him, you were captured. After that . . ." She breaks off, and I see tears streaming down her cheeks.

"I thought they'd killed you! For weeks, I thought you were dead. Then later our sources found out that you were alive . . . but changed. You were someone else. You didn't seem to have any memory of your past life. You thought you were the daughter of Eden's chief of intelligence. And what's more, so did everyone else. You and everyone else who knew about you seemed to accept that you had always been Yarrow."

She swallows hard, and wipes the tears from her face. Her eyes are shiny, and she looks at me so eagerly, so hopefully.

"But we know. The second children. And me. I know who you are. We think they can brainwash people through their eye implants. But second children don't have them. And my epilepsy seems to be the kind of brain glitch that keeps them from having much effect on me. We want you back, Rowan."

I both cringe and thrill at that name.

"We have the neurocybersurgeon who did the original procedure on you. She thinks she can reverse the effect. Sever the connection that the EcoPan seems to have with all of Eden's citizens. She says that might give you your memory back. It's risky, but it will be worth it if you remember who you are. And . . ." She hesitates a beat, and I notice. "And for other reasons. We need your help, Rowan."

I'm still sitting there, almost unmoving, even my breath so shallow that my chest hardly expands. Very carefully, I'm trying to construct a wall between myself and everything Lark has told me. I'm gathering up all the reasons why this cannot possibly be true, as if they were stones, and building them up into impenetrable ramparts. But no matter how hard I try, my construction is flawed. Her words find a way in.

What she said is impossible. At the same time, what she said is plausible.

The very fact that it is so totally unbelievable somehow makes it all the more likely. If Lark was going to lie to me, surely she wouldn't select a lie so extravagantly unlikely, would she? A lie has to be believable, and the fact that this isn't—not at all—perversely lends credence to it. No one would dare say such an outlandish thing unless it was true.

But it can't be! I know who I am.

I find that my hand has strayed to the pink crystal. I'm clutching it so tightly that I'm pulling the cord painfully into my neck.

"Lachlan gave you that crystal, when you were in the Underground," Lark says. I meet her eyes, and there is a mysterious pain there.

I want to tear it off, but the cord is strong, and pulling only causes me more pain. I let my hand flop to my lap, and the crystal bounces against my sternum.

No, it can't be true. I know one thing absolutely, above all else. I love my mother. I trust my mother. My mom would never hurt me. She'd die for me.

Your mother was killed. That's what Lark said. She died protecting me, trying to give me a better life. Of course she would, I want to scream. But she's not dead. She's not some other woman. She's in the Center now. I can see her anytime.

Suddenly Lark's last words pierce my confused brain. *We*

need your help, Rowan. And just before that she mentioned a mission.

This isn't true. She's made all this up to use me somehow. I don't know how, but this is all an elaborate trick. Or she's like Pearl, ambitious and manipulative, and she thinks this is a way to sow discord, to separate us.

It worked, damn her! I think of my happy life before Lark walked into the classroom. School and friends and boys, clothes and hair and a bright, beautiful, successful future looming ahead of me. I want that back. I want what Lark is trying to snatch from me with her supposed revelations. She's ruining everything!

Fury rises up in me. It's so much easier than the confusion, the sadness, the fear that are threatening to overwhelm me. Anger makes me strong. I know what to do when I'm angry.

It erupts all at once. "You liar!" I hiss at her. "You bikking liar!" My voice rises to a shriek. "You're just jealous of me. Of me and Pearl and all the people who really belong in Oaks, in the inner circles. You're just a piece of outer circle trash!"

"Rowan, I . . ."

"Don't call me that!" I cry. "I'm not . . . I'm not . . ."

But the very fact of my fury proves that I believe her. I should be laughing at her. Instead I quake inside, in the depths of my soul. Rowan. Who is Rowan?

Me.

I can feel her, that other girl inside me. Separate, but closer than ever before. The synthmesc I took last night made everything more confused, but maybe it also opened a door that some other force has so far kept resolutely shut.

Tears fall down my cheeks. Lark reaches a hand to brush them away, but I spring to my feet. "Don't."

"Rowan, I'm sorry. I know it's hard. Do you remember? Do you remember any of it?"

My head is pounding now, each pulse an agony in my temples. "I don't know," I say miserably. I'm succumbing to her words, her tricks. "I don't remember anything. Not really. But I *feel* . . ." It is a struggle to get out the words, as if some huge and powerful force is desperately trying to hold them inside me. "I feel like I've forgotten something. But I can't even remember what it is I've forgotten."

I can't be this other girl named Rowan. I can't be a second child. Second children are hunted, killed, imprisoned . . . or worse.

Oh, great Earth! It hits me like a sledgehammer: a memory—no, it's just a fragment of last night's dream—of being tied down to a table, of needles piercing my eyes. Of screams. My own screams, and worse, the unseen screaming of other people in other rooms. I'm being pushed down by mechanical arms into a tub of viscous gel. I try to hold my breath, but the machine punches me in the gut and I exhale and gasp, feeling the slimy gel fill my lungs . . .

"I can prove it to you," Lark says. "I can take you to the crystal cavern."

I want to say no. I want to order her to leave, tuck myself into bed, sleep long dreamless hours, and wake up to being a normal girl again.

But what feels like another part of me says, "Let's go."

10

THE STARS ABOVE us wink dimly
through the particulates scattered in the atmosphere that
are supposed to block some of the sun's radiation. I know—
because I've read—that the stars looked brighter when people
lived outside of Eden. But I've never seen them as anything
other than faint flickering specks. How could I, when I've
never been outside of Eden? No one could survive in that
scorching, poisoned, dead nightmare of a world. The world
that humans destroyed and a machine—the EcoPan—is trying to revive.

The ground lights up at our feet, illuminating with every
step and growing dark again once we pass. There aren't many
pedestrians in this part of town, far from the entertainment
circle. Our steps make bright flashes against the pale ambient
lighting coming from houses. Eden knows me. Oh, not me
personally. The automated, computer-guided city wouldn't
recognize me as Yarrow unless a securitybot happened to scan
my eyes. But it recognizes me as part of the city, lights up for
my convenience, goes dark when I'm gone. I am part of this
unnatural ecosystem.

"We are un-animals," I say to Lark, and for a second she
looks at me like I'm still high on synthmesc. But she soon

understands what I mean, and picks it up as though it were a thread of an ongoing conversation. For all I know, it is.

"We used to be part of something huge," she says. And I know that "we" isn't her and me, or anyone alive in Eden today, but our very species. "We were creatures, animals like you said. Part of the forests and the fields."

"Were we, though?" I ask. "Or were we meant to always be fighting nature, subjugating it to our will?"

"Like the Dominion believes?" Lark asks cautiously.

"Well, they're heretics, aren't they? A forbidden sect that thinks man should have dominion over the beasts and the land. That's what got us here in the first place. But . . ." I frown as we walk. I've never thought about these thorny issues before. "We learned in Eco-history that every species competes, every creature fights every other. For space, and food. They fight in their own species for dominance, for mates. If we're animals, why should we be any different?"

Lark taps the side of her head.

"Well, yes, we have big brains," I say. "But what did they get us?"

"They let us survive our own mistakes," Lark says, gesturing around to the artificial, sterile, clean world we live in. "They let us realize that if we ever return to nature, we have to do things differently."

"But will we?" I ask. "Or, in a few thousand years when it's safe to leave Eden, will we do the same thing all over again?"

"If we do," Lark says firmly, "we don't deserve a second chance."

We walk on into the night, and though I don't actually remember anything from my other life—if that's even true, which I can only barely believe—I have a strange sense of something like nostalgia. A sentimental longing for a past I can't recall. Walking with someone I like through the cool of the night. Happy couples here and there, murmuring secret soft words to each other. Where do I fit in all of that?

I look sidelong at Lark, now walking determinedly, her eyes fixed forward, hurrying to our destination. Where do *we* fit in all of *this*? How strange it is to know that she is my dear friend, but to only feel the feelings of a couple of days.

Friend? Or more? She hasn't mentioned the rooftop kiss again, and neither have I. But every time we look at each other it seems to hang there between us, that tender touch of lips.

Did I love her?

We walk a long time. I suggest the autoloop, but Lark seems wary of being scanned. She doesn't want any record of our travels. My sandal-clad feet are tired from slapping the hard pavement, but she suddenly grabs me under the arm and makes me walk faster until we round a corner.

"Look! Did you see that?" She peeks around the corner, and I stand on tiptoe to do the same, over her head.

"I don't see anything."

"I saw a pavement light flash. Just for a second, then it was gone."

"Is someone following us?" I ask.

She peers into the night. "It was far away, and I don't see anything now. Maybe someone just stepped out of their front door and then changed their mind and went back in."

It sounds plausible, and the street looks deserted, so we press on. But there's a new sense of urgency to Lark's steps. She hustles me along down unfamiliar routes. Eventually she steps into a darkened doorway and takes something out of her small pack.

"I hate to ask, but . . . Well, no, I'm not asking. I'm insisting." I realize she's holding up a hood. I shiver with a deep fear. Is that a suppressed memory? Or is it just natural that people are afraid to have their head stuffed in a bag?

"You don't trust me?" I ask, backing up a pace. "But I'm trusting you!"

"It's not that I—we—don't trust you. We don't trust your programming. What if you, the real you underneath it all, wants to keep our secret, but you've been programmed to reveal our location if you find it? What if you want to keep it in, but can't?"

"I'm not a robot, you know. I *can* think for myself."

She looks at me sadly. "Oh, Rowan. None of us know exactly what they've done to you. What they've taken away. I just hope we can get it all back. Get *you* back."

She might not trust me. But I feel like I trust Lark. I still don't know why, other than it's a feeling. But it's a stronger feeling than any I've ever known. Besides, I need the truth, and this is the only way, so I let her slip the bag over my head. In the close darkness I am utterly disoriented. Which is exactly the point. I know we're on deserted back streets—I don't hear anyone, and otherwise it would be too weird to escort a girl with a bag on her head—but within a minute I can't keep track of what direction we're going in. When she finally stops me and tugs the bag off, smoothing my hair down tenderly, I can only see that we're in a generic, featureless alley. There are no doors, no windows, no distinguishing feature to tell me so much as what circle we're in.

Lark kneels down and threads her fingers through a drainage grate in the ground. With a grunt of effort she jerks it loose and sets it aside. I peer down, and see only sheer walls and darkness. It's only a little wider than my shoulders.

"Here?" I ask, incredulous.

She winks at me. "You've done it before. Just tell yourself that and . . . jump!"

"Seriously?" I ask.

She takes my hand. "I know it's scary. I'd go first, but

there's a trick to getting the grate closed again as you swing in. It angles like a slide. You won't hit the ground hard. And I'll be right behind you."

I can't turn back now. Despite my doubts and fears, part of me knows Lark is telling the truth. The things I've seen at the Center, the things I've dreamed, all propel me forward. There is something huge here, bigger than me alone. I have to press forward, see this through.

"Do you promise?" I ask.

"I promise," she says, and I study her face. There's nothing but honesty there, and . . . what else is that? Caring? Concern? Worry?

Love?

"Go!" Lark whispers urgently. "While it's still clear. We can't take the risk that anyone might see. Hurry!"

I let my legs dangle over the edge, but I can't convince myself to leap into the void.

Behind me, Lark sighs. "Lachlan bet me ten credits I'd have to do this." Suddenly she puts her hands on my lower back and shoves me over the edge.

I'm in free fall! Straight like an arrow down the tunnel I fly, grabbing for the walls. But they're smooth and slick, with nothing to grab to slow me down. The passage begins to narrow, and I start to panic. Am I coming to a bottleneck? Will I get stuck?

All at once the chute begins to angle, cupping my body so instead of falling, I'm sliding. The angle slows me down, and then—what feels like a long time later—I slither into a chamber and land on the ground with the softest bump.

Awestruck, I look around. There is a gentle glow from recessed artificial lighting, allowing me to see the fantastic cave formations. Stalactites hang from the roof, each with a single drop of water forming with tantalizing slowness at its point, looking like fangs dripping venom. When Lark slides down behind me a moment later, she finds me touching the cool rock walls.

"Real stone!" I gush.

"It's beautiful down here, isn't it?" Lark asks.

I nod. "How far down are we?"

"I have no idea. It feels like we fall forever. All I know is that it's deep enough that none of it interferes with Eden's infrastructure, the building foundations or the sewage system."

I can see passages radiating from this central chamber. "It's a natural cave system?" I ask.

"Yes, though carved out and modified a bit, leading to . . . well, you'll see soon. If I can find my way, that is."

I think she's joking, but it proves to be a complex process. I don't know if she's faking confusion so she can lead me back and forth through the same passages to confuse me, or if she's really lost for a while. Eventually, though, she says, "We're almost there. Just down that corridor. Are you ready?"

"No," I say honestly, with a little giggle that borders on the hysterical. "But what choice do I have?"

She looks at me earnestly. "Apparently, you have plenty of choice, thank the Earth. Whatever they did to you at the Center, at least they didn't take your free will away. Maybe they couldn't."

I take a deep breath. "I'm nervous," I admit. Afraid is more like it, but I don't want to confess that.

"It's okay," Lark assures me. "You're among friends. Every single person down here will be overjoyed to see you."

I don't really believe that. Still, this is a necessary step, and I can see the eager anticipation in Lark's eyes. "I'm ready."

She presses a hidden panel in the wall, and the rock face of what looked like a dead end suddenly fractures down the middle. With a creak, two halves part, opening a cleverly hidden door. We walk along a corridor, which I can see opens up ahead. There are lights, faintly sparkling, and an enticing smell.

I hear a noise ahead of us, and shrink back. But it's the sound of children. Children, down here? Second children? The happy voices come closer, and suddenly I'm surrounded by a mass of children. They're carrying pencils and pads like they just came from school. Late lessons, maybe? They're being herded by an older woman, and have the sleepy-eyed, happily bedraggled look of children who have had a long day and are up past their bedtime. Though they are evidently headed somewhere, probably to sleep, one of them spots me and breaks from the group.

"Rowan!" a little girl shrieks, and hurls herself at me like a tiny cannonball. She wraps every single limb around one of my legs and looks up at me with huge eyes as I stagger into Lark, trying to keep my balance. "I knew you'd come back! Me and Lach, we both knew it!"

I peer down at her uncertainly. With her twin pigtails sticking unevenly from either side of her head, she's absolutely adorable.

Then I notice her eyes.

They're bright golden brown, shot through with a radiating sunburst. They look more utterly alive than any eyes I've seen. I realize with a shock that this little girl doesn't have eye implants. Everyone in Eden has lenses implanted in their eyes that filter out harmful radiation, prevent blindness, and have an ID link. They flatten out the eyes' natural color, so that every person I see has dull, slightly hazy, monotone eyes in flat brown or black or silvery blue.

This little girl's eyes sparkle! That, as much as her ebullient personality, makes me grin back at her. The other children all press around me, and though I feel a little strange and self-conscious, it is hard to be too afraid of children. "What's your name, precious?" I ask.

She lets go so abruptly that she slides down my leg, landing on her bottom with a thunk that makes her scowl. "You don't remember?" She scrambles backward like I've suddenly become a dangerous beast, and melds with the dozen or so other children, who range in age from four to early teens. They all look at me a little uncertainly now.

A plump, matronly woman steps up, her arms spread as if to gather the children to her like a mother hen. "Give her a moment, wee ones," she says with a low chuckle. "She's only just arrived, after what must have been at least one or two interesting adventures." She snips the little pigtailed girl's nose with teasing affection. "You must forgive her if a naughty little girl's name isn't the first thing in her mind."

The woman smiles at me, and holds out her hand. "I'm Iris, and yes, we like each other quite a bit, if you're wondering. They told me you might have some . . . memory problems. But what a lovely surprise to see you! We knew—or at any rate hoped—you'd be joining us again soon."

"Hello," I say tentatively. I like her right away, but it's a new feeling, with no trace of a memory of old affection. I look into her eyes. They are a pretty green with flecks of light brown. I peer into each childish face. Sparkling hazel, deep vivid blue, agate, green, and speckled gray. Eyes full of color and vitality.

Dangerous eyes.

Second child eyes.

The pigtailed girl seems to consider me, then holds out her chubby little hand. "I'm Rainbow. But you can call me Bow. Or Rain. Rainbow is a *really* big word. I can only spell the R so far."

I take her hand. "Do we like each other, too?" I ask.

She nods solemnly. "But not as much as I like Lachlan. Or as much as you like Lachlan. He's both of our favorite people."

I feel the heat creep up my cheeks, and I'm sure I'm a fiery red. People keep talking about this Lachlan as if we have something special, and I don't know a thing about him. Is he here? I look all around, but only see an anonymous crowd of people clustering around me. Word of my arrival has spread fast. The children were bearable, but now adults are pressing close, taking my hands, hugging me. Everyone looks happy, relieved. I am welcomed home.

By people I don't know, to a home I can't remember.

My breath is coming hard, and I feel unsteady on my feet. There are so many people! I can't bear the recognition in their eyes when I have none to give back.

Lark sees my agitation, exchanges a meaningful glance with Iris, and the older woman claps her hands sharply. "That's enough! Give the poor girl some space. She'll be here for a while, and we'll celebrate her homecoming tonight. For now, let her go to her room and gather her thoughts."

I have a room here?

The crowd disperses, with nods and waves and promises to catch up later. Iris takes the children away. I'm alone with Lark, to my immeasurable relief.

"Rowan?" One more person is coming. I turn to meet them . . . and think I'm looking in a mirror. I'm back at that party, high as a kite, looking in the funhouse mirrors that change things in unimaginable ways.

I'm staring at a male version of me.

"Ash?" I breathe.

11

LARK TOLD ME I have a twin brother, but she never told me his name. I conjure it up from somewhere deep inside of me. They couldn't erase everything, right? I remember how to read, and walk, and what objects are. I can envision a map of Eden's streets. The core of my knowledge remains. Ash is evidently in my core. I look at this boy, my mirror, and I know, in my gut, what to call him. I don't remember him—nothing about his personality, or our past together—but without conscious thought I know his name is Ash.

I feel a weird combination of panic and peace. Panic, because this is one more very powerful thing that confirms everything Lark told me is absolutely true. Peace, because I feel like I've found my other half, a half I didn't even know was missing.

I stare at him, devouring every detail with my eyes. I want to touch his face, hear his voice, his laughter.

But what I want more than anything is to remember him.

Everything else, I'm ambivalent about. I feel like my life, the one I know, is my own, like I'll be giving something up when I rediscover who I really am. I'm still going to do it—I need to—but it scares me. Finding Ash doesn't feel complicated at all. He belongs to me. I need to recover every single detail about my brother. And if I can't for some reason, I'll relearn it. Just seeing him floods me with a sense of connection, of belonging. I won't ever let that go.

I realize all of a sudden that I'm just staring at him speechlessly. But then, he's doing it, too, for reasons of his own.

"I never thought I'd see you again," he says, and his trembling, emotional voice is better than birdsong. His voice is beautiful. It is home. "I thought you were dead for the longest time. And then . . . I thought you were lost to me."

We stand a few feet apart, like we're frozen. Like we still can't quite believe this is real.

"I missed you," I say. "I didn't even know I missed you. But as soon as I saw you I knew it."

Then suddenly I fly into his arms. As soon as we hug, I know everything about him. Not events, history. But the sound of his breathing, the smell of his skin, warm and soapy. I know the texture of his hair when it presses against my cheek as I hug him.

I never want to let him go.

"Same old Rowan," he says, holding me at arm's length and looking at me with such kindness, such . . . I realize now what it is. Brotherly affection! How many people on Earth can say that they understand the love one sibling can have for another? Except for these second children, no one has a brother or sister. And most of these people hidden here didn't get to grow up with their sibling. They were shameful, dangerous secrets, hidden away, sold, or banished.

I'm crying openly now, with utter joy. I want to know everything. "Are we alike? Do you love bubble tea? Is your favorite subject Civics?"

I want him to gush, but a fine line creases the space between his eyebrows. "You hate bubble tea," he says. "So do I.

And you always said studying Civics was a waste of time after you learned the basics."

I'm disappointed. "Oh." I love bubble tea. I *thought* I loved bubble tea. But if Rowan didn't, how can I?

"It's okay," he says, and I think he's desperate to keep the mood joyous. "Are you still painting?"

I'm confused. "Painting? I've never picked up a brush in . . ."

Before I can get upset at the disparity between my old life and my new one, he grabs my hands, flashes a grin I recognize as exactly my own, and says teasingly, "Rowan, don't be ashamed at what happened to you! It isn't your fault."

I'm still crying, but there's sorrow as well as joy in my tears now. I'm crying for what I've lost . . . and what I've gained. "But I want to remember you—and myself. I want to so badly, and I just can't! I can't even remember Mom. Lark told me that she's dead, but in my head there's another woman who's my mother. I feel like I'm going crazy!" I start to turn away, but he pulls me into a tight, reassuring brotherly embrace. "I'm so sorry, Ash."

"Don't be sorry. We're together again. That's the most important thing. Once Flame gets here, she'll be able to examine you and see if she can reverse whatever they did to you at the Center. With any luck—and Flame's almost supernatural skills—you might be able to get all of your memories back."

Lark has slipped away a small distance, watching our reunion with sympathy, giving us a little time alone to reconnect. She joins us again. "You remembered Ash's name. That's a great start, and a good sign, I think. It's all in there." She taps the side of her head. "Just waiting to be unlocked."

"But for now," Ash says, "let's show you around. See if it sparks any more memories." Ash takes my arm, and Lark grabs the other, and we walk out of the antechamber where we first entered, onto a balcony.

I had been vaguely aware that we were up high (well, up high while underground) and that there was some sort of decorative foliage in the distance. There are fake trees everywhere in Eden. So when, out of the corner of my eye, I spotted the tree, I didn't think much of it. Ash was the center of my attention.

Now they lead me to the balcony, an overhanging shelf high above a vast open chamber that is ringed with multiple layers of walkways and stairs.

I look around me, and gasp.

The cavern is vast, maybe as big as the entire Oaks campus. Below are people chatting and walking, little tents in gaudy colors with flags advertising their wares—clothes, shoes, candy—like a fair. I see a long row of tables lined up, and people are laying out food—a feast! Some pretty amazing aromas are wafting all the way up to my high vantage point, including some I don't recognize.

But above, oh, the ceiling of the hall looks like a huge multicolored, faceted jewel. The arch of stone above our heads is ablaze with crystals in every possible shade of purple and pink and gold and ice-clear. It sparkles with simulated moonlight. It's so beautiful I feel a surge of happiness and hope. How can it be that such loveliness exists, unknown and unseen, so far below Eden? Eden is supposed to be a paradise, but already this feels more like the promised land.

And then, I see the tree.

Really see it.

It's huge, impossible to miss, but between the interesting people below and the vivid crystals above I glance over at it. Another artificial tree, so what?

But now, standing between Lark and Ash, looking down

on a deep green canopy that arches more than a hundred feet across, my knees start to shake. The smell of something rich and deep and vital hits me, and suddenly I know. I realize that there is no comparison between that and even the most realistic artificial tree. Those are sculptures and photosynthesis machines—attractive, but cold and dead.

How is it possible that there's a tree in Eden? All major life forms, animals and plants, have been dead for generations. Only humans, and a handful of algae, lichens, and fungi, survive. Yet here is a tree, huge and magnificent, growing belowground of all places.

"Can I touch it?" I ask, yearning to do so, but thinking it might be somehow sacrilegious.

"Of course," Ash says. "It belongs to all of us."

Without another word or thought I break free from them and dash down the steps, ignoring the stares of the few people I pass, unresponsive to their surprised greetings. The tree stirs something in me that will not be denied.

I break into a full run as soon as I hit the bottom. I've sprinted halfway across the cavern before I realize what I'm running on. The ground is soft and yielding beneath my feet. Dirt? It can't be! The soil is poisoned and sterile.

I skid to a stop and fall to my knees. The dirt is packed hard from so many footsteps, but I dig my fingers in and pull up twin handfuls. I feel the grains beneath my fingernails, and pull both handfuls to my face, breathing in the rich, musty, fertile scent. The entire chamber floor is dirt. And it must be deep, for the tree's roots to bury themselves in. I remember that tiny little bowl of earth they kept in the inner sanctum of the Temple. How paltry that little specimen seems now! What a mockery of what the Earth was, and what it should be.

But this! This is real. I stand, and my fingers open to let

the dirt slide back to rejoin the rest. Slowly at first, then with quickening steps, I approach the tree. Soon I'm walking on leaves, dried to a pale brown, and as they crunch under my feet an intoxicating smell rises. It is the same sharp scent that faintly permeates all the air down here—a strange cooking smell, I thought at first. Now I realize the sharp, cool, minty smell is coming from the tree.

How many years has this tree been here, shedding leaves into this rich soil so that they rot and become part of the soil themselves, the tree making its own nourishment? The tree is massive, its rough, gnarled trunk stretching so wide it would take a dozen people joining hands to encircle it.

"How is it possible?" I ask aloud. I'm asking myself, the world. I didn't even hear Ash and Lark come up behind me.

"Aaron Al-Baz, of course," Lark says.

I shiver, and feel a strange prickling along my spine. From the awe I'm feeling. From gratitude for the man who saved us all. It must be that.

"He made this place as a fail-safe," Ash says, "in case Eden wasn't ready in time, or if conditions were even harsher than he anticipated. He pumped in real soil before the Ecofail, and planted this camphor tree. It has environmental controls completely separate from the EcoPan and the rest of Eden. That's why the Center has never found us."

"Isn't it amazing?" Lark asks. "There's an artificial solar and lunar cycle built into the cavern roof, and water pumped from a deep isolated reservoir, filtered air . . . The entire place is almost self-contained. We—or they, because I'm just a guest—still have to go to the surface for food and materials. But we have a huge store of food and weapons now, and could hold out for months, easily, in an emergency."

I'm taking in their words, but all of my attention is on the tree. It is like I'm looking at one of the old dead gods people used to believe in, suddenly brought back to life. It is a giant, a benevolent monster towering over its tiny worshipers.

I feel an urge almost like the one I felt when I first saw Ash. A desperate need to connect. Before I know what I'm doing I'm hugging the tree as if it was another long-lost brother. I hear good-natured laughter behind me, but I don't care. I feel the bark on my skin, rough and vital, so much more real than anything else in my life. *This* is what we're all missing. *This* is why our lives, no matter how glorious they seem, have an empty pit at their core. To connect with another living thing—how marvelous it is.

Elated, I turn, with my back still pressed to the tree, unwilling to sever contact yet as I look across the cavern at my friend, my brother, at the dozens of people living a life so different from the one aboveground. I've been here less than half an hour, and yet already I feel more at home than I ever did at Oaks.

"Come on," Ash says, looping his arm across my shoulders. "The tree has been here for more than two hundred years. It will be here a little while longer whenever you want to visit. Before long, you'll almost forget that it is here."

"Never!" I swear, but let him lead me to the other second children, who are about to sit down to their communal supper.

It is a night such as I've never known. As one of the most popular, powerful people in Oaks I was always surrounded by friends. Or people I called my friends, anyway. And yet, never for one moment did I feel as accepted and welcomed as I do tonight. It's not even because we were all such close friends back when I was Rowan. From what Lark tells me, I've met most of these people but haven't spent a lot of time with them. At first I think it is because, despite my flat eyes, I'm a second child like them.

But as the night goes on, and the lights embedded in the crystalline roof sprout artificial stars, I realize that these people in the Underground are just fundamentally different than the first children of Eden proper.

Up there, everyone is separate. We come together, have friends, do things with each other, but somehow it feels like each person is in their own bubble. The bubbles bounce into each other all the time, but they never pop.

Down here, the bubble is around everyone. They're part of a community where each person is inextricably bonded to every other person around them.

As I look around at the happy people in their loose, flowing garments, their free-flowing hair, each with a piece of crystal at their neck or wrist, I have an epiphany: this is an ecosystem. The tribe, the tree, the dirt, the shared secrets and common danger. Maybe people weren't meant to live underground with only one tree and filtered air. Yet this is so much closer to what humans were meant to be.

We profess to worship nature and the lost environment, and yet up on the surface, every single action we take is in defiance of nature. Only down here are people really striving to live as our species should.

It breaks my heart that it is incomplete, that they can't have a forest of trees, real fruit, limitless expanse to run and dance and play.

It makes my heart sing to think that I am now a part of it all.

It is less hectic and loud than the raving parties I usually go to, but it makes me happier. I stick close to Ash—I never want to let him out of my sight—and Lark, but people keep coming up to me and talking about small, unimportant things that I somehow find delightful. I think Lark must have coached them not to expect too much of me. I can see the questions behind their pleasant chitchat, and I'm glad they're too polite to ask me the things they're really curious about.

When I yawn three times in a row, Iris spots it from the far side of the table and beckons me away. "She's back to stay," she tells the nearest. "You have plenty of time to get reacquainted. It's time this tired girl went to bed."

I hadn't really thought about that yet. I'd assumed that Lark and I would be going back to Oaks tonight. But when Iris, Ash, and Lark escort me to a room, I realize I don't ever want to leave.

Iris pushes open the door, and I step into a room without corners. It isn't exactly round, but close. The walls are stone, carved caves, and the craftsman left the walls smooth but a little uneven so that it looks almost like a natural formation. There's a bed with green sheets, and a bathing alcove. On the bed sits an unzipped backpack. A ragged stuffed animal lounges on the pillow.

"Oh!" I cry, and scoop it up, hugging the little chimpanzee to my cheek. I turn to find that Ash has tears in his eyes.

"Do you remember him?" he asks hopefully. "Benjamin Bananas?"

I look at the chimp's sweet little furry face, and there's no recognition. But when I cuddle him to my neck again, I feel inexplicably comforted.

"He was your favorite when you were little," Ash adds, and I nod. I don't say it, but I know I'll sleep with Benjamin Bananas tonight.

"We'll leave you for tonight, my dear," Iris says, giving me a quick hug.

"Will you be okay alone?" Ash asks. "I could stay. But I'm just next door if you need me."

"I'll be fine," I tell him. I kind of need to be alone for a while, to let all the mingled confusion and joy settle into my heart and mind and body.

They leave, and for a moment I feel achingly lonely and almost call them back. But I know they're just outside. All of them. My friends, my blood family. And my second children family.

I think I'll lie awake for hours pondering everything, but as soon as my head hits the pillow I feel my tired consciousness start to drift away. My last thought is: where was Lachlan? Why didn't he come to see me?

His absence hurts, and I'm not sure why.

I have an idea, though.

THERE'S A STRANGE moment right when you wake up, or maybe right before you wake up. Just on the edge of conscious thought, everything can be so simple. This morning, I wake up happy. That's it, nothing else, just happy. I'm not immediately thinking of any reason for my bliss, not counting on any person or event to supply it. I'm not thinking about who I am. I could be a girl or a molecule. All I know is I'm a happy one.

I lie there in my comfortable bed, the cool sheets soft on my body, letting that simple sensation fill me. I know it won't last, and I need to enjoy it while it does. In fact, the realization that it is finite is probably what breaks the spell. All too quickly the reality of my life rushes in.

Here's the funny thing: I'm still happy.

I should be frantic with worry, confused, afraid. Oaks must have reported me missing by now. Center officials are certainly searching for me. Not to mention my own personal extreme identity crisis. But all I can think of as I lie in bed is the positive. Ash. Lark. The tree. The welcoming village of second children.

Lachlan, somewhere . . .

As I shake that thought aside, I hear a knock on my door. "Come in!" I call.

Lark pushes the lockless door open and bounds onto my bed. Her lilac hair is mussed and her face is shiny. She looks absolutely beautiful.

"I waited as long as I could! Did I wake you up? Did you sleep well?"

I laugh. "No, and yes! I slept better than I have in . . . well, six months, at least. As long as I've been Yarrow. What's going on?"

"Everyone's gathering for breakfast, but it's informal. A big table, you grab what you like. You won't be on a service rotation yet, but eventually you'll take your turn cooking, serving, cleaning. Although, really, you've already helped the Underground so much just by being alive! By coming back! Every second child we save is a strike against the Center and their policies. And maybe, depending on how much you remember, you can do even more for us. For all of Eden."

"What do you mean?"

"You've been in the Center, in places none of us has ever accessed. You've probably seen things, heard things, that they never thought you'd be able to remember. Secrets. If Flame can unlock your memories of Rowan, she can probably retrieve all of your memories. You'll know what they did to you. More important, you'll know *why* they did it."

"You know, I haven't even really thought about that part yet." I've been too fixated on the *what* to worry about the *why*. "I thought it must just be to punish me for being a second child."

"Then why not kill you?" she asks, and I shudder. "Or imprison you for life? Or, if they just wanted to add another person to the population, slip you in without anyone noticing? Why go to all that trouble to send you to the best school in Eden? Make you rich, popular? The daughter of the bikking chief of intelligence!"

"There had to be a reason," I muse. "But what?"

"You're special in some way," Lark says.

I grin at her. "I'm glad you think so! But why would they?"

She reaches up to fleetingly stroke a lock of my hair. "Anyone would think you're special, Rowan."

For a second I have a bitter thought. It's Rowan who's special, not me. I'm a creation, an experiment.

I echo the last aloud. "I'm an experiment."

Lark nods. "Maybe. We know that other second children have gone missing. None of ours, but there have been others we didn't discover in time. And a few who didn't want to live isolated from Eden. Those who have black market lenses and try to pass up above. They vanish, and we always thought they were killed. But maybe they were . . . changed, like you."

"You said they are messing with everyone's minds, through the lenses. Maybe, with me and other second children, they want to see how far they can push it. It might be easy for them to tweak a few perceptions, alter a recollection here and there. With me, they wanted to see if they could change an entire person. Turn me into someone who isn't a threat to Eden."

"I think you're close to the truth," Lark says. "But still, I think there must be something about you in particular. Some reason the Center is especially interested in you."

"I just hope I remember something useful," I say.

"Don't think about that now. There's nothing we can do until after the surgery. Flame should be here sometime today."

I dress, and we go out for breakfast. I want so badly to ask about Lachlan, but I don't quite dare. Something about the way Lark prickles whenever someone mentions his name makes me wary.

The morning passes happily, with Lark and Ash telling me all about my old self. We play guessing games at the foot of the tree, perched on roots that rise above the earth like massive sinuous snakes. Guess what your bedroom looked like, Ash asks. I guess it had multicolored lights like my room at Oaks does. I realize now that it looks a lot like the interior of the crystal cavern. I wonder if my subconscious mind directed me. I'm disappointed to learn that my bedroom at home was simple, disguised as a storage or guest room to hide the fact that there was an illegal second child living there.

"Do you remember Mom?" Ash asks.

The image of Chief Ellena flashes though my mind, but I shove it aside and reach out for any tendril of memory. There are sensations of what a mother should be—warm and loving and protective—and I can't quite associate these with the Chief. So they must be from my real mom.

"I can't remember her face," I admit, and feel tears welling.

"It's okay," Ash says. "She's there, inside you. She loves you just as much whether you remember her or not. Even if she's not alive. That's what mothers do. They love you forever, no matter what."

Near lunchtime, Ash and Lark are called away to kitchen duties. I suggest joining them, but they want me to relax. "You should take a nap. Be relaxed for when Flame comes."

I agree, tying not to think about the prospect of surgery. Eye surgery. Ew. Just the idea of it makes me quiver.

I head toward my room, but when I'm almost there I have an impulse. I stop one of the second children passing me—a man in his thirties—and ask which room is Lachlan's. He gives me a knowing look that makes me flush pink, and I hear him chuckle when I walk in the direction he indicates. I wonder whether a lot of girls seek out Lachlan's room. I quickly force the thought away. I have no business thinking things like that.

His room is at the very top. When he steps out of it every morning he can look into the highest branches of the canopy.

I raise my knuckles to knock . . . and stop.

What am I going to say? I found connections with Lark, and reconnecting with Ash was easy. But the idea of meeting Lachlan makes me flustered.

You're being stupid, I tell myself. *He's a friend. He'll be happy to see you. And you'll like him because you liked him before, when you were Rowan. It will be easy.*

Through pure force of will I make my knuckles hit the door. Three slow, uneven raps.

Nothing.

I knock again, almost relieved that he isn't there. Maybe he's on a mission. Maybe I won't have to see him until I remember him, and know the reason why the mere sound of his name makes my legs a little weak.

I turn to go, but an irresistible force makes me whirl back almost at once. I lean my shoulder against the door, and casually, almost as if it were an accident, I push the door slowly open. My body sways into the empty space, and I peek in.

I breathe the air of his room, and the scent awakens a hunger in me, as if I'm a starving girl smelling food. The pervasive sharp smell of camphor mingles with a warm scent I can only describe as "boy" and a warm, woody spiciness. It's an exciting smell, and it draws me farther inside.

"Hello?" I call out, hoping at this point not to get an answer. Because now I'm unabashedly snooping. I flip on the light. . . . and find a museum.

Artwork covers every wall. Real canvases with vibrant oil paint, scraps of paper with pencil sketches. I'm mesmerized by the scenes. Animals, vivid and alive in dying landscapes. A minimalist portrait of the little girl Rainbow, with all of her vivacity captured in a few quick bold lines.

Then I turn and see the mural covering the wall directly opposite his bed.

It's me.

My hair is dark, long, and flowing over shoulders left bare by a gauzy white robe that seems to be less an article of clothing than a stray wisp of fabric blown across my body by a stray breeze. There are flowers woven in my hair, bright spots of white and pink in my almost black locks. The artist has positioned the image so that the contours in the stone walls mimic the shape of my body, making me look like I'm emerging from the rock itself like a magical woman.

Behind the mural of me are a hundred creatures, big and small, spread out like worshipers around a goddess. Each one is paired, like with like. A maned lion nuzzles against the flank of a golden lioness. A gaudy peacock spreads his tail protectively around a sleek brown peahen. Every animal is gazing at me with hope. At the very back, tucked in the shadow of a recess in the rock wall, is an image of another human. A man. I lean in close, but I can't make out his features. He alone isn't looking at the flowery goddess image. His head is bowed.

I step back and look at the central figure. Now I'm not so sure it is meant to depict me. The facial structure is the same— wide-spaced eyes, strong, angled jaw, the firm chin with a thumbprint dimple. But one thing is completely different.

The artist gave me kaleidoscope eyes. Vivid, vibrant, complicated second child eyes faceted with hues of green and gray and blue, with a starburst of gold radiating from deep black pupils.

Is that what I looked like when I was Rowan? Those eyes transform my face, make me look magical. I touch the contours of my own face, caressing my skin as I search for con-

firmation that this lovely creation is me. What skill the artist
has. It must be Lachlan who did all these pictures.

But why has he covered a huge percentage of his bedroom
with a picture of me. I must be the first thing he sees when
he wakes up, the last thing he sees before he falls asleep. I am
painted with such loving detail. He must spend hours looking
at my face, when I don't even have a clue what he looks like. I
don't quite understand it.

"What are you doing . . . Oh! It's you." The voice behind
me goes from aggressive to shocked to tender to confused all
within those few words. I whirl, and see a young man who
looks a few years older than I am. He has chestnut hair worn
a little long, cut haphazardly, pushed away from a handsome
face with a scar shaped like a long crescent moon slashed
across his left cheekbone. In the shadow of the doorway his
eyes look flat brown, and he could pass for a legal first child.
But as soon as he steps into the light, his eyes come alive with
nuances of hazel and gold speckled in the rich brown.

"Lachlan?" I ask in a whisper.

He doesn't answer, which I find incredibly frustrating. I
hold out my hand formally, a little stiffly. "Hi, I'm Yarrow."

"No, you're not."

"Well, yeah, but I mean . . . I am now. But I was . . ."
Everyone else in the Underground has made this pretty easy
for me. They completely understand that though they might
know me as Rowan, inside my head I'm completely Yarrow.
Lachlan is making me feel like I have to explain what ought
to be obvious.

But I can tell he's not having an easy time of it himself,
and I feel a flash of sympathy even through my annoyance.

It's strange to see such a big, strong man look so flustered.
He takes my hand, but I can tell he's not really aware of that.
He's looking at my eyes. I see his own gaze flicker just for a

second to the mural, to the girl who is so much like me but
with the exceptional second child eyes. When he shifts his
gaze back to me I swear he looks disappointed.

Offended, I jerk my hand away, but try to make myself be
pleasant. They say he was a good friend, once, so I owe it to
him to be civil. Though at the moment I don't know what I
could see in this tongue-tied, surly looking boy.

Lightly, I say, "I was admiring your artwork. It's amazing. They say that I was an artist, back when I was Rowan,
but I don't remember. Still, I can't imagine I was anything
like as talented as you." I gesture to the mural. "Take this, for
example. I don't think I've ever seen anything quite like it."

I turn back to him and say, more sharply than I mean to,
"Rowan must have meant a lot to you, for you to paint her
like that." I'm trying to provoke a reaction . . . and I get one.

"I . . . I can't." His voice is anguished. "This is just too
much. I don't know how to do this!" He turns and strides
swiftly out of his own bedroom, and I get the impression it is
only amazing self-control that keeps him from breaking into
a run.

"Lachlan!" I call down the walkway after him. He gives
no sign of hearing.

Other people do, though. In a moment Iris climbs the
stairs to this level, hiking up her skirts to take them two at a
time on her short, strong legs.

"So you've seen Lach at last, have you now?"

"Yes," I say, confused and cross. "And I can't imagine
what Rowan saw in him. He's strange, and not very friendly."

She sighs. "I look after the children of the Underground,
you know. For all that Lachlan may seem like a man, he's a
boy in many ways. The same angry, defensive boy I took in
when his family abandoned him. He's not good at showing
his feelings."

"But if we were friends, why can't he just—"

She doesn't even let me go on. "Friends to you, maybe. You never said, and I couldn't tell for sure in the time you were here. But Lachlan is in love with you. With Rowan. Of course it is killing him to have you back . . . and not her."

She pats me on the shoulder as I take all that in. "Be gentle with him," she says. "He's had a hard few months with you gone." She shakes her head. "A hard life, in fact."

She makes the little clucking sound I heard her make to the children, and leaves me alone outside the room of the mysterious boy who loves me.

It makes sense. Why would he paint such a picture if he didn't love me?

The thought makes me squirm with discomfort and happiness both. The happiness is instinctive. Some deep part of me is naturally gratified. But is scares me, too, to think that I might be loved by someone I don't even know.

PART OF ME now wishes I was back at Oaks. That life might not have been real, but it was real to me. It might have had its complications, but they were nothing compared to this. I love the Underground already, and the people I've met. Still, it was easier being a rich girl at Oaks.

I consider going to my room, but I know I'll just lie on my back thinking way too much. Luckily the children get out of class for midday break and, when they spot me, break into a run. They're intensely physical and wild, shrieking and clinging to me and patting my arms. One sturdy boy about ten years old pulls my head down so he can stare into my flat gray eyes. "Completely weird," he says, but without any malice.

"Have you ever seen eyes with lenses?" I ask him when he lets me go.

He shakes his head. "I haven't been up top since I was a baby."

"Yeah," Rainbow says as she clenches the loose fabric of my pants in one chubby little fist in a proprietary way. "The up-there is full of monsters." She thinks a minute, then her eyes dance. "Ohhh . . . have you seen any monsters?"

She looks at me hopefully, and the other children start to bounce up and down, shouting, "Monsters! Monsters!"

Mercifully, the children are distracting me from my worries. I'm caught up in the surging little bodies as if in a flood, borne to the base of the tree. They drag me down and beg me to tell them stories about the surface. "The other adults don't tell us hardly anything," Rainbow protests. "Make it good."

"Make it scary!" another chimes in.

"I'll do better than that," I say, getting into it. "I'll make it true."

So I devise the perfect monster for these eager little second children. As they cluster around me with their beautiful complicated eyes latched onto me, I tell them about Pearl.

I exaggerate a bit. Oh, okay, I exaggerate a lot. The kids eat it up.

"The best monsters are the most beautiful ones," I confide to them in a low voice. "Because then, you can't tell right away that they're monsters. They're so lovely they make you want to be with them. Want to be like them. That's how they trap you. And then, once you can't escape, they destroy you."

"Unless you fight back!" Rainbow shouts. There are cries of agreement. I like these kids.

"Exactly," I say. "And you should always fight back. Anyway, one day the monster Pearl saw a young woman who was as beautiful as she was, with lilac . . . no, pink hair." Luckily they're so excited about the story they don't notice my slip. "Only this pink-haired girl was kind and good and brave. So of course the monster Pearl wanted to end her. So that night she filled her fangs with poison, sharpened her claws, and . . ."

I fill their little heads with the most extravagant tales of the surface. Stories of securitybots stalking unwary second children and mowing them down. Rumors of the gangs of Greenshirts who snatch people and drag them away to unimaginable horrors at the Center.

None of it is exactly true, but it is true enough to thrill them, and give them enough to fear that they are happy to be safe in the Underground.

They are begging for another story when there's a commotion from the top-level balcony. High up, I see Lachlan standing with a lithe woman with fiery red hair. Down below, people are waving to her. From another balcony Ash calls out to me, "Rowan, it's Flame! She's finally here!"

So much for the distraction of scary fairy tales. Now I have to live the real-life story—strange boys, lost memories, surgery, and all.

With regret, I rise, and I'm smothered in hugs before I can get away. "You'll be fine," Rainbow says as she bestows a squishy, sticky kiss on my cheek. "Lach wouldn't let anything bad happen to you."

My feet feel impossibly heavy as I trudge up the steps I ran so blithely down before. I want the truth . . . but I know the truth is going to be hard.

Is this the right decision? I think about my life at Oaks. It isn't perfect, but it's mine, and I've seen just barely enough of the rest of Eden to know it's better than a lot of other possibilities. Even now I could just go back to my old life. Don't we all delude ourselves in one way or another? I was happy, more or less. Will finding out the truth make me happier? Maybe the truth is overrated.

Or maybe happiness isn't the most important thing.

I'm still torn by the time I climb to meet them. A crowd has gathered. Ash, Lark, and Iris have joined Lachlan and the cybersurgeon Flame, as well as a few people I don't recognize. There's an older man, hard and serious, with black hair streaked with silver and an off-center nose. He nods to me, then I see his eyes cut quickly to Lachlan.

"I'm Flint, leader of the Underground," he says as he

imposes his bulk between me and everyone else. "I'm sorry I wasn't here to greet you properly yesterday, sister." The word "sister" sends a little shiver of pleasure through me. "But these are trying times, and we're all busy. And on edge." He looks over at a powerful woman whose bare arms are twined with snake tattoos. "Are you certain she wasn't followed? Double the sentries, just in case. Now in particular we can't take any unnecessary risks."

He claps a hand on my shoulder. "You've been returned to us at an ideal time, Rowan. We've been gathering intelligence, forming alliances. We have plans that may alter the fate of second children."

"There's still the final vote," Lachlan growls from behind him.

Flint flicks a mere glance at him over his shoulder, as if he's no more than a troublesome child. "We've put enough resources into this scheme that the vote is a foregone conclusion."

"Your plan puts the entire Underground at risk!"

"We know the risk," the tattooed woman interjects. "If we succeed, everything will change for us. And if we fail, well, at least we'll go down fighting."

"And the children?" Lachlan asks. "Will they go down fighting, too?"

The woman glares at him until Flint barks, "Enough! This is a matter for future debate. For now it is imperative that Flame retrieve Rowan's memories."

"So you can use them to your advantage," I hear Lachlan say under his breath.

"So she can help us save the second children!" Flint snaps. "She's already accomplished more than you ever did, with your long-term plans for slow social change. She infiltrated Oaks, and the Center."

"She was placed there, by the government, and we don't know why," Lachlan says. "We need to slow down."

"Slow." The tattooed woman scoffs. "If it were up to you, we'd molder down here for another twenty generations."

"And why not, if that's another twenty generations when second children aren't killed, or tortured, or experimented on!"

Quietly but sharply, the red-haired surgeon says, "My time is limited, and my life is in danger every time I come here. Can we proceed?" Her voice cuts through the verbal melee like cold steel. "Furthermore, you're upsetting my patient. Neurological interventions don't tend to go as well when the patient's nervous system is in an uproar. Calm the bikk down and leave me to my work."

"I'm staying," Lark says, and Ash echoes her. Lachlan says nothing, but his stolid stance makes it clear he's not going anywhere.

Flint gives Flame a little deferential bow of his head and leaves, with his henchwoman following. "Notify me as soon as the procedure is over. Whether she survives or not, either way."

"Survives?" I ask with a gulp. "I was thinking success or failure, not life or death."

Flame stares into my eyes, and I can't tell if she's searching me or admiring her own handiwork. "I am the best cyber-surgeon there is," she says without a trace of bragging, only supreme certainty. "If you die, it won't be my fault."

Then she winks at me, and Ash hugs me. "Yup, your fault, sis," he says. "That's what I always told Mom anyway. Everything is your fault." His teasing is at least better than hearing Flint and Lachlan go at each other about things I don't understand.

"I'm Flame, in case you couldn't figure that out," she says, waving a hand at her fiery hair. "Not natural, and not dyed. I fiddled with the localized phenotypic expression a few years ago so my hair would match my name. And personality. Yes, I'm *that* good."

When I step into the room, I have a weird suffocating sensation. For just a second my diaphragm seems to lock up, and I can't breathe. Behind the others, I see Lachlan tense and take a step toward me. But the moment quickly passes and he retreats to the far side of the room, with the others, forming a wall between us. He won't interact with me . . . but he won't leave.

Flame gestures for me to hop up on the exam table. She holds a scanner up to my eyes.

"Great Earth, but this is beautiful work. I amaze myself sometimes. Are you sure you want to have these beauties removed?"

"Yes," I say with slightly more assurance than I feel. I make myself remember that I'm not just doing this for myself. If it was only me, I think I'd be frightened of the risks, and choose my safe old life. But me getting my memories back could help everyone in the Underground. I think of Rainbow's trusting eyes, and try to be strong. "But . . . you were just kidding about the risk of death, right?"

She sighs. "Mostly. Whenever someone is put under full anesthesia, there's always a risk they won't wake up again. And whenever you mess with someone's brain, there's a chance they won't be quite the person they used to be when they come to."

"Yeah, but this time, that's the whole point of the operation!" I say, and try to laugh, but it doesn't go so well.

"I'm the best there is," Flame says, "but even I can't guarantee that things will go smoothly. Once the lenses have been implanted for any length of time, they integrate with the neurons and become much harder to remove. And you probably have some . . . extras. I won't know exactly what they've done to you until I get in there. Your lenses might be booby-trapped with microexplosives."

"What!"

"Kidding . . . I hope. I'll do my best—and as I relentlessly point out, my best is pretty bikking fantastic. But there are no guarantees."

"You don't have to do this," Ash says.

"Yeah," Lark adds. "We can tell you all about Rowan, and even if you don't remember, we can recreate her, and . . ."

"No," I say, and I'm proud that my voice doesn't crack. "They did something terrible to me. They took away *me*." I strike my chest emphatically with my fist. "I want my self back." I look over at Lachlan, who starts to look away but then forces himself to meet my eyes. "And if possible, I want to punish the people who did this to me. The ones who say that second children don't deserve life, and freedom, and . . ."

I can feel passionate tears welling, and Flame says, "Beautiful speech, but we don't have all day. I need to prep you. Shoo, everyone."

She tries to wave them out the door, but Lachlan says, "Can I just have a minute alone with Rowan?"

Flame doesn't so much roll her eyes as roll her entire body. "Have I mentioned we're in a bit of a time crunch?"

"Just a minute, I promise," Lachlan says, and something about his voice makes her relent. She and the others leave, and we're alone again.

I anticipate awkward silence, and I try to think of something inconsequential to fill the space. The weather, maybe? But he launches right in. "I'm sorry for the way I've been behaving. This is just so hard for me." He gives a sardonic smile, and that flash makes me want to see more, to see him happy and carefree and smiling for all the right reasons. "Listen to me! Hard for me? You're the one who has had to go through all of this for the last six months."

"Yeah," I say, "but I didn't *know* I was going through it until a few days ago. You must have had it worse. Worrying about me. I mean . . . if you . . ." I bite my lip. "Iris said that you . . ." I can't bring myself to say it. "Lachlan, what exactly are we to each other?"

"Right now, new acquaintances."

"You know what I mean. Before."

"That doesn't count until you remember it. I would never force feelings on you. Until you feel them yourself again, they're not real."

There's such feeling in him, such suppressed emotion. I want to draw him out, to make him tell me everything he feels, everything he wants from me. I can sense his longing quivering just beneath the surface, and I think, *Even if I never remember him, I might very well fall for this boy.*

"I think I dreamed about you," I tell him. "And, well, I can't really remember, because I was on synthmesc at the time—against my will!—but I think I've seen you before, at this wild party."

"I was there that night. Other nights, too. I've done my best to keep an eye on you. You take some serious risks, girl. But then, that's nothing new."

I like thinking of myself as someone brave, and I'm glad he thinks Rowan had courage.

"Stalker," I tease, to lighten the mood.

He steps nearer, closing the distance between us. I can feel the warmth radiating from his body. Or maybe it's my own heat. I couldn't fall for someone this fast, but if it's true that we have a serious history . . .

My feet don't move, but I lean toward him, like a flower yearning toward the sun.

There's a rap at the door, and I instantly sway back and clasp my hands together in a ridiculously schoolgirlish way. I don't want to think where my hands almost just went on Lachlan's body.

Lark comes in.

"I get a minute, too," she says, a bit defensively. Lachlan looks like he's torn between shoving her out the door and quietly retreating himself. There's such a weird dynamic between the two of them. What's their story, their connection?

I have to ask. "Did you two used to date or something?"

They look at each other with amusement, the first sign of any camaraderie.

"Er, no," Lachlan says.

"He's not my type," Lark adds with a giggle.

"Well, what then? I just don't understand the strange vibes you two are giving off. Are you . . ." I gasp. Iris says Lachlan is in love with me. Lark kissed me. "Did I . . . Was I involved with you both?" I can feel my cheeks go pink. I'm embarrassed and slightly thrilled at the same time.

"Yes," Lark says.

In the same breath Lachlan says, "No."

I look from one to the other.

"You weren't really 'involved' with either of us," Lark says.

"There was never time," Lachlan says. "Other things were more important."

"I'm sorry," I say. I want to tell them that I don't want to cause anyone pain, that right now I have tentative feelings for both of them. But I know everything might change the moment my memories come back. What I feel now won't matter. So I don't say anything more.

"See you soon, whoever you wake up as," Lachlan says, and before I can think whether it is a good idea, he kisses me on the forehead, the softest brush of lips. Then he's gone.

Lark sits on the exam table beside me. "Well, that was intense." She chuckles and tucks her lilac hair behind her ears.

I take her hands in mine, and she leans in with her eyes full of hope. "Lark, I need to tell you something." I hear her draw in an excited breath. Oh no, she thinks I'm going to say something else. That I love her. But I can't. I don't. I don't love either of them. Not yet.

I talk in a rush. "I need to thank you, Lark, for everything you've done for me. I was so terrible to you at Oaks, from the very first moment."

"That wasn't you!" Lark insists.

"It *was* me. It was the only me I knew then. I was not a good person, but you persisted, you brought out the better parts of me. You risked your life for me! Now, and in my past as Rowan. I am so grateful for you."

It's not my gratitude she wants, though. But I can't give her more. I need to wait until I'm whole again. Then I'm sure I'll know my own mind.

"Oh Rowan, I'd do it all over again!"

Then she's kissing me. And it's not a chaste kiss on the forehead. My lips part, and I feel the flicker of her tongue on mine.

The next instant she pulls away and is halfway across the room when she says, smiling through tears, "See you in a while. I'm excited for you to meet Rowan!"

14

"LIE DOWN. AND try to relax. Yeah, I know, easy for me to say. No one is going to be carving up *my* eyes. If it's any consolation, you won't feel a thing." She clears her throat and looks away before saying in a lower voice, "During the procedure, anyway."

"Afterward?" I ask.

"Look, we're dealing with a lot of unknowns here. Literally, just about anything could happen."

"Including microexplosions?" I ask, joking.

"This is the Center we're talking about. I wouldn't put anything past them. In theory, it should be a straightforward surgery. And it would be, probably, if I'd gotten to you a couple of months sooner. But by now your lenses have had a chance to almost fully integrate with your system. Effecting a full severance is going to be problematic."

"But you think you can do it?"

She nods. "Wouldn't be here otherwise. Now just lie back, and I'll see you in a while."

She picks a syringe from the table, but when she comes near me I instinctively curl into a ball. "No! I can't!"

I'm having memories, visions, of real life, of a dream, I don't know. The woman I called Mother, and other people in green scrubs, holding me down, injecting things into my veins that burn like fire . . .

Flame sets down the syringe. "I'm not going to do this if you're not willing. You know the risks. I need your consent." I stay curled up, focusing on my breathing. She glances over her shoulder and then whispers, "Are they making you do this against your will? If that bastard Flint . . ."

"No, I want to do it. I need to. For myself, and for all the second children." I force myself to uncurl. "I'm sorry. Go ahead. I'll try to be braver."

It's easy after the injection. For a few moments I feel a light-headed calmness. Then I seem to be floating up toward the ceiling. Then . . . nothing.

* * *

I'm small, and sitting on a woman's lap. I look up at the most beautiful, serene face I can imagine. She strokes the hair from my eyes and says, "Hush, and I'll tell you a story. Once upon a time there was a girl with kaleidoscope eyes, imprisoned in a castle."

"By an evil stepmother?" I ask.

"No, the evil stepmother will come later. This girl was imprisoned by her loving mother, who wanted to keep her safe."

I settle back into her lap and listen as she tells me a tale alternately joyous and sorrowful. A tale of long waiting, and rash impulsive action. A tale of adventure and love and heartache.

The girl, locked behind high stone walls, knew all about the outside world from her brother. She was safe in her prison, but lonely and bored. Her loving mother found a way for her to be free—but it meant leaving her family behind. Angry and afraid, the girl climbed the wall, and met a princess with lilac hair. She felt as if she'd known her all her life. In a way she had, because the princess was her brother's best friend, and she had heard everything about her.

For a while, life was beautiful. And then the monsters in green shirts came. The girl and her mother fled, and her mother was slain. Before she died, she told her daughter two terrible truths. Her own father had tried to kill her in her mother's womb. And she was firstborn—it should have been her brother behind the walls all along.

The girl ran through a mechanical city without plants, without animals, without so much as the smallest insect, until a prince disguised as a beggar found her and fell in love. He took her to a magical city where trees grow beneath the Earth, and gave her an entire family to replace the one she lost. Then, just when she thought she might be happy, the girl found out her brother was stolen by the evil ogre. The prince made a bargain: if she would give up her kaleidoscope eyes, he would help her save her brother.

"And they did," my mother coos to me as she rocks me in her lap. "The girl with kaleidoscope eyes, the lilac princess, and the beggar prince all saved her brother. But the girl gave up her freedom to save him. For just a moment, she escaped the mechanical lifeless city, and glimpsed paradise. But she was captured, and the monsters tortured her, changed her. Throughout it all, she never revealed her secret knowledge of paradise beyond the lifeless city."

"Mother," I ask, "what happened to the girl?" It's a very important question, but I ask it so calmly, because my mother's eyes make me feel absolutely safe.

"The girl? Why, she wakes up."

FROM VERY FAR away I hear another voice. "She should be awake by now. Hold on, I'm going to give her something."

I feel a flutter on the inside of my arm, and suddenly I'm being pulled away from my mom's loving arms. I try to hold on, but she vanishes.

I'm in a meadow. The sun is warm on my back, and a gentle breeze lifts the tendrils of my hair. There is tiny life all around me, the hums and clicks and buzzes and trills of a thousand small creatures crawling and flying in the flower-filled field. Just before me is a forest of just-turning fall foliage, still mostly green, but kissed with scarlet and brilliant gold.

A deer prances lightly from the woods, sniffing the air. I freeze, unwilling to scare it, but it sees me and steps on its delicate hooves across the meadow. Songbirds startle before it. The deer stops right before me and sniffs the air, reaching out its long, graceful neck until it is almost touching me with its nose. I reach out a hand and the deer speaks.

"I see you, Rowan."

THAT OTHER VOICE now: "She's still not responding. I'm going to increase the dose."

Then with blinding pain, blinding light, I'm viciously ripped from that beautiful, peaceful place and thrown into a world of nothing but agony. Daggers are stabbing into my skull, someone's thumbs are pressing on my eyeballs. I scream, and the terrible piercing sound only makes my eyes hurt worse.

But the physical pain is the least of it. Because I remember.

I remember everything.

And I'm not just remembering. I'm crashing into every single thing that ever happened in my life, all at the same time.

Every event of my life is happening to me *now*. I'm crushed by it, layer upon layer collapsing on me. I see my mother being shot. I turn away from my first sight of Lark . . . and turn back again. I'm being swallowed by nanosand. I see the beggar's golden starburst eyes in the handsome young man who saves me. Another memory pushes that one away. I see the wild, fertile world beyond Eden . . .

But I can't even think about that because there are other memories, worse things, from the time between Rowan and Yarrow. From the time when I'm just a slab of meat and neurons, strapped down on a steel table for the Center officials to play with. I can see the Chief of Intelligence looming over me, and, horrifyingly, she is both my mother and a stranger. I see her through both Rowan's and Yarrow's eyes. And, oh great Earth! I remember who else was always in the room, performing the surgery alongside of her. My father! Not some implanted false memory of a father, but my real father, the one who betrayed our family.

I can *feel* them scraping away at my brain. I can hear them discussing me impersonally, as if I weren't a being with consciousness and will.

By the time they were done with me, I wasn't.

I can feel each piece of Rowan being stripped away bit by bit, pounded down by their relentless treatments until the last traces of the person I was are gone. No, not gone, but hiding so deeply in the darkest recesses of my brain, quivering in terror, that they might have been lost forever.

Now they're back, and I'm Rowan again.

Only, I'm Yarrow, too.

I'm not one person with memories of before and after. I'm two different girls living in one body, sharing one brain.

The pain in my eyes is excruciating, but I try to open them, just to figure out what is going on. I am in a million places at once, with a billion things happening to me. But when I open my eyes, the world is dark.

I rub them, and feel someone grab my wrists. "You can't do that!" a woman shouts at me, and I pull back, staggering against something cold, metal. An operating table. That woman's voice, could it be?

I'm back in the lab again, and that woman I thought was my mother is trying to torture me again, to take away my self, my soul! My eyes are wide open and staring, but I can't see a thing. I'm blind! She's carved out my eyes!

"No!" I scream, a single word to protest every single thing that has been done to me, everything they are planning to do. I'll never let them steal my identity again. I'll never let them meddle with my brain. I'd die first.

I'd kill first.

When hands touch me, I flail wildly at first, but as soon as I can grab a hank of material I pull the person in and start pounding them with my fists. I can tell from the meaty resistance that I'm not hitting anything vital, maybe a hip or a thigh, so I keep tight hold and drop to the ground, wrapping my legs around them. We roll, and as soon as I end up on top I start swinging.

"Rowan, stop!" the woman's voice says, but I'm an animal fighting for her life. I hear a muffled *oof* and a snap of bone. Ribs, I think.

Suddenly I feel arms around me, big, strong arms, and I'm being lifted off the ground. For a moment my legs kick, and then I'm enfolded in an embrace that is part straitjacket, part hug. I still can't see a thing, but I know the touch of him, the smell.

"Lachlan," I breathe into his chest. "Help me!" I plead, my voice muffled and desperate.

He says those sweet, comforting nothings, and I feel the

fire drain away. I just want to be comforted. His arms make me feel safe.

"It hurts, Lachlan. It hurts so much . . ."

He kisses my brow, softly, reverently, like he did before. "I know, Rowan. But it will pass. Do you remember anything?"

I look up at his face with wide, unseeing eyes.

"Lachlan, I remember everything."

Then I pull him closer so that my lips brush against his earlobe as I speak. Of all the things I remember, one thing outshines all the torment, the pain, the loss. One glittering beacon of hope.

"There's life outside of Eden!"

15

"WHO'S HERE?" I reach out a hand, and feel the answering pressure of fingers I'm sure are Lark's. I'm on the ground, my back pressed securely against Lachlan's chest.

"I'm with you, Rowan," Lark says.

"Me too," echoes Ash.

"I can't see!" I manage not to shout, but nothing can hide the edge of hysteria in my voice. Lachlan holds me a little tighter, and I feel the slightest nuzzle of his cheek against my hair. My panic is held in check—barely.

"Things didn't go quite as well as I'd hoped." I hear Flame's voice, flat and cynical as ever. "Your eyes and nerves didn't respond quite the way I'd anticipated." She's disappointed, with her own skill, I suppose, but she makes it sound like my eyes were the ones who deliberately let her down. Well, sorry.

"But . . . you remember?" Lark asks, breathless with hope.

"I remember everything," I say, and rub my thumb over the knuckles of the hand I'm still clutching. I'm almost glad I can't see the expression on her face, and Lachlan's. The two people with feelings for me, both holding me, wanting to comfort me. They've waited for me to remember them for so long. Even amid all the other chaos of our lives, I know they've waited for me to choose. And I can't. I love them both. My feelings for Lark are fresher, since we were friends when I was Yarrow. But that's all we were in that incarnation of me: friends. Rowan loved her, Yarrow . . . might have, soon. And the second I remembered Lachlan, my feelings for him hit me like the tackle of a securitybot, hard, fast, devastating.

I can't think about this now.

Part of me doesn't want to think about anything else. Hard as that is, everything else is so much harder.

"Why can't I see?" I ask. Because that seems to be one of the top ten important things in the ten thousand important things going on right now.

I hear Flame suck in her breath, and I think it almost kills her to have to say, "I don't know. You should be able to see just fine. In theory. But . . ."

"What?"

"One of the lenses came out without a hitch, and it looks like I managed to undo all of the damage and excise all of the connections the lens made."

"*One* of them?" I have a bad feeling about what is coming next.

"Lefty was fine. The right eye, though, presented more significant problems. I found I couldn't completely sever the connection, so I had to be a little more aggressive. Unfortunately . . ." I can almost hear the shrug in her voice. "Hey, in my defense, I don't think there's a person in Eden who could have done what I did with old Lefty, even the people who were messing with your neurons in the first place. Do you realize that your lenses were intricately linked directly to your brain? Most lenses have a slight connection via the optic nerve to the brain, but yours were almost fully involved. I've never seen such a tangle of real and artificial nerves. If those lenses had stayed in a few more months, it would have been irreversible. We're lucky we got one out, and your memories back."

I process this for a moment. "You mean," I ask slowly, "I still have one of my lenses?"

"Yes," Flame says. "The right one."

"And . . ." I gulp. "There's still a *connection* in the right lens?" Lachlan must be able to feel my pulse accelerating where my back presses against his chest. He starts to stroke me soothingly from my shoulder down my arm.

"I took out a lot of the connections, nearly all of them, but yes, there are still some there."

I feel my control waver, and say much louder than I mean to, "You mean they can still access my brain? Get inside my head and mess with my memories?"

"No, no," Flame reassures me. "Well, yes. A bit. But they'd have to have you back in the Center." She pauses a beat. "Probably."

"You're never going back there, Rowan," Ash says. "You're safe now. You can stay in the Underground. No one will change your memories again." His voice sounds unexpectedly strong and resolute. I think living down here has been good for him. Come to think of it, I haven't heard him cough more than once since I came down here. "I'm not going to lose my kid sister again."

I flinch at that, because now I remember that I'm really the oldest one. When he was born second, with a lung condition, my parents chose to make him the firstborn. He needed medical treatment. If they'd hidden him away, he would have died. I love my brother. I'd give my life for him. Still, resentment for that decision, for the long years of isolation I bore, smolders under my love for him. I hate that about myself, but I can't help it.

Now, if I'm actually blind, I'll be trapped again. I've gotten my memories, but without working eyes I won't be able to leave the Underground. I'd need help, I'd be too conspicuous, I'd put everyone in danger.

Trapped again.

First trapped behind a wall. Then trapped under Yarrow's personality. And now trapped deep below the surface by blindness.

"Your sight might return," Flame adds, sending a surge of bright hope through me. "Your optic nerves have suffered severe trauma. Right now you need to rest, close your eyes, and wait. I'll give you something to help you sleep. When you wake up, I'll evaluate you and we should have a clearer picture about your prognosis."

Sleep sounds heavenly. Just to drift away from all my problems, from the onslaught of memories. But . . .

"I have to tell you something. Who else is here?" Because I hear the murmurs and movement of other people who haven't yet spoken aloud. And the thing I whispered to Lachlan isn't meant for every ear. Oh, it should be. I should shout it from the highest algae spire in Eden. But I worry about the chaos it might inspire. I think this is something that has to be handled carefully at first.

"Flint," Lachlan breathes into my ear. Maybe I should get up, but I feel so comfortable here. Without my sight I'm better on the ground, with someone I trust completely at my back. "Iris. And Adder." He drops his voice to a whisper. "The woman with the snake tattoos you saw earlier."

"And that's all?"

I feel him nod, and I wonder if he's using it as an excuse to brush his cheek against my hair.

I take a deep breath, aware that this is perhaps the most momentous moment of my life. Briefly, I tell them what happened after we broke Ash out of the Center. To give them the best chance to escape, I realized at the last moment that I had to stay behind, a distraction. I tell them of my manic flight through the city, to the very edge of Eden. How I passed the wall of refuse into the camouflaged forest of towering artificial trees.

"Then an earthquake came. The ground heaved up, and the trees started to fall. A huge split opened in the ground."

"I don't remember an earthquake that day," Ash said, looking at me confusedly with his flat lenses.

"We think the Center can erase some memories through the lens interface," Flint says. "No one on the surface remembers the earthquake. Only second children."

"And I remember it," Lark chimes in, then chuckles. "When your brain randomly zaps itself, it's hard for anyone to take it over, I guess."

"When the earthquake happened, everything changed. The desert stopped being hot. There was no nanosand. And when the Greenshirts came after me and I ran out across the sand, I saw . . ."

"Go on," Lachlan urges me gently.

"I saw a wilderness." My voice is full of wonder. It is unbelievable, even though I clearly remember seeing it with my own eyes. "Trees! A whole forest of trees! A meadow with flowers and bees and butterflies. A deer! It came out of the forest and looked me right in the eye!" My voice is rising with excitement. I know I sound like a fanatic, but how can I not? It is what the people of Eden have been anticipating for generations. The Earth has healed itself.

When I finish speaking there is utter silence for a long moment.

"That's amazing," Lark says, though there's something off about her voice. Does she believe me? Or does she just care about me so much she wants to support anything I believe, even if she thinks it is a delusion?

But nothing can dampen Ash's enthusiasm. I hear a thud as he drops to his knees in front of me and takes my hands.

"You've seen our salvation, Rowan!" he says. "This makes everything we've been through worthwhile."

Everything, I think. My prison, and all of humanity's prison in the city of Eden. Our mother's death. Our father's betrayal of us. Was all of the suffering the price we paid for the paradise that awaits us out there?

Then there's another silence. At first I think it's surprise and awe. Then the realization sets in. "You don't believe me?" I ask, incredulous. I didn't expect instant belief, but at least I thought they'd be curious, ask questions. Aside from Ash and Lark, though, they all seem to dismiss what I've said outright.

"Rowan," Flame says with a gentleness unusual in her. "Your brain has been through rather a lot. They've done things to you I can only guess at. You've gotten your memories back, but there might be other things left behind."

"What do you mean?" I ask, growing nervous.

"They implanted a whole new person, and a new personality. I couldn't actually erase anything they might have added to you. I could only unlock the things they had banished from your memory."

"So you're saying that among all of the things I remember, things about my real life, they might have implanted more false memories? Not just Yarrow's personality?"

I stare into the blackness. She's right. Although I can remember everything from my life as Rowan, I can also remember the memories of being a young Yarrow. That birthday, the day in the rain. But I know, rationally, that those are false memories, like a vivid vid I watched over and over so many times it became ingrained in me. I might feel like I remember those Yarrow memories, but my brain can rationally decide that they aren't real.

But they still feel real. Could it be possible that the fertile land I saw outside of Eden is a false memory, implanted by the Center?

No.

Maybe.

No! I can remember the smell of the wildflowers, of the herbs I crushed under my feet as I walked. I remember the dark liquid eye of the deer. It is real!

I hate the tiny trace of doubt that haunts me, and I react with anger. "I saw it with my own eyes!" I realize too late the irony of this, but forge on. "I was there. It wasn't the result of a neural interface or implanted memories. I walked across a meadow. A bee landed on my arm. There was a forest, deep and dark, and a deer walked out of it." My voice is getting louder and louder, and I can feel Lachlan squeeze me gently, in warning. Does he believe me? I couldn't bear it if he didn't. But he doesn't say anything.

I hear Adder's voice next. "Does she expect us to believe that nonsense? She's delusional. Or still drugged. Flint, let's see what she knows about the Center and take it from there. We don't have time for this kid's stories." She doesn't even respect me enough to talk *to* me. Just about me, to Flint.

Flint is more diplomatic. "Rowan, try to look at things clearly. If the Earth is healed, if all that is really out there, we'd know about it. The EcoPan has sensors out there, monitoring the air and water and soil conditions, looking for signs of recovery. What you're describing would take centuries to happen. Millennia. Eons. Scientifically, it isn't possible. There are no more plants. There are no more animals. The land has to heal, and then they have to evolve. Or, at best, we can hope that some of the seed banks survived the fall of mankind and the Ecofail. Bioengineered plants and mechanical bees. In any case, the most we can hope for is a clean but empty earth. Not trees and animals. It's simply impossible."

His voice is so calm and reasonable, his logic so persuasive.

"I know it doesn't sound likely," I say, and I'm ashamed that my voice is faltering. "But it was there!" I'm breathing hard and my voice rises again. "I saw it, and it was . . . it was . . ." I break down. The memory of that wild beauty, combined with my burgeoning doubts about its existence, is overwhelming me. I can feel tears welling in my eyes, and I try to blink them back, but I feel one fall from my right eye.

Lark gasps. "Rowan! You're bleeding!"

The tear feels strangely heavy, and when I wipe it away it has the viscous feel and metallic smell of blood.

"That's enough!" Flame hauls me abruptly to my feet. I feel bereft without the comfort of Lachlan's chest at my back. "She just got out of surgery, and you're overtaxing her. She needs time to recover." She guides me across the room, and my thighs bump the edge of a bed.

"We need more information from her!" Adder says. "Real information we can use, about the Center, not those deranged babblings about a forest."

"Your rebel work can wait," Flame says coldly. "I'm responsible for her health, and I insist she be left alone."

I hear Adder mutter, and Flint whisper that there's still time before their plan is fully operational. Then I feel the prick of a needle in my arm. By the time Flame and Iris have me tucked in, the voices have all faded, and I'm drifting away . . .

SOME TIME LATER—an hour, a day, a week—I wake up and open my eyes. I'm in what must be a recovery room. It looks partly like a medical unit, and partly like a bedroom. It takes me a moment before I realize I can see again.

I start to grin . . . but something is wrong. When I reach for the glass of water waiting at my bedside, my fingers fumble and I almost knock the glass over. I stop and look at it, then at everything else in the room. Things look a little flat and . . . I can't quite define it. Not quite right.

It is a full minute before I realize I'm still blind in my right eye.

I have to talk myself down from panic. I can see—that's good. Losing sight in one eye isn't the end of the world. A mirthless chuckle erupts. The end of the world already happened with the Ecofail, so there's nowhere to go but up.

I try to count my blessings, but I'm scared and upset as I cross the room to look in the mirror. I hear the door open. "Rowan, you're awake!" It's Ash, with Lark on his heels. But I don't even look at them. I'm fixated on my image in the mirror.

My left eye is my own, the one I've known my whole life. Blue, green, and gold, sparkling where the light hits it.

My right eye is a flat, dead gray. The lens is still implanted.

Both of my lives, my selves, are represented in my eyes. Rowan on the left, Yarrow on the right. I'm still both girls. Does that mean I'm accepted in both worlds, the Underground and the surface? Or that I'll forever be an outsider to both?

From somewhere very nearby, I seem to hear a voice whisper, "I see you, Rowan."

"What did you say?" I snap, whirling to face Lark and Ash.

"You're awake," Lark says, looking a little confused. "Can you see me?" She peers more closely at me. "Oh!" Her hand flies to her mouth. I close my eyes.

"No, it's okay," Lark instantly says to soothe both of us. "It looks beautiful! Interesting!"

"I don't care how it *looks*," I say, though that's not true. I want to be wholly Rowan again. I resent that the other person is inside me against my will. And that voice. Is that an echo of Yarrow speaking to me? Something else? Just a confused false memory?

Once they know I can see out of one eye at least, they are relieved. My half blindness doesn't seem like a big deal to them, nor does my strange appearance. They're just happy I'm alive and here, with my memory intact.

"Where's Lachlan?" I ask after a while. I feel like I need him right now. I love Lark—one way or another, I'm not sure which—but with her privileged life as a first and only child I don't know if she can understand what I'm feeling as well as Lachlan can.

When I ask, though, Ash looks at Lark . . . and Lark looks quickly down.

"What's wrong?" I ask. "What happened to him?"

"Lachlan's gone," Ash tells me. "He went to find your forest."

16

"HE DID *WHAT*?" I shout. "He went off on his own to cross the desert?"

"There was a big argument after Flame sedated you," Ash says. "Lachlan wanted to immediately call for volunteers to try to cross the desert and see if what you remember is true. Oh, I believe you! *We* believe you. But Flint and the others don't. Flint wouldn't authorize it. So . . . Lark suggested he go without authorization."

Lark is still staring at the floor.

No. She wouldn't do that. She'd never stoop so low.

But why won't she look at me?

"*You* suggested that?" I ask with venom. I turn to Ash. "Didn't you try to stop him?"

"Of course," he says. "But you know how he is. Once he has his mind set on something he's not just going to wait around for permission."

I know that, but even Lachlan wouldn't do something so foolhardy, would he? Not unless someone pushed him into it.

"Look at me, Lark," I say, and finally she does. Her eyes are wide and innocent, caring and concerned. But it could be just an act. I've seen Pearl often enough acting nice to get something she wants. She could be as sweet as anything to

someone's face, and then tear them apart as soon as their back
was turned. Lark might be dissembling just as well.

My voice steely, I ask her, "How long has he been gone?"
I have no idea how long I've been asleep.

"Almost a day," she says in a small voice. I'm sure I hear
guilt in it, and see guilt in the slump of her shoulders.

"You sent him away," I hiss at her. "I don't know how
you convinced him, but you talked Lachlan into going to
look for the forest, didn't you?"

"No, I . . ."

I don't let her finish. I'm so convinced. "I saw the look in
your eyes when I got my memory back, and I remembered
everything I feel for Lachlan. You couldn't stand it, could
you?" I feel a little of Yarrow coming out. I want to make her
suffer. "You saw me in his arms, and it drove you crazy. You
hated him for it. You wanted him dead."

She's shaking her head, and Ash is stammering *no, no.*

But I'm still two people. Rowan's feelings for Lachlan
are mixing strangely with Yarrow's need to dominate any girl
that's a threat. Some rational part in the back of my brain is
whispering a warning that I'm behaving badly, and just about
to step over a dangerous edge. Once I do, there may be no
going back again. But somehow, I can't stop myself.

"You're bikking jealous," I say in a slow voice. "Ever since
you found out about Lachlan, you've hated him. You've been
planning something like this all along, and now you finally
got your chance to get rid of him." As I speak, Lark's face goes
from uncomprehending to incredulous . . . to furious. I don't
care. I can't stop myself.

I lean closer to her and whisper, "You sent him to his
death, so you could have me all to yourself!"

Lark gasps, a sound of pure astonishment. Then, almost
in the same instant, she slaps me and runs out of the room. As

the door slams behind her, I hear a sob. But it's the angriest sob I've ever heard.

My cheek is stinging, and Ash looks at me dumbfounded.

"She didn't send Lachlan away," Ash says, looking at me like I've lost my mind. "She thought we should all go. Her, me, Lach. You when you were feeling better. Flint said no, and when he left, Lark said we should all go anyway, that Flint might be the leader but he didn't actually have the power to control us. Then Lark and Lachlan had a big argument, with him saying it was too dangerous for her to go. That you'd never forgive him if anything happened to her."

"Oh," I say in a small voice.

"They said they'd save the argument for after you woke up, see what you thought. But then when I went to check on Lachlan, he was gone. So was one of the survival suits. Lark wanted to go after him right away, but I talked her into waiting until you woke up. You're the only one who has been out there. I figured we had a better chance of helping him with you there, too."

What have I done? Lark tried to stop Lachlan, then wanted to save him. And I accused her of wanting him to die in the desert, burned or swallowed by nanosand.

I have to apologize. To accuse her of such a thing is almost unforgivable. My cheek burns from her slap, but more than that, I burn with shame. After all of the brave, generous, loving things she's done for me. Lark saved me from a prison I didn't even know I was in.

The person who said those horrible things—it wasn't me. Was it? Was it Yarrow's artificial personality coming through? Or is it the real me? How can I really know how I act within a society, when I've been hidden away all of my life? Maybe I'm really a terrible person who believes the worst of everyone. Maybe I can't trust, or love . . .

I need to make this right.

"Rowan," Ash begins tentatively as I tie back my hair and pull on my shoes. "What did you mean, when you said Lark wanted you all to herself?" His voice is so careful, as if he's afraid of the question, and even more afraid of the answer.

Oh, great Earth, he doesn't know. He doesn't realize.

"Ash, I'm sorry." I didn't think it was possible for me to feel any more awful, but I do. "I know you have feelings for Lark, but . . ." How can I say it gently but without leaving him in any doubt? "She loves me," I say at last, simple and stark and unequivocal.

He stares at me. He knew it was coming, I can tell. He must have seen it in the way Lark looks at me, heard it in her voice. Still, he seems taken aback.

"Are . . . are you sure? I know she likes you. A lot. I just thought . . ." His voice breaks, and he clears his throat to pull himself together. It ends up with him coughing.

"I'm sorry," I say again, miserably. I don't know what to do. How can I be responsible for someone else's feelings—his or Lark's? All the same, I feel sick and guilty.

"Do you love her back?" he asks.

How can I even answer that question? Even Rowan didn't know, really, and I've only just become her again. And the Yarrow in me still has guilty flashes when she—I—view Lark as an outer circle intruder into my elite life. I'm not proud of those thoughts, but they come unbidden. I have to study every thought that pops into my head, trying to figure out if it is really mine. Rowan's. But Ash needs an answer. "I . . . I think so. I don't know."

"What about Lachlan?" His tone is a little defensive now, a little sarcastic. "Do you love him, too? I know how he feels about you."

I sigh. "The same answer. I think so. I don't know."

"So you get two people who love you, and I get . . . no one."

"You have plenty of people who love you!" I say, even though I know it's not what he wants to hear right now.

"It's not the same," he says. "I've liked Lark for so long. We're so close, we talk about everything. Well," he adds with a mirthless laugh, "obviously not everything. I like her so much, Rowan. I love her. I can't help it! What's wrong with me?"

"Nothing, you're perfect."

"Just not for Lark."

"She loves you, I know she does. Just . . . not like that. I don't know if she could love a boy in that way."

"And you?" he asks, curious now.

"Oh Ash, I honestly don't know how to answer!" I tell him. "For sixteen years, I didn't meet anyone but you and Mom . . . and our father." Just thinking of him fills me with bitterness. "I didn't know anything about people, how to be with them, how to be friends or how to love them or anything. I met Lark, and I thought she was the most wonderful person I'd ever met. But she already felt like my best friend, because she was your best friend, and you told me so much about her. When I finally met Lark, it felt like the conclusion of a story I'd been telling myself for years!"

"And when you met Lachlan?"

I chuckle. "He was the first second child I ever met, and that made a strong bond between us, instantly. Beyond that . . . he made me angry, and confused, and excited. Usually all at once! He made me feel like life was an adventure, but that with him I'd be safe. Loving Lark was quiet, expected, wonderful. Loving Lachlan was like a thunderstorm, an earthquake. And also wonderful."

I've said it now. I love them both.

Ash hangs his head. I think he may be fighting back tears. In a moment, though, he pulls himself together and looks up at me, smiling. "I'm happy for you, my cockeyed sister."

I gape at him, then realize that if he's teasing me, he's going to be okay. So I revert to our old brother-sister relationship and punch him in the shoulder.

"Ow!" He says, rubbing his arm. "I mean it, sis! I want you to be happy. One of us should be." I shoot him a look. "Sorry, sorry, that's uncalled for. So, in love with two people, eh? What are you going to do about that?"

"I have no idea," I admit. "But right now, I have to apologize to Lark. And then go and find Lachlan."

"Too bikking right," Ash says. "Otherwise, the only one left who will love you is your boring old brother."

He's trying so hard to act like he's okay, but as I leave I can hear him sigh.

I enter Lark's room without knocking. I'm afraid if she knows it's me, she won't let me in.

"Lark, I'm so sorry," I say immediately, then stop. She's packing things into a satchel. "No! You can't leave! I was stupid, I admit it. So very stupid. I don't know what came over me. It wasn't me—it was Yarrow. That sounds like an excuse, but I swear as I was saying it I didn't mean it. I tried to bite it back and I couldn't. It was like Rowan was just watching Yarrow mess everything up." I'm talking all in a rush, desperate for her forgiveness. "Please forgive me. Please don't leave the Underground. I . . . I don't know what I'd do without you."

"I'm not going," she says, and I beam.

"Does that mean you forgive me?"

"It means I'm not abandoning you—all of you, the second children. I'm going to search for Lachlan."

"I am, too!"

"No" she says firmly. "You just got out of surgery. What's

more, Center officials are probably looking for you all over Eden. I'm not on their radar. I'll be safe. You need to stay here." She swallows hard, and adds, "Don't worry, I'll get Lachlan back for you."

"I can't lose both of you!" I cry. "And it's not your job to get Lachlan back . . . for me. Oh Lark, I'm so confused!"

Before I can start to weep, she has her arms around me. "It's okay, Rowan. It's not your fault. Hey, I like Lachlan, too. He's a wonderful guy, and the two of you . . ." She makes a little hiccuping sound. "If you love him, I'm happy for you."

"I love you both," I say starkly. It feels easier to say the second time.

"I . . . Okay. Well, that's . . ."

I start to laugh, I can't help it. "That's messed up, that's what it is!" I say. Then I shrug helplessly. "I just don't know what to do about it."

"Well, let's ask Lachlan." She tosses me a tightly compressed package.

"What's this?"

"A survival suit. There are hundreds of them stored deep in the cave system. This place was originally meant to be used if the conditions were too harsh to survive on the surface, even with Eden's atmospheric shields and climate control. They're meant to keep people safe in extreme temperatures, radiation, toxins—all the stuff we killed the Earth with."

"But they're so old. Do they still work?"

"They should, in theory," she says. "Only one way to find out." I pack my survival suit in her bag and together we leave. We'll sneak out and find Lachlan.

Ash catches us before we do. His eyes are a little red, but he's carrying a pack and looks excited and eager. "You're not leaving me behind."

"No way," I say. "I went to too much trouble to save you. I'm not going to risk you getting hurt, or captured again. And with your lung condition you're less likely to survive as long in the desert, if the suits fail or anything goes wrong."

"My lungs have been a lot better since I came down here. The air seems cleaner, or maybe it's something about the tree." He takes a deep, full breath. The sharp smell of camphor is all around us from the huge, fragrant tree. "I'll be fine. You can't keep me from going with you. I'm tired of being treated like the victim. I want to be the one doing the rescuing for a change. And I am the older sibling," he adds with a grin.

He's not, but I won't tell him that. He's had enough heartbreak for one day.

"Okay," I say with a resigned sigh. "But be careful. And if I say run—you run!"

17

"IF YOU HADN'T agreed to let me go with you, I had one more card to play," Ash tells us as we make our way carefully to one of the exits. We're doing our best to look nonchalant, but as three of the newest, and therefore most interesting, people in the Underground, we have all eyes on us. We have to walk aimlessly around for a long time before we manage to get to an exit unseen.

"What's that?" I ask.

He holds out a little case. It sloshes when I shake it. "I swiped it from Flame's bag when she was doing your surgery. It's a pair of the temporary lenses she makes for the second children when they have to go to the surface."

"Who will it say I am if I'm scanned?" I ask.

"It's programmed to initially read as a glitch. The scanners and bots don't always get a clear read, so if you just get caught in a neighborhood sweep or random scan, it will tell them that you're an official citizen, but not who you are. Then it's programmed to give a false identity on the second scan, like if you're actually stopped and individually questioned. Glitch mode is usually enough to get someone by, they say." He winks at me as he holds up a little pocket mirror for me to fit the lens over my naturally colored eye. "The Center doesn't know how dangerous you second children are!"

When he moves to put the mirror away, I grab his wrist. I feel like I'm meeting myself anew every time I see my own image. Who am I now? I look like Yarrow, and seeing myself with the flat silvery-gray eyes makes me feel more like her again. I should probably wish that she was gone, thoroughly eradicated from my memory. But I almost miss her. She was me, in my mind anyway.

The lens dims my sight slightly, a disconcerting thing when that's my only functioning eye. The circuitry must have some effect on my vision in this model. I don't remember that from the temporary lenses my mom got for me, before she was killed. With my flattened depth perception and the slight blur to my vision I feel very vulnerable as we make our way to the surface.

I trust Lark and Ash with my life. Still, like Lachlan, I feel it should only be me taking the risk. I saw the oasis, the fertile land where everyone expected desert. It should be me who goes looking for it again. Of course, with my messed-up brain, no one quite believes me. I think maybe even Lark and Ash believe me more out of loyalty than an actual rational conviction that I saw the forest. So really, someone other than me needs to see it. If Lachlan comes back with a tale of trees and flowers and birds, they'll believe him.

I remember walking with Lark at night on the streets of Eden. Such glorious nights of freedom and new experiences! I was afraid the whole time, but giddy with excitement and the joy of discovery. Now I've experienced life as a fugitive, and as a legitimate member of society. I find I still walk with Yarrow's confidence, the assurance of a pampered, sheltered, rich girl, whose status will always protect her. Though I'm the one in the most danger, with the most to lose, I find I'm moving with more confidence than either my brother or Lark. Ash is new to this kind of adventure. And even Lark, who has been doing clandestine missions around Eden for years, seems nervous today. Maybe it is the residue from our emotional talk.

Since the journey is long, we risk the autoloop. Lark pays our fare with a flash of her lenses. There's a tense moment when a couple of Greenshirts on patrol come on board right behind us. At first I'm afraid that Lark has been flagged. But they sit far away from us and seem more concerned with catching up on their sleep during the ride, than looking for second children or escaped prisoners.

When they get off a few stops before ours, Lark explains in a whisper that she shouldn't be on any of the Center's lists. "I forged a letter from my parents, saying that they were withdrawing me from school for a week while I recovered from the trauma of my friend's attempted suicide."

"Sorry," she adds when my eyes go wide. "You know the Oaks administration. They hate scandal, and the thought that any of the Oaks parents might know about the drugs and bullying and suicide risk made them bend over backwards to accommodate me. And of course my parents think I'm still at Oaks. I figure at least one of us needs to be completely legitimate."

It works. We make it to the outer circles without incident. We disembark just before the outermost circle. We'll walk the last part of the way.

But something is different. The last time I was here, I was shocked at the rampant poverty. The buildings were dilapidated, the people near starving. I was astonished that there was such disparity between the inner circles, where the elite live, and the outer circles. While I'd been aware that social status declined the farther one got from the Center, I had no idea that our Eden could have a place filled with crime, hunger, desperation.

So as we move farther out, I'm braced for that again, for the pity, the anger that we can't take better care of our population.

Before, people walked around looking nervous, dejected, scared. Now the people I see appear to be relaxed and happy. There is no look of desperation in any of the eyes I meet. Before, people would avoid eye contact with strangers, but now we get a few casual smiles. There are fewer people on the street, too, which at first I think is a bad sign. But soon I notice that more of the stores are open and stocked. The windows in the offices and businesses are clean, not cracked, and I see light and movement behind them.

People are working.

They're fed. They're safe. They're happy.

While there is still an obvious discrepancy between the inner and outer circles, this place that used to resemble a war zone is now comfortable, I'd almost say prosperous. We pass by a place where there once was a deep crater, where the surrounding houses had crumbling, leaning walls from a long-ago blast. Lachlan once told me that there had been an uprising. The poor had taken up arms and tried to fight for their rights to work and food. The Center had crushed them, violently, devastatingly. No one but the second children remembered. I mentioned it to Lark, and she had never heard of it before. It had happened before we were born, but the second children in their twenties and older clearly remember hearing the explosions, seeing plumes of smoke.

Now, though, there is no sign of the crater I once skirted while the Greenshirts fired on me. The road is smooth, free of debris. The buildings are whole. What's more, they don't look like new construction.

I'm utterly confused, and ask Lark about it.

SHE LOOKS AROUND. "Looks about like I remember," she says. "Though admittedly I don't go to the outer circles all that often."

"But it wasn't like this," I insist. "It was dirty and dangerous." What does she mean she doesn't go to the outer circles? She came from the outer circles, and she went back as part of her work with the secret group the Edge, which sought to unify rich and poor, inner and outer circles.

Lark looks at me skeptically. "That was the first time you ever saw poverty," she says. "After being sheltered, and then only seeing the inner rings, I'm sure this was a little shocking."

No, I want to say. This is certainly different from the elite inner circles, but the people look normal and happy. This is nothing like the scary place I remember. What's wrong with me? Why don't my memories match up with reality? Or are my memories fine, and Lark's faulty?

I don't want to deal with this now, so I drop the subject. Finding Lachlan is the only thing that matters. Still, I can't help but wonder exactly how much Lark's epilepsy protects her from whatever memory manipulation the Center is inflicting on people through their lenses. Maybe she has a clearer vision of the world than most . . . but they might be able to get to her in some ways. I look at her out of the corner of my eye as we walk. I trust her completely. But could she be dangerous without even knowing it? How can any of us trust each other in a world where the government can meddle with your mind?

Lachlan could have tried to make his escape anywhere along the vast perimeter of Eden. This might be a fool's errand. Lachlan found me easily when I was out in the artificial giant beanstalks. He said he sometimes hid out in the fake forest. He could be anywhere. Still, it would make sense for him to try it in the same place where I escaped, to retrace my steps in hopes of finding the same thing I did. So we head that way, passing the soup kitchen where I once saw Lachlan disguised as an old beggar.

Only, it's not a place where the desperately poor receive a modicum of bland, filling food. Now it's a restaurant. A sandwich board out front declares their menu and modest prices. The outdoor cafe tables are filled with people who look like they're on their lunch break, grabbing a cheap, good meal.

It's all so . . . normal.

A hostess sees me pause, and asks if my friends and I would like a table. "No," I start to say, then confusedly ask, "Do you know a man . . . a young man, or an old man with a cane, who helps the poor people in this circle?"

She looks at me quizzically. "The poor? There are no poor in Eden."

I leave before she can say anything else. I don't want her to get suspicious at what was apparently an odd question. No poor in Eden?

Lark sees my befuddlement, and says, "Don't worry, it will probably be a while before you can tell what really happened from what they tried to implant in you. You have memories of terrible poverty? I wonder why the Center would give you those memories. After all, there are no poor in Eden."

I catch my breath. Her words are exactly the same as the restaurant hostess's. As if they both are reading from the same script.

Finally we come to something familiar—the wall of refuse from the civilization that existed before Eden. It is a tangle from another world, made up of concrete beams and rusting bars, obsolete electronics, and things that defy description.

Things that must have been useful back in the age when humans believed they were lords of the Earth. Now the EcoPan regulates all of our lives, from oxygen consumption to water to food, to make sure we have what we need without causing harm. Everything is efficient, recycled. The computer program and its bots take care of everything. Our lives have zero effect on the planet.

Before the Ecofail, though, people needed all sorts of strange implements and inefficient vehicles just to get through their everyday lives. Those are among the artifacts in the wall. The garbage of our past lives, keeping us secure in this one.

Secure . . . or trapped?

I have to be right. I know what I saw.

There are no guards around the wall of refuse. Why would there be, when beyond them lies death? At least, as far as anyone knows. Surely some people have crossed, those whose curiosity overrides caution or control, or the people like Lachlan, who live on the fringes and need places to hide.

Even the trash looks somehow . . . neater. Before, it was obvious that the locals in the outer circle had added their own garbage to the wall over the years. Now, though, that has all been stripped away, no doubt sent for recycling. All that remains are the artifacts, and their strangeness makes it look more like a museum piece than a wall of leftovers.

The difference makes it hard to find the spot where I crossed the last times. They weren't ideal circumstances, what with my life being in grave danger, so it is hard to visualize the details. The longer it takes, the more frustrated I get. Every obstacle in this search seems like one more shout in my face that I must be wrong.

I sniff the air. In the Underground, the smell of that single tree permeates the air. If there was a forest not more than a mile away, couldn't I smell something? The trees, the flowers, the dirt itself? Wouldn't a bird fly overhead one day? Wouldn't some hardy insect manage to get past the desert?

Nothing. No smell of life, no sign of life other than humans.

"Here it is . . . I think," I say. There's a place where the pattern of the jumble looks familiar, where three massive concrete beams cross. I see a little nook at the intersection that looks wide enough for us to slither through. "Yes, this is where I crossed before. I'm sure." *Almost* sure, I add silently. I doubt myself enough. I don't want to seed any more uncertainty in Lark or Ash, no matter how supportive they seem.

"I'll go first," I say, and start to wiggle my way through. They follow close on my heels, which I have to shout back isn't a great idea. It's not like there's a designated path through here. We have to double back a few times when we get stuck, which involves a lot of wiggling, and occasional pokes on sharp corners of things I can't begin to identify.

Finally, I squirm free into bright sunlight dappled with shadow. "No," I breathe.

"Wow," Ash gasps as he exits behind me. "This is amazing. If I hadn't seen an actual tree, I'd be sure those were real."

"It's wrong," I breathe as I crane my neck up to look at the massive creations. "So much of this is all wrong." They look like trees, but they are artificial bean plants like the giant's beanstalk in children's stories. Their stems are as thick as the camphor tree's mighty trunk, and they tower hundreds of feet high. They are covered with tendrils that twine to follow the sun, their broad leaves actually solar catchers that make energy with artificial photosynthesis.

"Great Earth, this is intense!" Lark says as she crawls out behind Ash. "They're so tall, so beautiful!"

Suddenly I snap. "They're not supposed to be tall, don't you understand? Most of them fell during the earthquake—

smashed and destroyed on the ground. They can't have gotten them repaired so fast. How could they?"

I clutch my head in my hands and mutter, "They're erasing things. They're taking them out of my brain and out of the world, and no one notices."

"Rowan, are you okay?" Lark asks.

"No!" I shout. "And these trees aren't beautiful at all. They're fake! I've seen real trees."

"So have we," Ash says, trying to calm me. "We just mean that they're impressive."

"They're wrong, just like everything else in Eden." I feel like I'm losing control. The doubts that swirl in my head make me lash out at the people I love. My need to prove myself makes me feel reckless . . . and lose my reason. "The real trees are out there!" I fling my arm to point through the trees, past the desert we can't yet see. "A forest, maybe a whole world of forests, while we're trapped in this fake world of lies and delusion."

And then I'm running, dashing through the impossibly tall beanstalks, while they call for me to wait, to stop. I don't care. I have to see the forest again. It's like something is calling out to me, summoning me home. Out there—that's where I belong. I won't let anything stop me.

Not even the merciless heat that hits me the instant I cross that sudden transition from dappled shade to glaring light. Reality slaps me in the face with the sudden heat. Within a few steps I stumble to my knees. My shins feel like they're on fire where they press against the sand. What was I thinking? Something hits my back. Lark has thrown me one of the survival suits. She's standing on the edge of the desert, hopping on one foot as she struggles into hers as quickly as possible. I tear my pack open and step into it, feeling the seals automatically bond to make an all-over covering that shields my body from the worst of the heat. At least, at first. After a moment I can feel the temperature start to rise again, though it is by no means as bad as when I was unprotected. Still deadly, I think, just not quite so quick.

Soon, Ash and Lark are suited up and hurry to join me. "What is it?" Ash asks. "Did you see Lachlan?"

"No, I . . ." How can I explain that I had to get to the forest, that a primal pull was tugging at my very soul? The forest that, for all I know, only exists in my mind, fed to me by the Center for unknown reasons.

Before I can explain myself, we're interrupted by a jarring beep. "Nanosand!" Lark calls out as she checks a device clipped to her hip. "It's a motion sensor, one of the spares they use to guard the entrances to the Underground. I figured it would work for moving nanosand, too."

I can see a shimmering in the distance. It looks like heat rising, that watery effect. Soon, though, I can tell it is the sand itself shifting. A patch of the mobile death trap that can swallow a human whole—and digest them, if what Lachlan says is true—is moving slowly toward us.

"They don't move very fast," I say, remembering my last experience with the nanosand. "But more will be coming, and they can easily surround us if we're not careful, and don't keep moving." Lark's motion scanner might prove a lifesaver. Nanosand is easy to outrun, as long as you know it is coming.

"How long do we have?" Ash asks as we hustle away from the creeping sand.

"Twenty minutes, maybe half an hour," Lark says. "I *think*. These suits were designed for the highest end of normal temperatures in Aaron Al-Baz's day. Death Valley could get to 130 degrees Fahrenheit. This suit could take that." She checks a scanner. "But I'm getting readings of 150 to 160 out here. This isn't normal heat."

"After the earthquake, the heat vanished just like that."
I snap my fingers. "And the sand shifted, and I saw what
looked like vents. This desert is man-made. Fake, just like the
bean trees. Just like the rest of Eden." I wish I could wipe the
sweat from my brow, but the suit covers my face. "This isn't
what the rest of the world is like, I just know it. They made
this desert."

"To keep us inside Eden?" Lark asks.

"To keep us outside of the wilderness," I realize. "Come
on!" The urgency is back. "It can't be more than a mile. We
can make it if we run!" I take off, and hear them following
behind. I'm sure they're doing the same calculations as I am.
Twenty or thirty minutes. Even I, a fast runner, can't reach
top speed in this deep sand. The heat is slowing me down
a lot, too. And Lark and Ash aren't nearly as fast as me. If
my memories aren't playing me false, we can make it a mile
through the desert without a problem. But if there isn't a
cool oasis at the end of it where we can recover, we might not
make it back.

WE TALK TO keep our spirits up. Out loud, I manage—for now—to shut out my doubts. Shut them out, but not shut them down.

"I can't wait for you to see it," I gush. "The camphor tree is amazing, but it's like . . . seeing a prisoner in a cage as opposed to seeing a happy family. Oh, once you see it, you'll understand."

"If there is a living, healthy world out there, there would be no need for population control," Ash says. "No more second child laws. People could do what they wanted."

"We did that before," Lark says gently. "Uncontrolled breeding, expansion, land clearing, mining . . . all those things and more destroyed the planet."

"But did they?" I ask. "I mean, what people did was thoughtless, reckless, terrible . . . but did they really kill the planet? What if it is all a lie?"

"If what exactly is a lie?" Ash wants to know.

"All of it!" I've read Aaron Al-Baz's journal. I know that no matter how much damage humans did to the planet, *he* was the one who killed off most of humanity.

"I never did get to tell you," Lark says. "I didn't tell anyone. I wasn't sure what it meant, and I wanted to tell you first.

I discovered something. Remember the photo you gave me? The one from your mother?"

A lifetime ago, I gave Lark a rare relic of the pre-fail days, an old-fashioned photographic image printed on plastic paper of a starscape over a great rocky rift in the Earth.

"The technology of the plastic paper dates it to right before the Ecofail. Back then, everything was nonbiodegradable plastic. Since we came to Eden, we haven't used that. So I know the photo was made within a decade of mankind's collapse."

The collapse that was sparked by Aaron Al-Baz, who decided there was no hope for humans, and created a virus to hasten their end just as the global ecosystem was collapsing. Lachlan is the only one other than me who knows this, though. We decided to keep it secret. Aaron Al-Baz is a hero. We didn't know what unmasking him might do.

"You can't imagine how many hours I've spent gazing at that photo. I love it, because you gave it to me." I can see her cheeks flush through her protective suit. "The more I looked at it, the more I started to notice details. When we lived in the outer circles, my dad would always take me stargazing on the rooftops."

I remember. I had my first kiss on one of those rooftops.

"My dad taught me about the patterns of the stars, the movements of the planets. Each planet travels a different distance, at a different rate. You can predict where planets will be hundreds, thousands of years in advance. And . . . you can look into the past and figure out what the night sky would look like on any given day. And Rowan, I figured out that the stars in the photo you gave me were in that position more than a thousand years ago!"

It takes a moment for this to sink in. "You mean . . . that photo was taken a thousand years ago?"

It's Ash who says what I'm thinking. "But that would mean that the Ecofail happened a thousand years ago, not two hundred."

Another lie from the government. Should I still be surprised?

"We have to tell people. They deserve to know! We've all been told that it will take a thousand years before the Earth is inhabitable again . . . and that time has passed. We think we're only two hundred years in, so we're content, patient. We think it will be generations before there's any hope of freedom, so we never question anything."

"Yeah, but . . . ," Ash begins. "That's not possible. You can't just take away eight hundred years from people." He laughs. "We have history books. We have family stories. They tell us that the Ecofail was only about two hundred years ago. You must have made a mistake about the stars, Lark."

"I checked and double-checked," Lark insists.

"Then it must be a forgery." Ash sounds complacent, so sure he must be right. Content in the beliefs he's been told all of his life.

Of course. He has the lens implants.

I think he *can't* believe it. Literally can't.

"Ash," I ask carefully. "Tell me the truth. Do you believe in the forest?"

He starts to nod . . . and then it is as if I can see the neurons firing in his brain, changing his mind mid-nod. "I believe in *you*, Rowan. That's why I'm here. And I believe we need to save Lachlan. But . . . trees? A whole forest, with animals, and clean air? How could that be?"

I feel tears prick my eyes. It's not his fault. He must be being controlled. Just like everyone in Eden with lenses.

"And you, Lark? The complete truth."

I watch her narrowly, and I can tell that for her, too, it

is a bit of a struggle. But her epilepsy interferes with a lot of the connection, resetting it, so it would seem, whenever she has an episode. "I believe the stars," she says. "They can't be changed. I believe the proof I found in my mother's job, the tallies that showed that we wouldn't run out of food or water or air even if the population doubled. I believe that no one but the second children and a few people with lens problems remember the earthquake. Put that all together, and it's clear something is very wrong with Eden. It's clear we're being lied to and controlled."

She sighs and takes my gloved hand in her own. "I don't know if there's a forest, or a whole living world out there. But if you saw it, I'll believe in it. I want to believe in it." She squeezes my hand quickly and then lets it go. "We need hope, Rowan."

We walk in silence for a time. I want them to hurry, but they don't seem able to go any faster. Sweat starts to drip into my eyes. The world around me is hazy and shimmery. I can't tell if it is from the inside of my suit fogging up, or the desert mirage of waves rising from the horizon, or the slight dimness the lens imparts. I feel like I'm walking in a dream, sluggish in the overwhelming heat. Just like in a dream, everything feels a little off.

I feel like I'm falling asleep on my feet. Ash gasps out something breathlessly that I can't make out. Bikk! The heat and exertion are giving him breathing problems. I knew we shouldn't have let him go.

"We should turn back," I say, even though every fiber of my being is urging me toward the trees I *know* exist right beyond the horizon. "No," I amend, "Lark, you need to bring Ash back." I make my voice firm, hard, commanding. "If one of us gets into trouble, the other two might die trying to save them. We can't have any weakness or hesitation." I ignore

Ash's wounded face. "Look, we'll never find Lachlan out on the desert. There's not time in the suits. It's too vast. The only chance is if he made it through to the forest. You two go back, and I'll run the rest of the way. If he's there, I'll have plenty of time to find him. And probably enough life left in my survival suit."

"I'm not letting you go on alone!" Lark says.

Instead of answering her, I look at Ash. She does, too.

"I can survive. Ash can't."

Ash protests angrily that he isn't weak, that he's not a burden, that he won't be treated like a child. But I lock eyes with Lark, and we understand each other. He has been her best friend since long before she met me. Many of the things she loves about me are the things she first came to love—though not in a romantic way—in him. Her friend, my brother. We join forces to keep him safe. Lark and I are survivors. It might wound him to think it, but Ash is not. The desert will kill him.

"Come on, Ash," Lark says, taking his arm. "We're going back."

"No!" Ash protests, but there's a whining, childish quality to it, as if he already knows he's defeated. "I'm not going."

Lark puts a spin on my tactic. "If you don't go now, you're putting us all at risk. The longer you stand here arguing, the less time Rowan has to cross the desert."

"Then we should *all* go back," he begins, but even as Lark starts forcibly dragging him away, her proximity alarm sounds.

"There's movement!" she shouts, looking down at the reading, then whirling frantically to scan the desert all around us. "Is it Lachlan?"

But he's nowhere to be seen, and a moment later we see the undulating disruption in the sand that means a patch of nanosand is approaching.

"It's okay, stay calm," I say. "You head back toward the bean trees. That's what it wants, to chase you out of the desert. If you leave, its job is done. If I keep going it should follow me. You'll be safe. It can't catch you if you keep moving."

Lark nods and pulls again at Ash. The motion detector keeps sounding. "Bikk! There's another one."

I see a patch approaching from our flank, like a shimmering blob just beneath the surface. "Go!" I shout, and Lark takes off running back toward the bean trees. But before long Ash breaks free and tries to run back to me.

"Come on, Rowan! I'm not leaving you behind. I can't lose you again!" His feet sink into the soft sand and he runs painfully slowly.

"Go back!" I cry, and almost run to him to force him to turn around. But no, better if I just run away from him. He can't catch me, can't keep up. He'll have no choice but to go back with Lark. It seems like the most efficient way, and with the heat seeping inexorably through the suit, speed is of the essence.

Only, Ash doesn't realize this fast enough. He tries to run after me, even though it is obviously hopeless, and Lark trips as she spins and runs after him. For a long moment we're all spread out in a line, me at my top speed, glancing over my shoulder at the other two as the motion sensor continues to wail.

Then I see it.

The alarm barely detects motion. It can't tell how many things are moving. My senses dulled by the heat, the lenses, by the myriad uncertainties in my own brain, I'm slow to see the other patches of nanosand approaching. Two are close; Ash has seen those.

He doesn't see the third.

Like a predator it has circled around behind him, and now

moves in for the kill. I skid to a halt, sending up a plume of sand, and race back to him as fast as I can. I point, I shout, but my voice is muffled by the suit and I'm sure he can't hear what I'm saying. But he knows something is going on, so he stops to figure it out.

The worst choice.

I know what nanosand feels like. First the stealthy nibble around the edges of your feet, feeling almost like the rest of the normal sand. Then a suction as it becomes a little bit harder to move. At first you'd think you just stepped in a patch of looser sand, and you'd stop, trying to pull your feet out. This is what it wants.

Nanosand doesn't just trap you. It *eats* you.

That's what Lachlan told me. Each individual particle is a synthetic organism. Together they act with a hive mind, pursuing any living thing foolish enough to enter the desert. The particles grab you, adhering to every surface of your skin and clothes. Then a billion tiny artificial creatures draw you slowly underground to your doom.

Then, Lachlan said, they start to digest you. Flesh, bones, and all. I don't know how he knows this. Maybe it is all a legend. But I was almost killed by the nanosand when it swallowed me. It filled my nose, my mouth, tried to choke the life out of me. I would have died if it hadn't been for Lachlan.

Now I skid to a stop just outside the reach of the nanosand and stretch my arms out for Ash. He's looking at the ground in perplexity, as if he can't believe this is happening to him. He bragged about being ready to face danger, but now that it is here he doesn't know what to do.

"Hold on! I'm coming!" I hear Lark call out. Then she shrieks. Beyond my slowly sinking brother I see her dodge sharply to the left, a look of panic on her face. There's nanosand all around her! She plants her feet and stops abruptly as a patch seems to erupt in front of her, then hurls herself backward out of its reach, sprawling on her back in the sand. I drop Ash's hand and take a step toward her.

"No!" she shouts to me. "I'm fine. Help Ash first!"

She looks like she can evade the sand for a moment longer, and this patch has swallowed Ash to the thighs by now. I grab both of his wrists and pull as hard as I can, but the suit is slick, and my gloved hands slide off, making me stumble back. When the tension of my pull releases, he falls back, too, and the nanosand seems to lurch hungrily around his hips.

I hear a sharp cry from Lark and risk a glance at her as I skitter around this patch, looking for a safe place to stand so I can grab Ash again. Bikk! No! It's got her, too!

For a moment I'm frozen, as Lark and I lock eyes across the shimmering, sweltering sand. Who do I help? Who do I save? How can I choose her over my brother? But how can I let her die?

"Help him first!" she shouts. "I can hold out. I'm on the edge—it just has my legs. My top half is on regular sand." I squint against the glare. It looks like what she says is true. "Hurry! Help him!"

With a sob I turn all my attention back to Ash. I clench the sleeves of his protective suit in a tight grip and heave, shifting him a few inches. But the nanosand seems to be pulling back. I lean backward, using the weight of my body for leverage, and shift him a little more. But it's as if he has weights on his legs, pulling him deeper. For every inch I drag him out, the sand sucks him down two more inches.

"Ash, please, hold on!" I cry desperately as my hands slip. I can't even risk a glance at Lark. He's sunk so deep now, and the sand keeps moving closer to me, so I'm dancing here and there, trying to find solid ground.

"No!" He slips down to his shoulders . . . his neck. I'm

not strong enough! I grab his face in my hands, and feel him slide from my grasp. "Ash!" I shriek, and as I lunge forward to reach for him I don't know if I'm trying to save him, or to join him. *I can't fail. I can't lose my brother.* Anything would be better than that.

Suddenly a hand reaches over my shoulder, plunging deep into the nanosand and grasping Ash by the shoulder.

"Lark!" I gasp with relief, certain that she managed to escape.

But it's Lachlan. His face is barely visible beneath the fogged-over mask of his protective suit, but his golden second child eyes seem to glow. He shoves me aside and lies on his belly, reaching both hands into the killer sand. Even though he's much stronger than me, it takes all his effort to haul Ash halfway out. As soon as I can grab his arm I help, and we pull him free, scrambling out of reach of the sand.

All I want to do is lie panting on the ground, overcome with relief. But the sand is still moving inexorably toward us, trying to surround us. "I'll get him out of reach of the sand," I shout. "You get Lark!"

I scan the desert as I stumble away, supporting Ash on my shoulder. I'm dizzy with heat, disoriented. I can't find Lark against the shimmer of heat rising all around us. "Lark!" I scream. "Where is she?"

Ash tumbles to the ground, out of reach of the nanosand for a moment at least as the shifting patches of deadly sand re-group and resume their hunt. I start to run toward the nano-sand, but Lachlan's arm loops around my waist and he jerks me off my feet, whirling me around. "We have to go. Now!"

"But Lark! I have to save her!"

Lachlan pulls my head to his chest and holds me tight. "She's gone, Rowan. She's gone."

MY SCREAM ECHOES across the scorching dunes. I crawl toward the place where I last saw Lark, when she assured me that she was fine, told me to focus on saving Ash. Why did I listen to her? Why didn't Lachlan come sooner? I scramble to my feet and run the rest of the way. Lachlan is calling to me but I can't hear what he's saying. I don't care. My heart is broken.

I claw at the nanosand. My knees are being slowly engulfed by the predatory grains, but I don't care. I'm searching for one single lock of lilac hair, anything I can grab hold of to save her.

But there's nothing.

My screams fill the air, and beneath them, the motion detector is still wailing as if it, too, is mourning Lark. I feel an arm around my waist, and Lachlan scoops me up. I flail in midair. "We have to save her! I have to reach her!"

But the nanosand almost has us surrounded. With one arm around Ash to help him, Lachlan carries me away, kicking and crying and screaming for my lost friend. My lost love.

By the time we get far enough from the nanosand to be safe for a few minutes at least, Lachlan is almost carrying us both. Ash is near the end of his strength. Weak with sorrow,

I realize there's no time to mourn Lark now. Ash's breathing is ragged, and his face beneath his protective mask is pale. I was a fool to believe that he was well. The medicinal camphor in the air in the Underground might have soothed his lungs, but they were damaged before he was born—when our father tried to kill me in the womb—and nothing can fix him. The exertion and heat have brought on his symptoms more quickly, more strongly than I've ever seen before.

"We have to carry him," I say when Lachlan releases me. "Hurry! He needs help!" All I want to do is curl up into a ball and cry until I pass out, but I have to pull myself together. I can't lose them both.

Ash is on his knees, drawing ragged breaths so shallow I can barely see his chest expand. The heat is seeping into our suits. Even with them on, it must be 120 against my skin. Outside it has to be much hotter. We can't last much longer.

"I'll take his feet," I offer, but Lachlan brushes away my efforts and without another word kneels in front of Ash and pulls him over his shoulder, so Ash's arms and legs dangle. It isn't dignified and can't be comfortable, but Ash is beyond complaining. He dangles there limply, looking frighteningly lifeless.

"I know these symptoms," I tell Lachlan.

"So do I," he says. "Ash was like this the night we rescued him. The night I lost you."

Lachlan is panting and sweating. How long has he been in the desert? Did he make it to the forest? I can't ask now. I need all my breath just to keep going. Even when I was being chased for hours through the streets of Eden I never felt this weak and breathless. The merciless heat is draining my strength, my will.

Even the tears that fall from my eyes feel boiling as they roll down my cheeks.

Finally, we make it to the shade of the giant artificial bean plants. The difference is instant. We cross the sandy border, and all at once the temperature drops by half. There is a fleeting instant when I can feel the pleasant coolness bathe the front of my body, while the back of my body is still in the scorching desert. Then we're safe, cool.

Lachlan stumbles to his knees and I cushion Ash's head as he goes to the ground. Quickly, Lachlan strips off his protective mask and I feel my brother's pulse. It is weak and slow, but steady. But there's a wheezy rattle in his breathing. His lungs are so irritated that they're filling up with fluid. He's prone to that, and the resulting infections, but that is a fairly slow, chronic process. If it were just that, we could get him to help in time. But an asthma-like condition makes his lung problem worse. When his lungs react too badly, his throat begins to close, too, almost like an allergic reaction. I can tell from the gasping squeak in his breathing that his windpipe is tightening.

If it closes all the way, he won't be able to breathe.

I pull off the rest of his protective suit and check his pockets. "Where's your inhaler?" He's unresponsive.

"It's hard to get medical supplies in the Underground," Lachlan explains. "He ran out a few weeks ago, but when I offered to steal him another one he said he didn't need it anymore. He was breathing just fine down there."

Ash's eyelids flutter open. "Shouldn't . . . have . . . come . . . ," he manages, then he's overcome by a cough that makes his eyes roll back in his head.

"Stay with me, Ash. Do your breathing exercises. Remember?" I try to do them with him, the careful, controlled breathing that would always buy him some time if he had an attack in the house. Now, though, every breath of mine threatens to become a shuddering sob. Ash isn't doing much

better. I don't know how much it will help, anyway. At home
the breathing would keep him calm until someone could get
his inhaler, in a mild case, or a syringe if he needed stronger
drugs. So far, medicine has always been able to reverse the
symptoms. This time, though, he might have to be intubated,
or . . .

No, can't even think about that right now.

His eyes are closed, but I know he can hear me because
he's trying to match his breathing to mine. I fill my lungs
fully of the refreshing cool air, but he's only getting a fraction
of that volume into his own lungs. I wish I could breathe for
him.

Oh, great Earth, not both of them! Not in pursuit of a
forest that might only be my delusion. This is my fault . . .

"Can Flame help him?" I ask as I strip off my protective
suit, and then the rest of Ash's.

"She saved him before," Lachlan says. "But it was touch
and go for a while. She's used to nerves and brains and chips
and wires. This isn't her specialty."

"Leave . . . me . . . ," Ash gasps out.

We ignore him. "Can we get him to the Underground?"
I ask.

Lachlan shakes his head. "It's too far, and carrying an unconscious person though the streets, on the autoloop, would
attract too much attention. But there's a place we might be
able to go, close by. If it's still there."

With a grunt of effort he hauls Ash back over his shoulder
and we march through the fake forest. It takes more effort and
frustrated tears than I could possibly have imagined to ma-
neuver Ash back though the tangled wall of relics, but finally
we reach the other side. Ash is completely unconscious now. I
kiss his clammy cheek, grateful to feel the smallest movement
of breath against my skin. He's just barely holding on.

What will I do without him?

No, I don't dare think like that. Ash will survive.

We have to take a risk carrying him through the street in broad daylight. Before I was captured, it wouldn't have been an issue. I had seen several people openly passed out on the dirty, dangerous streets. Drug use was rampant, illness common and poorly treated. It wouldn't have been by any means unusual to see someone carrying an unconscious friend somewhere.

Now, though, we stand out a bit on the obviously poor but clean and orderly street.

"What happened here?" I murmur.

"I don't know," Lachlan says, shaking his head. "A little while after you were captured, they sent in construction bots to renovate the neighborhoods, one section at a time. The people were all evacuated, I don't know where. It happened amazingly fast. There were guards posted at the radial streets to whatever circle they were working on, but I managed to sneak past and . . . Have you ever seen vids of an anthill? It was like that. Swarms of thousands of bots scurrying around, cleaning, repairing, rebuilding. Each circle was done within a week. Then the people came back and . . ."

"Let me guess," I say grimly. "They don't remember how it was? They think this is normal?"

He nods. "It's better. Safer, cleaner. No one starves. But . . . why?"

I have no idea. But the Center is obviously messing with people's minds again. Part of me is awed that they can change the memories of tens of thousands of people so easily. Most of me, though, is disgusted. And frightened. They made a good thing—helping the poor—ugly.

The mind, the self, is the most important thing we have. How can a human exist if their basic sense of self is threatened?

Lachlan takes us through a neighborhood I'm not familiar

with. "Whose place is this?" I ask as we take the back entrance into an apartment complex.

Lachlan gives me a half smile. "A mutual friend's," he says, and I can't begin to guess before we knock on a door and are greeted by a cheerful square-jawed face.

"Rook!" I cry, and throw my arms around him. When I let him go, he's blushing. But the second he sees Ash he scoops him up and carries him inside.

I wish I wasn't seeing Rook in the middle of terror and tragedy. He's helped me so many times. I'd love to just do something normal with him—introduce him to my brother, then sit around with him and Lachlan talking about our childhoods, our hopes for the future. I feel like Rook could easily be a dear friend. But right now he's all business. He disappears into his bedroom and comes back with a bag full of assorted medical supplies and medicine.

He dumps them on the floor and tears through them. "I don't know much about these. What does he use? Is there anything here that will help him?"

There are drugs to stop blood clots, to lower blood pressure, to halt heart attacks in their tracks. There's gauze that stops bleeding instantly, and salves that heal burns within days.

"Here!" I cry, seizing an inhaler that I'm almost sure is the same as the one he used at home in emergencies. Fumbling, dropping it twice in my haste, I hold it to Ash's lips.

"Come on, little brother," I plead. He's conscious, looking at me, and his lips move to take the inhaler into his mouth. I nod to signal, and then press on the button to release the aerosol medicine that will help his windpipe open and his lungs clear.

But it's too late. I can see his eyes widen in panic as he realizes he can't inhale deeply enough to even take in the medicine. In a tragic feedback loop the panic makes it harder to breathe, which causes more panic, until he's just making horrible retching, creaking sounds as he tries, and fails, to get the tiniest breath into his lungs. His face flushes red, then blanches white as he looks at me with wide, desperate, pleading eyes. *Save me*, they say.

Then his head falls to the side, and he stops even trying to breathe.

"Oh, great Earth! No!" I grab Ash and start to shake him. "Wake up! You have to stay with me. You have to breathe!" My voice falls to a whisper. "You have to try . . ."

Lachlan grabs the inhaler out of my hand and tries to spray it down Ash's throat. But it's too late. I watch numbly as Rook tries rescue breathing, but nothing is going in past Ash's swollen airway. I know his lungs will still be functioning, barely, but nothing can reach them.

Unless . . .

The doctors told Mom about a last-ditch, emergency procedure she could do if Ash had an attack so severe, so quick that medicine didn't help and the hospital would take too long to reach. A thing to do when all other hope was gone.

But it is a desperate act, and it terrifies me.

"I need a knife!" I cry, and instantly Lachlan hands me a folding blade from his back pocket. But it is a heavy knife, dull from utilitarian tasks. I have no doubt that in a fight he could shove it between someone's ribs, but it won't work for this. "I need something very sharp and fine. In the kitchen, hurry!"

Rook is halfway there before I call, "Wait! And a tube, a straw, a baster—anything hollow. And alcohol!"

He's gone, with a look of frenzied determination, and I count the seconds. How long since Ash took his last breath? How long until it is too late? Past a certain point, his brain will be damaged, his organs will begin to fail from lack of oxygen. A minute longer than this, and he'll be gone.

It feels like forever, but it can't be more than a minute before Rook comes back with a slim, sharp paring knife and a long fancy straw twisted in a figure eight, the kind they use for tall, fruity drinks. In his other hand he has a bottle of anisette liqueur. Low proof, but it will have to do.

"Open it," I command, and when he hands me the open bottle I pour it over the knife and straw.

I don't let myself think about what I'm doing. I just force my body to go through the motions. This isn't Ash on the verge of death. This isn't his pale throat I'm slicing into.

I feel along his skin, finding the bulge of his Adam's apple, the dip below, and the smaller lump of cartilage. The dip is where I must cut. Steadying my hands, I press the knife into his flesh. Too gently! His skin dips beneath the point of the blade, but the knife doesn't make an incision. I remember another time when I wasn't tentative or timid with a knife. The time I opened a Greenshirt's throat before he could kill Lachlan. So much blood . . .

I can't be timid. I can't hesitate. Steeling myself, I press harder, and see his skin part in a fine line, half an inch wide. I cut half an inch deep. I remember what my mother told me. Just a little bit too deep, and his windpipe could be severed.

I pinch the wound from the side, making it gape open. There's hardly any blood. Then I slide the straw in, angling it down. If only the obstruction is up high. If only his entire windpipe isn't swollen shut. I say a silent prayer to the Earth before I blow gently into the straw. It feels like the air is moving into his lungs. I pause, and blow again.

Three more breaths, and he begins breathing on his own, sucking narrow streams of life-giving air through the twisty straw.

He's alive. For now.

ASH IS WHEEZING through the straw. His eyes are closed but I don't think he's actually unconscious. I think he's exhausted.

I am, too. Physically and emotionally drained.

"Lark . . . ," Lachlan begins.

I shake my head. "Not yet." If I have to talk about her loss right now, I'll break down. I have to keep the last reserves of my strength—physical and emotional—to help Ash.

"Rest a little while, and make sure he's stable," Lachlan suggests. "Then when he can walk we can bandage him and make our way to the Underground."

I nod, and smooth the hair away from Ash's pale and clammy brow. Rook goes to get us some water. "What did you find out there?" I ask in a low voice. I want to ask the crucial question: *did you find my forest?* But that is too blunt. I can't bear a no, so I make it open ended and wait.

"I found sand," he says. "Sand, and heat, and death. Oh Rowan, I'm so sorry about Lark."

I stare at the floor, trying to push the emotion away. I've managed to stay strong so far, to help Ash. I told myself I wouldn't mourn for Lark until I was alone, until Ash was safe in the Underground. But my grief is so overwhelming I can't fight it anymore. The tears begin, but they're quiet ones.

This is my fault. All of it. Ash's trauma, and Lark's death. If I hadn't led them on this suicidal mission into the desert . . .

No, the blame started long before that. I became responsible for all this tragedy the moment I poked my head over the wall of our family compound. If I'd just done what I was supposed to and stayed hidden, I would never have met Lark, never put her at risk. Ash would still be a student with an impossible crush on his best friend. Mom would still be alive.

I start to sob at last, the sorrow for Lark joining the great ocean of things I mourn. Even stronger than the sorrow is the guilt I feel. Lark would still be alive if it wasn't for me.

From the corner of my eye, I see Lachlan move as if to hold me. He stops himself. I can tell he feels helpless. He's a fixer. He wants to take whatever is wrong and make it right. Or better, at least. But there's nothing he can do for this pain.

"Tell me what you need, Rowan," he says softly.

Lark, I want to say. *Mom. Safety. Security.*

"Time," I say at last. How many meanings that word has. Time, as in space to process and heal before I have to talk about her loss. Time, as in more with her. Time, as in why didn't you come sooner, Lachlan?

I dry my tears. There's still work to do. "You found nothing, then? No sign of the forest I saw?"

He shakes his head. "But that doesn't mean it's not there. How far out did you run the day of the earthquake?"

"It felt like less than a mile, but it could have been more. I don't know."

"I couldn't make it a mile. The suit started to fail, and I had to turn around. I didn't see anything." His voice is gentle. He doesn't want to hurt me with the truth. But he knows he has to tell me. "I made it maybe three-quarters of a mile from the bean trees. If there had been a forest a mile away or a little more, I should have been able to see it."

"Not if there's some kind of camouflage, or shielding technology," I say, grasping for any possibility. The bean trees have mirror tech so no one from inside of Eden can see them even though they tower all around the border. Every cell in their artificial surface reflects an image of the exact opposite side, so that no matter what angle you look at them from (from far away) they are invisible. Maybe there's something like that at the edge of the desert, so no matter how close you get you can't see beyond it to the rest of the world until you actually cross the boundary.

"It's possible," Lachlan says. "But for now I think we have to accept that we can't prove it. We can try again, when things are more settled. Now isn't a good time, though."

I look at him narrowly. "You don't just mean until Ash is safe, do you? There's more going on."

"Yes, but I shouldn't talk about it."

I feel my anger rising. "After all I've done, all I've been through, you can't tell me what your big plans are? Don't you owe me that much at least?"

"It's not that I don't want to. But . . ."

"Oh, I know. The Center might still be in my brain. You can't trust me."

"I trust you completely, Rowan," he says. "I don't trust them. I don't entirely like what Flint is planning, but if it works, it could mean an incredible change. And if it gets discovered before it is put into action, it could compromise the entire Underground. We've been safe down there for generations. I can't do anything to put it at risk."

I think of Rainbow and the other kids, the trusting second children who would be killed or maybe experimented on like

I was if they were discovered. "I get it, Lachlan, I really do. It's just . . ."

"I know. You've lost so much. You want to fight, too. Believe me, I know."

After that we wait in silence until Ash comes to. He has a moment of panic when he can't breathe normally, but once he figures out what I've done he slowly calms. When he can walk, Lachlan bandages his throat in such a way as to make the straw less noticeable.

"Thanks, big brother," Lachlan says as he hugs Rook tight.

"I'll come with you," Rook says. "It might be easier traveling with a Greenshirt. Anyone gives you trouble, I can always badge 'em." He flashes his open, affable grin.

"If you don't mind," Lachlan says.

Rook punches him playfully on the shoulder. "Mind? Get real. I . . ."

He's interrupted by a beep, and checks his com. "Bikk, they're calling me in to work. I'm not supposed to be on duty for another two days. Want me to call in sick?"

"That's okay," Lachlan says. "We should be fine."

Rook looks uncertain, biting his lip, then he nods. "Okay. Whatever you say. Hey, when you get a chance, bring this lady over for dinner. I'd say invite me to your place, but . . ."

Lachlan laughs. "It's not that I don't trust you . . ."

"I know, I know." Rook gives me the tiniest peck on the cheek. "Good to see you again, Rowan. Take care."

"You too, Rook. And thanks."

And then, very slowly and carefully, we make our way back to the Underground.

By the time we get there, Lachlan is carrying Ash again. It attracts stares, but we don't have a choice. It would have been better to make the descent by night, but I case the side streets for half an hour, making sure no one is around when I finally beckon Lachlan. We lift the grate and I slide down first. A moment later Ash slithers down, and I pull him out of the way before Lachlan comes right behind him. Strangely, there are no sentries on duty along the passageway through the cave system.

When we finally enter the vast crystal chamber, Lachlan is near his end. His knees are shaking, and his voice is ragged when he calls out to anyone who can hear him, "We need help!" When he puts Ash down—a little more roughly than he intended—I see his hands are shaking, too.

People rush to our aid. "We need a doctor," I say. "We need Flame!"

But before anyone can properly help us, Flint shoulders his way through the crowd, the ever-present Adder at his side. He looks furious. I spring up with my hands on my hips before he can utter a word.

"No!" I say loudly and firmly to him. "Whatever you have to say, it can wait. Right now my brother needs medical help." Around us, a crowd is gathering. I can tell they are anxious to help us but don't quite dare pass Flint.

"You bring trouble wherever you go," he says to me in a voice filled with contempt. "And you lead our people astray." He glances at Lachlan, who for the moment looks too exhausted to care. "How dare you steal our resources, risk the life of a second child, defy me, all to chase some delusion that was planted in your cerebral cortex? We took you in, Rowan. We risked a lot to save your brother, and later you."

I stifle a near-hysterical laugh. "You let Lachlan try to rescue Ash because you wouldn't mind if he was killed! He's the only one here who stands up to you. And it was Lark who saved me when I was at Oaks and didn't know who I was. You've done nothing!"

He looks at me grimly. "We let you live. I'm beginning to think that was a mistake."

"Please, just help Ash," Lachlan says, rising unsteadily to his feet. "We can argue and play power games later, but right now he needs a doctor."

"Well now, I don't know if I feel inclined to help your big brother, Rowan," Flint says, folding his arms across his chest and smiling unpleasantly. "What is he to us, after all?"

I hear grumbles from the crowd, which has swollen to at least a dozen. "But it's Ash," I hear someone say. "Help him," another murmurs. They look confused, upset. This isn't what the Underground is about.

"We help our own," Flint says, steel in his voice. "He's a first child. He's not our problem."

Iris steps up out of the crowd. "We took him in, Flint," she says. "We made him our problem. He needs us." She forces her way past him and bends to examine Ash. "We can't just care about second children, Flint. We have to care about all children if we want humanity to survive. All children, and all people."

Flint doesn't even have the decency to look ashamed. "We'll help your brother, and then he's out of here. Second children first—that's the way it has to be. He and that busybody friend of yours, Lark, have to go by dark." He doesn't even notice she's not with us.

Hearing her name sends a stab of pain through my heart, but I hold firm. "You can't kick Ash out. The Center will find him. They'll put him in prison. He won't survive!"

"Not our issue. From now on, only second children are under our protection."

I take a deep breath and finally say it. "Ash *is* a second child. I'm the firstborn." I tell them how my mother was carrying twins, how his respiratory abnormality made it necessary to pass him off as the firstborn. I hear gasps, murmurs of sympathy.

Not from Flint, though. "Then come nightfall, you both leave. You're no longer welcome in the Underground. Not after the trouble you brought to us."

"What trouble?" I ask.

"We caught a trespasser trying to break into the Underground." Before I can ask what that has to do with me, he turns and stalks away, and as he leaves I hear him say, "Help the boy, then send Rowan to the interrogation chamber. She has a lot to answer for."

I try to tell myself all that matters is that Ash gets help. Interrogation chamber? I vividly remember my first moments in the Underground, feeling like I was drowning with a soaking wet bag over my head, while Flint hurt and frightened me. It was a test to make sure I wouldn't break if I was caught, to see if I could be trusted. I guess I still haven't proven myself trustworthy. Me, and whatever else besides me is lurking in my brain. What's going to happen this time in the interrogation room? Is it for the trespasser . . . or for me?

Ash first. Iris is directing people to help him up, and two of the stronger men scoop him up. Before they take him away, Ash's eyes flutter open. He holds out a hand to me, and I ask the men to wait.

"*You're* the firstborn?" he asks weakly. Bikk! He heard! I thought he was too out of it to notice. I never wanted him to know.

There are so many things in his face now, and I know him so well that I can read them all. Pity for me at having been forced into a life of imprisonment and danger as a second child. Guilt that he had the privileged role he wasn't meant to have. Anger that this important information was kept from him.

And, what he doesn't want me to see, resentment that his privileged place might be stripped from him.

We all have unworthy thoughts we would never say aloud, the thoughts that make us feel unworthy every time they cross our minds. We don't all have a sister who knows us so well she can read our mind.

I don't blame him for that thought. When I found out, I couldn't help feeling angry that I was cheated out of my rightful place in the world. But it was for Ash. I'd give up anything for him, just as he would for me.

I wonder if it is harder for the winner than for the loser, for the one who got a better deal than fate had mapped out for him?

As they're taking him away, I feel a tug on my clothes. It's little Rainbow, looking up at me. She has clutched in her hand a messy pale purple flower made from scraps of fabric.

"Rowan, where's Lark?" Rainbow asks me. "I made this for her to wear in her hair."

That's when I break down for good.

THERE IS NO Rowan, or Yarrow, or whatever else is in my head. There is only grief. I cling to Lachlan and hardly even know who he is. There is only loss and emptiness.

I don't hear it when Iris comes to tell us that Ash is stable, but Lachlan tells me a little while later when the well of tears seems to have run dry. "I guess I have to face Flint now," I say, taking a deep breath that ends in a shudder and one slow final tear. I wipe it away and stand up straight.

"I'll be with you," Lachlan says. "Always. I won't let him kick you or your brother out. He's loved. So are you. The other second children won't stand for that."

I don't know. People get scared, and that makes them clannish. They want to follow a leader, even if they don't totally agree with his decisions. Lachlan will stand against him, on our side, but will that be enough? Flint has already proven he has no problem being merciless when it suits his cause . . . or him. His very nature is brutal, I think, when there's nothing to hold it in check.

I walk in first, without knocking or announcing myself. I think the flashbacks will be about me, about my own torture in this room, and I've steeled myself to bear it unflinchingly.

But when I see the pale outflung arm covered in bruises I don't think of myself, but of Lark when she was captured and interrogated. There's a girl strapped to the table.

Adder stands over her, on the far side of the table. Her knuckles are bruised. She could use a club, but she prefers to use her fists.

Flint is on the near side of the table, and turns when he notices me, revealing the strapped-down figure.

Long silvery hair matted with blood. Vivid blue eyes half-shut, glazed over, staring, appearing lifeless until I see a blink. A svelte curvy frame gone gaunt. The most expensive clothes her parents' credit can buy, torn and filthy.

It's Pearl.

And despite everything that has happened between us, everything that she's done, I feel an overwhelming surge of pity for her. I want to protect her from Adder's fists, and Flint's plans.

But I've gotten to know the world pretty well by now, and I think no matter what I want, it's not going to go well for Pearl.

"What is she doing here?" I ask. I feel Lachlan move up beside me.

"That's exactly what I want you to tell me," Flint replies. "Were the two of you working together? Concocting some little scheme with your Center handlers?" He turns to Lachlan. "I told you we couldn't trust her."

I almost have to smile as I say with utter frankness, "Pearl and I would *never* work together on anything." *Not now.*

"She came at the same time you did."

"We weren't followed, I'm sure of it," I say. But am I? I tried to keep watch, but mostly trusted Lark to do it. She was under a lot of stress. If she made a mistake, maybe Pearl had been able to follow us when we left Oaks. But why would she do it?

I step closer and look at her battered face. She seems to be unconscious. Both of her eyes are purple-blue and swollen nearly shut. Her lips are bruised and split. Her nose, which had been at such a perfectly refined angle it was hard to imagine it was natural and not the result of a surgeon's skill, is now bent at a horrible angle. There are bruises all over her body, finger marks, and larger marks from the grit-filled tube Adder's associate wields as a club.

"Did it really take so much to make her talk?" I ask, glaring at Adder.

"No," Adder admits with silky pleasure. "But it never hurts to be sure." She chuckles unpleasantly. "Well, it doesn't hurt *me*, anyway."

"Pearl," I say gently. "Can you hear me? It's Rowan." Her eyes try to focus. I wonder if she has a concussion. Then I remember she has no idea who Rowan is. "I mean Yarrow. From school." She's dazed, and it takes a long time before she recognizes me.

"Yarrow!" she gasps. "Help me!" She moans when talking reopens a recently split lip. "I'm so sorry, Yarrow. She didn't give me a choice."

"Who didn't give you a choice?" I ask.

"Chief Ellena. I tried to say no. I swear I did. But she knew things about my parents, about me. She would have told everyone. We would have been cast into the outer circles. But I didn't want to do any of it." She looks at me like she's drowning. She starts to cry, the tears washing tracks through the blood on her face.

Flint got her story out of her easily enough, but she tells me again in a pained whisper as I bend close. Not long after we left to look for Lachlan and the forest, sentries found Pearl wandering through the cave system. She'd followed us to the secret entrance.

"Why did you follow us?" I ask.

"Your mother—"

"Don't call her that!"

"Chief Ellena, the head of intelligence, she wanted me to keep an eye on you. All the time, from the first day you came to Oaks. She told me to take you in, be your best friend . . . and tell her everything you did and said."

"You were her spy!" I say accusingly.

"What choice did I have?"

"Everyone has a choice," I snap. "You could have told me. You could have lied to her." But I can imagine how hard it must have been for her. A privileged girl who had never had any hardship, suddenly faced with disgrace and poverty? Of course she would have yielded. And if the brain manipulation started on her, as it had on me, is she really responsible?

But this is Pearl, horrible Pearl, who tormented so many people. There must have been some innate aspect of her real nature that allowed her to act so badly. Just as there must have been of mine.

"After the . . . incident on the rooftop, she was so mad at me. Half her bikking research budget almost fell off the roof, she said. After that, she told me to never let you out of my sight."

In serious trouble with the head of intelligence, Pearl had to find a way to get back in her good graces. "When I saw you go underground, I didn't know what it was all about. But it had to be something she wanted to know about. Something big. Yarrow, I have no idea what's going on here! I swear I don't. I just wanted to give her something so she'd leave me alone."

She thought about running back to the Center to tell

them, but what if it was just some secret party? What if she summoned the chief of intelligence and a bunch of Green-shirts and it was just a bunch of kids dancing? So she did what was probably one of the bravest things in her life and slid into the blackness after us.

"I thought I was going to die," she says bleakly. I can't help glancing up, and Flint catches my eye. She is going to die, I realize. She's an enemy who knows their location. She can't live.

"You and Lark weren't there," she goes on. "There were passageways everywhere! I thought I heard you and went in one direction, but I never found you. The caves went on for-ever . . ." She drifts into a daze, and Flint continues her tale.

"When we found her she was severely dehydrated. She'd been wandering down there since you came. She told us every-thing in exchange for a sip of water." He adds with grudging admiration, "She's not strong like you or your friend."

I catch my breath. Lark was so strong. She gave me the world. She gave me myself . . .

Flint interrupts my reverie. "What do you think we should do with her?"

He's kicking me out, he claims, so why is he asking my opinion? It must be a test. If I pass, I can stay. The right an-swer, the strategic answer, the one he's looking for, is that she can't be allowed to live. She could lead the Center directly to us. In one way, I know this is the right answer. Even if she's being blackmailed by the Center, she's still working for the enemy. Her release could mean the death of every single sec-ond child, from the ancient grandfathers to tiny Rainbow.

But what if we kept her a prisoner here? It is almost funny to think of snooty Pearl living hidden away from the limelight, wearing secondhand clothes, never doing anything fashion-able. She'd never be popular again! Who knows, maybe she'd even change after a while down here. The second children wouldn't put up with her bullying. Her insults wouldn't hurt them. She might learn to be a decent human being.

But that would mean she was still a risk. What if she escaped? And a strategist would think of the drain on resources. She would be one more mouth to feed, and a useless one at that.

She left me to die, dangling by my fingertips off the roof. She drugged me. She made dozens of people miserable all her life. She is a dire threat to the people I love. Does she deserve to die?

Flint holds my gaze, and I can almost hear him willing me to be merciless. To believe that the ends justify the means. To be like him. I could . . .

I feel Lachlan's warmth at my back, and know there is always a better way.

"We let her go," I say resolutely.

He shakes his head. "I'm disappointed in you, Rowan."

"Why should I care about that?" I snap. "Look, you can give her a huge dose of whatever you gave Lark." I have to clench my jaw when I say her name, but I force myself to go on. "Make her confused, wipe her memory."

"That doesn't always work," Flint says.

That's true. Lark was fuddled and uncertain, but the next day she still remembered chunks of what had happened when the second children captured her. Once we talked about it, she eventually remembered almost all of it.

"Maybe Flame can try something. If the Center can manipulate memories, surely she can, too. She gave me my identity back. Maybe she can take enough away from Pearl that she can go back. So she doesn't even know who she is anymore!"

I had my real self stolen. *I* had another person stamped over the core of my own nature. How could I allow that to happen to Pearl?

Would that be, in its own way, even worse than death?

I don't think Flint is even considering it. He dismisses me brusquely. "You can go now."

"But what are you going to do with her?" I ask.

"You should be more concerned about what we're going to do with you," he replies.

"But you can't just kill her!" I cry. "She's young, she's being controlled . . ."

"This is war, Rowan," Flint says. "Bad things happen in war. Kill or be killed. It's human nature."

"But it shouldn't be!" I gasp out. Before I can object any further, the entire Underground is shaken by a deep tremor, and a grinding boom echoes through the cavern. I run to the door and look out over the huge chamber. The tree's leaves are trembling as if rustled by a breeze.

"What was that? Another earthquake?"

For a moment there is silence.

Then, from all around us, an alarm begins to sound. Somewhere, a desperate voice shouts, "The Center! The Greenshirts! They're here!"

22

SUDDENLY PEARL CEASES to matter to everyone in the room except me. Flint and Lachlan exchange a quick glance and then Lachlan says, "Stay here, Rowan, I'll be right back." He looks keenly alert and hard and fierce in a way that I immediately recognize. He's ready to do anything it takes to protect what he loves.

Within seconds, I'm alone with Pearl. I want to follow the others, to do something to help. I know where the weapons are, I remember the security drills Lachlan showed me in case of an attack. I could be up the camphor tree in minutes, ready in a concealed sniper position. Not that I know any more about firing a weapon than which way to point it, but still, I might be able to help a little bit. Or I could get the children to safety.

But if it's not a false alarm, if it's really true that Center officials are here, is any place safe?

"What's going on?" Pearl asks in a small voice. She looks so fragile and frightened that most of my remaining animosity melts away. There's no doubt in my mind that Flint will kill her. Even Lachlan might side with him on this, though he'd be deeply conflicted. The safety of the second children comes first.

But if we're under attack, anything could happen. Maybe

it is a false alarm after all. Maybe there's just one curious Greenshirt who stumbled onto an entrance and is about to pay for his curiosity with his life.

Or it could be an army.

The best case for us is the worst case for Pearl. If things calm down, Flint will remember her and come back to end the threat. If I want to take matters into my own hands and save Pearl, this will be my only chance. The Underground has many systems in place to repel an attack, and the second children are well trained in what to do, even down to the youngest. I probably can't do anything to help them—I'd just get in the way. The only life I can save is Pearl's.

"We're under attack from the Center," I tell her. I can see the conflicting emotions flit across her features. The word "attack" has her scared. But for her, the right word might actually be "rescue."

"If you stay here, Flint will kill you," I tell her bluntly. "I don't know if you're a victim, or guilty as hell. But I hope that if you make it to the surface and get back to Oaks you remember that you would have let me die, but I'm saving your life. You owe me. And the price for my help is your silence. You will never speak of this place. Agreed?"

She nods. Of course, what else would she do? Am I being stupid, trusting her? But trust has to start somewhere. I have to be the one to make the leap. Flint never will.

"There are children down here," I say, leaning close and making her look at me so she realizes how important this is. "Little kids, and families, who will be killed or imprisoned if they get caught. I don't know what is happening out there, but if we make it through, you have to swear to keep this secret. To keep the children safe."

"I never wanted to hurt anyone," Pearl says miserably. "I didn't have a choice."

"Don't dare say that again!" I shout. "I know you were scared, and felt helpless, but you had a choice. There's always a choice. Sometimes the choice means you suffer so someone else doesn't have to. Sometimes it means you give your life so someone else can live. But you can always choose to do the right thing, even if it's also the hard thing."

She bows her head, chastened. "I'm sorry."

Sorry doesn't help now, I think. From somewhere far away, I hear another muffled boom, and feel the stone beneath my feet shiver.

Letting Pearl go is risky, but it's right. I just hope if anyone has to suffer for my choice, it's me, and not the other second children. I unstrap her wrists and ankles and help her to her feet.

It is so typically Pearl that even under these dire circumstances, just a breath away from death, the first thing she does when her hands are free is to smooth her eyebrows, pinch her cheeks to give them color, and push her disheveled silvery hair away from her face. Live or die, the most important thing is that she look good doing it. I almost laugh at the thought that someone so vain and shallow could be actually maliciously evil. She's weak, that's all. She's a victim of stronger forces.

Then I notice her earrings. She's still wearing the ones Chief Ellena gave her. They're teardrop faceted emeralds—not real, of course, but their facets glint with more sparkle than a real stone could. The inside seems to dance whenever she moves her head. What an idiot I've been. Pearl lives for fashion, never wears the same outfit twice, changes her jewelry three times a day. And yet since the day the Chief gave them to her, she's never taken off these earrings.

And now, those gems aren't just glittering when they reflect the light. They're gently pulsing a slow rhythm. Comprehension suddenly dawns on me. "Those earrings, they're from the Chief. She told you to always wear them?"

Pearl touches the earrings and nods, smiling uncertainly as if she's just received a compliment. But I'm not fooled any longer.

"Oh, Pearl, you played a good game. You had me convinced that you were just an innocent victim. When all along you were a scheming harpy who was happily following the Center's every order." My voice is so soft that she doesn't catch the danger as fast as she should. "Those earrings, they're trackers, aren't they?"

Pearl shakes her head and tries to back away, but bumps against the interrogation table. There's nowhere to go. Another boom rocks the cavern, but I can't think of anything beyond my hate for Pearl, who abetted the monstrous things that happened to me.

I grab her by the collar, the soft material of her luxurious, impractical inner circle clothes tearing beneath my rough touch. "You knew I was being experimented on!" I shout into her face. If it wasn't for the tracker earrings I'd be swayed by the utter confusion on her face. But I know how well Pearl can lie and manipulate people. I won't be fooled.

I shake her as I scream at her. "I was a test subject! They strapped me down and went *into my brain*!"

"I didn't know . . . ," she tries to say, but I slam her back against the table. She trips, and I go down on top of her, straddling her. She's squirming, but not fighting back. I don't care. All the rage that has built up inside of me for years comes pouring out. Everything seems to be her fault—hers, or people like her. The rich, privileged, secure first children who think they rule Eden, who despise anyone unfortuate enough to be born different or poor. Or second.

I pick her up by the collar as I shout, "You helped them

take away everything I had, everything I was!" I think of my mother, shot by Greenshirts as she tried to make a better life for me, and I blame Pearl for that, too. "They made me into another person, and you went along with it. You didn't tell me I wasn't really Yarrow. You didn't try to help me. I'm not buying those phony tears now. It's too late for that!"

I slam her head back into the floor, and she groans. "I know who I am now! They robbed me of my identity, hid my memories, gave me new ones, tried to make me believe I was Yarrow. But I'm not, do you hear me!" I slam her down again. "I'm Rowan!"

Suddenly Lachlan's back in the room. He takes one startled look at us and then hauls me off her. I keep screaming at her. "You did this! You helped them break me! You helped them strap me down and put needles into my eyes! They got into my brain and made me do things I would never, ever do. Because of you, I lost myself!"

Pearl painfully drags herself up to her knees. She's staring at me in bafflement while Lachlan holds me back.

"Who is Rowan?" she asks, and I'm taken aback.

"Me!" I say, jerking myself free of Lachlan but not immediately resuming my attack. "I'm a second child. See my eyes?" I open them wide so she can see the one kaleidoscope eye, the other flat gray and blind. "They made me forget who I am. They turned me into someone I didn't want to be."

"But . . . why?" she asks. I shrug, and before I can say anything else she asks in a peculiar, frightened voice, "Can they do that to anyone?"

Lachlan breaks in. "There's no time. We're under heavy attack. There are Greenshirts pouring in through the labyrinth. Those booms you heard . . . When they couldn't find the way through, they just blasted a new passage. We have to go. We have to get the children to safety."

Suddenly, Pearl ceases to matter. I start to dash off with Lachlan. As I reach the door, Pearl calls out, "What about me?"

I pause long enough to look at her angrily. "These are your people. You called them here. You have nothing to worry about." I turn to go again, then call back over my shoulder, "Unless Flint has a spare moment to come back for you."

In the crystal chamber beneath the tree, there is chaos. I don't see any Greenshirts down there yet, but our people are running around with guns, trying to organize. I can see that the drills mean little in the face of actual attack. Everyone knows where they should go, but the reality of defending a family is somehow different. People who were trained to report to a certain post are delaying so they can check on friends to make sure they're safe. People are arguing that they should fight while the younger people should hide. Teenagers are boldly trying to take on more dangerous roles.

And small children are looking lost.

"Lachlan, go!" I say. "You're needed elsewhere. I don't have a post. I'll take the children. But where?"

He shakes his head. "Getting them to safety is more important than saving the others. More important than saving the tree. I'll have to show you the secret chamber. I should have before now, but . . ."

I know. No one fully trusted me.

We dash amid the chaos on the ground and start rounding up kids. There are more explosions, and now the sound of sporadic gunfire echoes through the caves. It is still muffled by the stone walls, though. They haven't broken through to the main caverns. Someone is still putting up a strong defense.

I spy Rainbow, and oh, the little hero has done half our job for us. She has her hands on her hips and she's shrilling orders to a bunch of terrified-looking children, some of which are a few years older than she is. She's clearly in charge, and though I can see her relief when Lachlan and I run up, I think if she had been left on her own she would still have gotten the kids to safety. And maybe even brought down a Greenshirt in the process. She has a gun strapped to her hip on a belt that is so big she had to double knot it instead of buckling it. I'd bet anything she liberated it from one of the older children.

How did we humans allow the world to be so terrible that tiny hands need to fumble with deadly weapons? No civilization should permit this.

"Where are the others?" Lachlan asks. There are still at least a dozen small ones unaccounted for.

"I don't know," Rainbow says. She has the steady voice of a little warrior. "Class had just let out before the alarm, so they could have gone anywhere."

Lachlan and I exchange a look. Get these to safety first, or try to account for all of them? Save these kids and risk the others . . . or try to save them all, with the possibility that by the time we round them up it will be too late, and we'll lose everyone?

He makes a fast decision. "Come with me," he says, grabbing Rainbow's hand. He takes us behind the giant camphor tree. The roots rise above the ground, snaking across the cavern as if the tree is reaching out to us. At the base of the tree, where the trunk branches out as it touches the earth, making almost a cave, he starts brushing away crunchy dead leaves and loose soil. There's a panel with a handle. He jerks it open and ushers the children inside.

"It's dark," Rainbow says, with a little quaver in her voice for the first time. She's trying to make it sound like a simple comment, but she doesn't want to go down there. It must be hard for a person who has lived underground all their life to suddenly have to go someplace deeper, darker, even farther from the bright surface they must yearn for.

"Dark, but safe," Lachlan tells her. "The tree will protect you."

"How long do we have to be down here?" Rainbow asks.

"Stay until someone comes for you," he says. "No matter how long that is."

I see all their worried little faces looking up at me with hope and fear. Then Lachlan slams down the hatch. They must be so scared down there in the darkness.

There's gunfire, from much closer this time. I'm scared up here.

"I have to go to my post. I think they've breached the defenses." Lachlan presses a gun into my hands. "Remember how to use it?"

I nod.

"Good. But don't. Not unless you absolutely have to. You look for the rest of the kids."

He kisses me, quickly—a goodbye kiss. We both know how this will likely end.

He starts to go away, then turns back to me. "It's not enough," he says, his voice husky. He cups the back of my head and pulls my whole body close. "Not enough time. Not enough *you*." He kisses me again, tenderly, lingeringly. "Promise me you'll stay alive."

For some reason I can't just say it, can't give him the reassurance. I don't want to promise something I can't deliver. "I promise I'll try."

"You have to live, Rowan. I can't lose you again." His eyes are glistening. "Stay with the children."

"No," I say. "I'm staying here to fight."

"The kids need someone. If the adults are all captured, they'll be alone."

I hesitate just a moment, and it is a moment too long. It's too late.

Greenshirts have stormed through the Underground's defenses. They're swarming the crystal cavern. While the second children are running around desperately, exposed, taking potshots at the troops, the Greenshirts are in a tight formation, with shields, and weapons suited to long range.

They open fire, and second children start dropping to the ground. There are screams, curses, crying. A haze from their gunfire fills the air, and an acrid smell.

"Get up the tree, Rowan!" Lachlan cries.

I don't know whether he wants me up there to keep me safe or, like we practiced one day, so I can be in a good sniper position. I just follow orders, shove the gun into my waistband, and start climbing.

Quickly, I reach a high branch with a good vantage point. Hidden in the leaves, I straddle the broad branch and look for a target. There are bodies everywhere. A few Greenshirts are down, their blood slowly seeping into the earth at the camphor tree's roots. But far, far more second children lie sprawled on the earth. They lie motionless, but I can't see any blood.

A few Greenshirts stand alone, still, shouting commands, and I could probably pick one of them off. But I'm not good enough for the shots I need to take. Down below me, more Greenshirts are coming out from behind the main troops and scooping up screaming children. Methodically, they drag the children away.

"No!" I scream, but my voice is lost in the chaos.

They're not killing the children. I don't think they're killing anyone. There's no blood. They're stunning them all.

This is so much worse than I could have imagined. Death would have been bad. But they want us alive.

To experiment on.

I picture little Rainbow with needles jabbing into her

eyes, wires going into her brain. I envision that brave and lovely personality being twisted into something filthy.

I can't let that happen. I slither from my branch and start to climb down. I'm so enraged I'll fight any Greenshirt with my bare hands. I feel like an animal protecting her babies.

I see Lachlan among those still standing. He's using the tree for cover and shooting at a trio of Greenshirts. Lachlan's gun is deadly, but they're heavily armored. Some of his shots hit, but the Greenshirts only stagger back for a moment and keep coming.

I need to get to him. I need to help him. But I'm still twenty feet up.

He breaks cover to try to get a better shot at them. That's when a Greenshirt he didn't notice opens fire from his flank. Lachlan's body seizes up, frozen and stiff. Then he goes suddenly limp and falls to the earth.

23

I THINK THERE are no heroes in this world. Not for long, anyway. Aaron Al-Baz, who everyone in Eden knows is a hero, was a mass murderer who eradicated our species in his attempt to save the planet. Heroes deceive. And heroes fail. Lark, the bravest person I knew, died on a fool's errand, from a careless moment. Another hero gone. Now Lachlan is being dragged away by Greenshirts, along with dozens of other second children—men, women, old folk— who also lie stunned. Or maybe dead, I can't tell. There is no blood, but their bodies are lifeless, their eyes staring. Lachlan would have died to save the Underground. Now he will die, and the Underground will, too.

And me? Will I be a hero? I want to jump out of the tree onto the back of the nearest Greenshirt, shoot him, claw out his eyes, choke the life out of him for daring to violate our peaceful sanctuary. I want to be as brutal as they are, as merciless as the Center. And if will and dreams could bring success, I would be a hero.

But I would be throwing my life away. Part of me feels an urge to do just that. Lark gone, Lachlan captured . . . what is left for me?

Ash, I think. I don't see him among the captured.

The children hidden among the roots of the great camphor.

I watch Lachlan's body being dragged away, looking so powerless, and wonder if the situation were reversed, would he would risk it all for me? No, he would protect the children. He would know there is no shame in hiding or running instead of fighting, if that's the best way to protect the innocent.

And later when the children were safe, he would come for me.

"Be strong, Lachlan," I whisper under my breath. "Stay alive. I swear I will come for you."

The cavern floor has cleared out as the last of the unconscious second children are dragged roughly out. The fight is still raging in the rooms and passageways overhead, though. Gunfire from our side bounces in endless echoes around the cavern, along with the more muted sounds of the Greenshirts' stun weapons. I drop down to the roots and crouch hidden behind the tree. The kids are safe for now, so I need to find Ash.

I'm sure he's still in the hospital room, recovering. I just hope he's recovered enough that he can walk, or better still, run. If he can hold a gun, even better.

The simulated sun that drifts in its daily cycle across the crystal roof of the cave system shows late evening. The fading golden light casts long shadows on the ground, the branches reflected in blackness below. I use these to my advantage, slipping through the darkest spots as I make my way to the infirmary. No one spots me.

I fling open the door . . . to an empty room.

Was he captured? Was he strong enough to evacuate? A bed that must be his is mussed, the sheets thrown back. There is a spot of blood on the pillowcase. From his tracheotomy, or from a new wound? I search the room for clues but find none, other than more beds that look like they were left in a hurry.

I don't know what to do! Search for him and risk capture? Risk leaving the hidden kids alone under the tree? They're brave and resourceful, but what will they do alone down there if no one comes for them?

As I hover at the door, undecided, the Greenshirts make my decision for me. I hear several of them outside, their heavy boots stomping.

"Did you see their creepy eyes?" I hear one of them ask.

"They're unnatural," another says. "Like they're not quite human."

Another pair of boots stomps up, and I risk a peek through the cracked door. They salute the newcomer.

"We're just in the mop-up stage, Sarge. Still dragging a few more bodies off . . ."

"Bodies?" the sergeant asks sharply.

"Figure of speech. No casualties that I know of, sir." He chuckles. "Quite a few teeth knocked out. That stun we started using hits 'em hard, and they go down stiff. Had teeth crunching under my boots since . . ."

The sergeant has no patience for frivolity, and interrupts him. "Is this level clear?"

"The lower level rooms have been searched, up to the fourth level." That's good and bad. It means that if Ash was in here, he's been captured. But it means that they think this room is clear. They probably won't open the door and find me. Carefully, I pick up a scalpel and some kind of pointed probe from one of the surgical tables, clutching them both in one hand. The other slides the gun from my waistband. If they do come in, I won't go down without a fight.

"Sarge," the Greenshirt says, "I don't get why we don't just kill them all. I mean, they're going to be executed anyway, right? Why not just gun them down? Or leave the stunned ones to be burned. Less mess, less paperwork."

"Those kinds of decisions are above your pay grade—and mine," he says. "We can just assume that the Center has a good reason for it."

"And if we miss some, no problem," the Greenshirt says, and I see him pointing upward. "My plan can be the backup. Barbecued criminals!"

The sergeant presses his ear to hear something crackling in his earpiece. "The upper stories are clear," he says. "The fire is well established." He raises his voice. "All troops, clear out. I repeat, clear the cavern. We have ten minutes until total involvement."

Fire? They're setting the Underground on fire? How can that be? It's solid rock. The only flammable thing is . . .

Oh, great Earth no!

They couldn't! How can they not be overawed by the presence of a real live tree in a world they think is dead? How is it that when they saw the camphor tree they didn't immediately stop the attack and fall to their knees?

I get my answer an instant later. "Are you tellin' me these subhumans think that's a real tree?" The Greenshirt who joked about shattered teeth is laughing even harder. "They must be a pack of idiots. Worshiping a fake tree? I might as well worship my lamp and call it the sun."

They're being manipulated. They aren't being allowed to see the truth. Their lens implants won't let them, despite the evidence right before their eyes.

"Second children don't have the advantages that we do," the sergeant says. "They're criminals, outcasts, without education. I'm sure most of them are mentally subpar. You and I can clearly see that this is a synthetic tree. Oh, a decently crafted one, but fake nonetheless. The poor deluded second children see what they want to see."

"You sound like you feel sorry for them, Sarge."

"Maybe a little," he replies, "when I think of the reasons why the Center might want them all alive."

Finally, an eternity later, they walk away. As he leaves, the sergeant shouts, "More accelerant on the trunk! Move lively now!"

I wait, making myself count to thirty to be sure they're gone, then step out into a nightmare.

The tree, the beautiful tree, is a fireball.

The entire canopy is engulfed in horrific dancing red. The flames kiss every leaf, making the fragrant oils in the tree sizzle. Fire licks the trunk, too, but it can't get a purchase in the thick moist bark.

It's sacrilege. It's a sin.

The children!

The vast chamber is filling up with smoke. It rises in acrid gray clouds to hover over the top half of the cavern. Down here the air smells like a sickening combination of sharp melting camphor resin and smoke, but the air is still breathable. The cloud of smoke makes a thick wall so any Greenshirts up there won't be able to see me. Small mercies.

I run to the base of the tree and stomp out the nearby flames with my feet. My toes are singed, but I hardly notice. "Rainbow!" I scream as I dig among the roots, trying to find the handle. I hear a muffled voice from below and finally grasp the handle. When I open it I see her little face looking up at me, worried but stoic beyond her years.

"The tree is on fire. We have to go! Get everyone out." She's a natural leader and marshals the terrified children. "Rainbow, is there an exit down here? Or a safe place we can hide?" She knows this place much better than me. She's been running around exploring every nook and crevice almost since she was born. This is her world. She has no memory of the surface of Eden.

She takes my hand. Hers is ice cold, and she squeezes tightly. But she says with decision, "Come this way."

She leads us through the kitchen, and down twisting corridors I've never explored. There's a passageway so low to the ground that I have to crawl, though most of the kids just hunch over. The way is pitch black, but Rainbow leads us unerringly. "I wouldn't show you 'cept for a 'mergency," she says. "It's my best hiding spot. No one ever found me in hide-and-seek."

When we enter, an automatic gentle glow illuminates the large chamber. There are barrels marked with names that make no sense to me. Some kind of chemical names. There are blocks of what looks like putty, like something a child would play with. And wires everywhere, linking all the unidentifiable substances.

"What is this place?" I whisper.

"They call it the Boom Room," Rainbow says, then slaps a little boy's hand away when he reaches for a block of pink putty. "No touching! It's a self-instruction room."

Self-instru . . . Oh! I see the panel on the wall, high above the reach of children, with a very simple, obvious red button. I have no doubt about what would happen if I hit that button. I grab the two nearest kids and start to back out.

"Iris said absolutely no touching. I'm not supposed to go here." For the first time she seems in danger of breaking down. "They took Iris. They didn't see me, but they shot her and she fell down and . . ."

"It's okay, sweetie. I promise, I won't let anything bad happen to you. To any of you." I think she believes me. She looks at me with such trust! I can't let her down. I've made a promise. "But I don't think we can stay here. Is there an exit? The cavern will fill up with smoke, even down here, eventually."

"I *think* there's another exit," she says, scrubbing her cheek with her fists.

"You're doing great, Rainbow. I know you're scared. Just do your best."

She leads us back out through the low, twisting corridors. "We have to go out into the cavern," she says. "Just for a bit. The secret tunnel is through another passage. Is it safe?"

I peer out, fighting back my choking as the acrid smoke hits me. The smoke is so thick I can't even see the fire in the treetop. I pull the front of my shirt up over my mouth and nose. "I think so," I say. "I don't see anyone."

I step out first, and remember the deer I saw coming out of the forest into the meadow. The steps tentative at first, then bold. Was that real? "Come on." I beckon to the kids.

Then I feel like I've been punched in the gut, and every muscle in my body cramps at once. I stiffen, and topple like the bean trees did in the earthquake. I can't turn, I can't move my arms to break my fall. I'm utterly powerless as I fall on top of Rainbow.

She screams and struggles out from under me. Then I see her face freeze in a horrible grimace as she's hit and paralyzed, too. Greenshirts are charging us. They grab the other children by the arms, the legs, the hair, dragging them out and shooting them at point-blank range.

My eyes are open. I can see, and think, and breathe. But beyond that, I have no control of my body. I'm a living corpse.

By chance, Rainbow falls so that we're staring into each other's eyes. She can't move either, but I can see the expression frozen on her face. *You promised us, Rowan. You promised you'd keep us safe.*

I can feel the hands that grab me roughly and roll me to my back. The Greenshirts are wearing respirators now as they clear away the last survivors—us.

Suddenly I hear a familiar voice shouting from across the cavern, getting closer. It is shrill and imperious, a voice that is used to being obeyed. "Not her, you idiots. She's one of us!"

Pearl is running up, coughing, bruised, and bloody, but somehow managing to look regal. She's an inner circle elite, and these Greenshirts instinctively defer to her. "If you've harmed her, you'll be working security at a recycling facility for the rest of your career!"

She bends over me, letting her silver hair fall over us, making a shield. Her hand comes toward my face, and I can't flinch away.

"Be Yarrow!" she hisses as she slips a dull gray contact over my kaleidoscope eye.

24

I WAKE UP in a dimly lit room with sparkling lights above me. I smile to myself. The crystal cavern. I'm warm and comfortable, with an overall lethargy making my body feel heavy. My eyes are just barely slitted as I lie in a daze. I can't see anything except the bright spots against the darkness.

Maybe it's not the crystal cavern, I think lazily. My brain seems to be working in slow motion. Maybe I'm back in my dorm room at Oaks. The glittering could be coming from the lights I have tacked on my wall. This gives me hope. I can hold on to things, no matter how they try to change me.

It's the raw scratching in my throat that makes me remember. Smoke. Fire. Death. It feels like a dream. But so does most of my life at this point, hovering between reality and implanted memories, between Rowan and Yarrow. Maybe if I close my eyes the raid on the Underground will really be a dream. I remember being captured, paralyzed. I remember a sharp sting in my neck, and then the world went black.

I don't want to face whatever reality this is, the reality of imprisonment and humiliation, torture and fear. I don't want to forget who I am again. But I have to be strong. I survived being brainwashed once. I have to do it again, to make myself hold on to some scrap of who I really am, so I can save Ash, Rainbow, Lachlan—everyone who matters to me.

Resolutely, I open my eyes . . .

. . . into exactly the hell I feared most. I'm in the Center, strapped to a metal table. The flickering lights aren't the beauty of the cavern or the comfort of my room, but rather the winking lights of monitors and scanners, of mysterious, vile machines with wires coming out of them, of the artificial light glinting off scalpels and probes.

I remember Pearl bending over me, whispering in my ear. *Be Yarrow.* Sure enough, the vision in my remaining good eye has that slightly hazy quality that tells me the counterfeit, temporary lens is in place. Maybe I can bluff my way through this. I have to try.

There's no time to prepare myself, though. A movement across the room catches my eye, and I see Chief Ellena rise gracefully from a swivel stool. She's swinging something dangling from her fingers, almost playfully, a little smile on her face. It's my pink crystal necklace, a piece of the Underground.

It takes all my effort to say blearily, "What happened, Mom?" I don't dare reveal anything yet. I want to wait for her to commit first.

Chief Ellena drops the crystal on my chest. I want more than anything to clutch it in my hand, to keep it away from her prying eyes. But I'm strapped down at the wrists and ankles. Not too tight, and this in itself almost seems like another kind of mockery. You can wiggle all you want, but you can't get away.

"Sounds like you had a terrible few days," she says. "We didn't know what to think when you disappeared." She snatches back the necklace and slips it into her pocket.

I feel like an actor shoved on stage without ever having read the script. What did Pearl tell them? I decide to act confused—which isn't really an act.

"I don't remember everything that happened. I snuck out of Oaks for a party, and . . . I don't know. Maybe I was drugged?"

She narrows her eyes at me. "Seems to be happening a lot lately."

"I'm sorry . . . Mother." The false word sticks in my throat.

"I expected better from you, Yarrow. I've devoted a great deal of time to your . . . upbringing. What a disappointment you are."

"I'll try to do better, I promise," I say, trying to sound like a contrite child. I sneak a look at her face. Maybe she's buying it . . .

"Your reactions are surprising. Of course, it's not entirely your fault." She presses a button, and the door is opened by two guards. Pearl walks in between them, leaving them outside.

Her reaction is perfect. "Great Earth, Yarrow, you look disgusting. I can't tell you how happy I was to wash off all the filth from that place." Her face is bruised, but she carries herself like a particularly snobby goddess. Her hair is clean, covering her shoulders in a perfect silvery cascade. She's wearing flowing white.

"Chief Ellena," she goes on, "when can Yarrow come home? Back to Oaks, I mean. And, pardon me for saying so, but when can she take a bath?" She turns up her delicate nose, which, although several shades of purple, has been set straight. "No offense, but she stinks! Not her fault, being in that horrible place. And thank the Earth she was there!"

She's chatting so smoothly, in her typically superior Pearl

fashion, that even I almost believe her. She's blithely ignoring the fact that I'm strapped down, and the Chief's suspicious looks.

"How did she manage to save you?" the Chief asks.

Pearl and I exchange looks. I gulp, and come up with something they can never prove didn't happen. "I remember now. It was Lark who took me down there. She has some connection with those criminals. Well, Lark has a crush on me, so I was treated nicely." It kills me to use Lark's name like this, but I don't think she'd mind saving me one more time. And whatever I accuse her of, it can't hurt her now. She's beyond the reach of the Center. I feel the pricking of tears, but blink them back. "But Lark always hated Pearl, so they were going to kill her. I distracted them, and then set her free."

"She was amazing," Pearl says, still managing to sound a little bored, as Pearl would. "She saved my life."

"Of course!" I say. "You're my best friend. I'd do anything for you. Mom, why am I here? I'd really like to get cleaned up. I need to get back to school."

"What small concerns you have, Rowan," she says. "When you should really be thinking about things that matter, like I do. The future of Eden. The future of humanity."

She slips it in so casually that I don't notice it right away. When I do, I gasp, and try to hide it in a wince. Should I ignore it? Should I ask who Rowan is?

No. I can tell by her eyes that she knows everything. She leans in close. "You've been unconscious for a while, Rowan. Plenty of time to tap into your memories and learn the truth."

I tug desperately at the restraints, but this time they react to my struggles, automatically tightening and locking my arms and legs down against the cold metal slab.

"You were always a gamble. A first-generation experiment. I mean, anything can happen when you get too deeply into someone's brain, their psyche, their personality. It's all very tricky business. A lot of trial . . . and error. Oh, Rowan, I wish you could see some of the errors. It would give you a whole new appreciation for the work we did on you. The others didn't react so well to having multiple personalities superimposed on each other. Some of them went mad, and tore their own faces off trying to recapture what we took from them. Some went catatonic, utterly unable to cope. But you, Rowan—you're special. Why is that, I wonder? Because you went so long without lenses, perhaps? Everyone gets a little tweaking, almost as soon as they're born."

Pearl, realizing the danger she's in, backs toward the door. "I should go. My parents will be worried."

The Chief shoots Pearl a sharp look. "My dear, your parents have already forgotten that they even have a daughter." Pearl gasps. "Wiping one memory is easy."

"I . . . I . . ." She shakes her head in confusion. "I'll just be going . . . ," she tries again. The elite queen is crumbling, and there's a scared girl standing in the room with us. Because she knows that the things the Chief is saying are not meant for her ears. Secrets. And those kinds of secrets only get told to people who won't be in a position to repeat them much longer.

The Chief presses a button and the guards come swiftly back in. They've been told what to do ahead of time. Instantly they grab Pearl and slam her onto another metal table next to mine. The restraints snake up automatically, coiling around her wrists and ankles.

"Let her go!" I scream. "She didn't do anything!"

"Is that what makes you different, Rowan? That urge to save people? All the things I programmed Pearl to do to you, and you still want to help her. And the cruelties she urged you to participate in? You went along, for a while. I tried to give you no choice. But Rowan kept coming through Yarrow no matter how hard I tried to keep her down. So you were a success and failure both, Rowan. What about you, Pearl?" The Chief cocks her head to the side quizzically. "How do you think you would fare in Rowan's place?"

"As . . . as a test subject?" she asks, confused. She tries to come up with an answer that will keep the Chief happy. "I hope I'd make you proud. But I'm a first child, a citizen of Eden. You only experiment on the . . ." She wants to end that sentence with a slur, an insult, but I think she sees me as a real person now. She's seen second children, knows they're people just like her, and she can't bring herself to insult us. "On the unfortunate second born," she says at last.

It's a mistake. The Chief regards her with scorn. "Rowan, at least, shows strength. A strength we would like to crush, true, but strength is admirable. What are you, Pearl? A reed that bends in the wind? You have no spine, no core, Pearl. You are a hollow creature. And the hollow are ready to be filled up. Still, all in all I would count you as an utter failure as a test subject."

"What do you mean, test subject?" Pearl cries as she pulls against her bonds.

"Oh, little Pearl . . . did you really think someone could be as horrible as you all on their own? You were my first success, in the beginning at least. When the Chancellor and I realized that the EcoPan technology could be taken further, we saw the possibilities immediately. Humans are sheep at heart. They follow . . . but they bleat, too. There has been far too much bleating lately. Outer circles complaining about their lot in life. Privileged inner circle brats chaffing at confinement within Eden. It was a volcano bubbling below the surface, on the verge of cataclysm. Until I stepped in."

She tells us how she found a way to use the EcoPan's neural connection through the lenses to gain a deeper access to the brain. They learned how to change a person's entire personality by layering a new one on top of the old. It wasn't even that hard, she said. People believe whatever is easiest to believe, and who would ever believe that they weren't themselves? It was simply a matter of implanting a few key false memories. The human brain was remarkable at being able to fill in the gaps.

I think of the few sharp memories I have of Yarrow's childhood—the birthday, the Rain Festival. She's right. I took those few things that seemed real and built a whole plausible life out of them. I did most of her work for her.

"People *want* to conform," she says. "They *want* to obey. They just don't like to admit it. My technology just makes it a little bit easier. It's not perfect, we'll still lose a few subjects, I'm sure. But now, thanks to you two, we're ready to proceed with the next stage of testing. Before long, all of Eden will be peaceful and obedient. And happy. Oh, don't think for a moment I don't want people to be happy. But happiness and freedom don't mix, I've found. Too much thinking leads to discontent. Now wherever we see discontent, we can simply take it away. Are you a person who resents being trapped inside our paradise, eating synthetic strawberries and sipping algae smoothies? Well then, we'll just change you into someone who doesn't have that resentment." She snaps her fingers. "Simple as that."

"You can't do that to people!" I rage at her. "You can't take away who they are!"

"Oh, but I can. We will be a city of peace and tranquility and utter contentment as we wait for the world to heal. We won't be the unruly animals who got us into this mess in the first place. And now that I have dozens of new test subjects, it is only a matter of time before I open this up to the rest of Eden."

"Test subjects?"

"All those other lovely second children you delivered to me! What a treat, what a boon! And like you, not a one of them ever had the implants. I think we will learn some very interesting things from this batch of test subjects. Especially the children. Their minds are so . . . malleable."

"No! Leave them alone! You can't!"

She ignores me, and turns to Pearl while I helplessly struggle and curse. "You were always my favorite though, Pearl. Do you even remember what you were like when you first came to me? It was four years ago. You were such a shy, quiet, kind thing."

I almost laugh when I hear this. Pearl? Quiet and . . . kind? But then I fully realize what she's saying. The Chief had been manipulating Pearl's brain, taking away the person she really was, turning her into the Pearl that all the students (and half of the teachers) at Oaks envied and feared.

That girl Yarrow followed and worshiped, that girl Rowan hated? That wasn't the real Pearl.

"She's in there, somewhere, though, isn't she?" the Chief asks. "That's why you helped Rowan, in the end. And here I thought our control of your mind was so perfect! We expected glitches with Rowan, the second child. But you were supposed to be a good, obedient girl. You're the gold standard of Eden citizens. The model for the others. But you went off script, Pearl. And I had written your script so very carefully."

She gives a sad little shrug, like a mother chastising a wayward child. "When the subject becomes aware of the experiment, the experiment is over. You're no longer of use to us, Pearl."

The Chief turns to me again. "The subtle brain manipulation we used on you and Pearl is delicate. It requires the finesse of our best surgeons and scientists, and the help of the

EcoPan. But there is a much cruder form of brainwashing we used at first. Instead of creating a work of art like you, layering paint onto a person's life to make a masterpiece, we can just wipe them clean. It's a simple, brutal procedure. It leaves the basic functions. They remember how to walk, and talk, and feed themselves. But the personality is gone." She grins at me. "Forever."

She goes back to Pearl and calls in the surgeons. "Luckily you still present some mystery to us, Rowan," she calls across the room. "You have information we will find useful, like the identity of whatever surgeon undid all my lovely work. And you present unique challenges. Your mind has been meddled with so many times, so intensively, yet you can still function apparently normally with both personalities intact. That will take some studying. Oh yes, Rowan, there's lots of fun to be had with you before you join your friend!"

She strokes Pearl's cheek. "Goodbye, Pearl."

Pearl and I both scream as the surgeon goes to work. After a moment though, Pearl's screams stop. It's a quick procedure. For a moment I can see Pearl's wild eyes, begging me to help. Then . . . she's gone. She's still the same beautiful, battered girl, physically. But I see the moment the light of her personality fades from her eyes. The part that makes her *her*.

She smiles at me and blinks heavily. "Where am I?" she asks with the fearless innocence of a person with no past, and no future.

25

THERE'S NOTHING I can do for Pearl.
There's nothing I can do for myself.

I remember once hearing the phrase "ignorance is bliss."
I didn't really understand that before now, didn't believe
it. But now I think of all the other times I must have been
strapped down to a table, when I had no idea that anything
bad was happening to me. Those times in the sensory deprivation room when subtle messages were being implanted in my
brain. The days when I ran to the woman I thought was my
mother, for comfort. I was a prisoner who didn't know she
was in prison. I was an unaware experiment. I was happy.

No, I wasn't. I wasn't anything, because I wasn't me.

Fear is the price I have to pay for knowledge. Death is the
risk I take for being truly alive.

Oh, but I know now there are things so much worse than
death.

I try to catch Pearl's eye as I'm wheeled out on the table,
but all I can see is a placid blank-slate stare. Then I'm being
pushed down a long corridor. One side has shining metal
doors. The doors on the other side are all glass. They're cells.
I crane my head as far to the side as I can and try to see in as
we speed by.

There are people I don't recognize. Then . . . an old man I met once or twice in the Underground. He's shuffling in his tiny, bare cell, his back a little hunched. What will they do to him?

There are more now. I get blurry images of people I know from the Underground. A long row of second children, captured and helpless, laid bare for any of the Center's experiments.

And then, most horrible of all, I catch a glimpse of Rainbow. Alone in a cold cell, she's standing defiantly in the center of the room, right by the door, her hands clenched in little fists. Her face is slick with tears, but she has a fearsome scowl on her face as she shouts, defying the world.

"Rainbow!" I shriek, but the glass is soundproof, and neither of us can hear the other.

No, no, no, not Rainbow. Not the children! What kind of sick person would do experiments on little children?

We pass more second children: little ones, old people, families lined up, separated in their own cells. I try to count. Dozens. A hundred at least down this seemingly endless corridor. All new test subjects for the Chief's twisted experiments in mind control.

But I don't see Lachlan. Or Ash. Could they have possibly escaped?

I make myself think the worst, to protect myself from the cruelty of hope. If they're not here, they're probably dead.

If they're not here, they're probably the lucky ones.

Then the gurney slows, and I catch a malicious smile on the Chief's face. "I think she might be a friend of yours."

There, sitting on a chair in the middle of an otherwise empty cell, is a girl with long lilac hair.

"Lark!" I yell, jerking at my bonds so violently that the rolling table pitches and almost tips over. The orderlies pushing me grab at me like I actually have a chance of escaping.

No, I tell myself. It's a trick. They're already in my mind and making me see things that aren't there.

"You can't fool me," I say, struggling to keep my voice steady. Struggling to keep hope at bay. "I saw her die. This isn't real."

The Chief looks at me with sick amusement. "What did you *really* see?" she asks. "You saw her swallowed by nanosand, that's all." She laughs, and the sound echoes through the long hallway.

"Nanosand eats people," I insist bleakly. "There's nothing left of her now."

"Or, perhaps, that's what we tell people. Carnivorous sentient sand that consumes even the bones, leaving nothing even for the grieving family? That's a pretty frightening story, isn't it? Perfect for keeping curious citizens from exploring the desert."

She leans closer and whispers in my ear. "Oh Rowan, haven't you realized by now that Eden only survives because we control what people think, and even what they see? The EcoPan began it, using the lenses to make people not see the obvious. It is amazing how easy it is to make people not notice something. Even something as huge as a looming forest of bean trees, no? But most manipulation is much more simple. The power of a story, Rowan. Spread a rumor, and before you know it, it becomes truth."

"You mean the nanosand doesn't kill?"

"The desert will kill quick enough," she says. "The nanosand is actually a rescue system. Thinking colonies of nanobots that rescue anyone foolish enough to go into the desert. But . . . you can't just spit out survivors and leave them to tell their tales. They get sucked into an underground holding cell, with food and water and nice cool air, and then they wait until we pick them up. Oh, we don't get very many, but I must say the ones we collect make very interesting test subjects. We know they are bold people with strong wills." She chuckles again. "The very subjects that give us the greatest challenge. Like you. And, I believe, like your friend Lark."

"Don't you touch her!" I shriek. "Lark! Lark! Look at me!" Her face is strangely blank. Has she been sedated . . . or erased?

"Oh, the glass is one-way, and soundproof. She can neither see nor hear you. And what good would it do her? Do you want to torture her more by making her think about all the things we're doing to the girl she loves? Oh yes, she told us that and a great deal more besides. Very cooperative. Not that we gave her much choice."

"Leave her alone! Don't you dare—"

She grabs my chin in a vise-like grip and makes me look at her. "You're not in any position to threaten me, my girl. Oh, your Lark is going to be a very fascinating subject. Her epilepsy makes her brain unique. She's the only person we've encountered so far who had lens implants at an early age but can still resist their programming. Do you know, every time she has an epileptic episode, her brain resets the EcoPan programming? She's resisted us so well . . . so far. But we have all the time in the world, and I promise we will conquer that pretty little brain of hers yet!"

The Chief is amused by my anger. I wish I could control it. I wish I didn't give her the satisfaction of seeing me beg and squirm.

"Please don't hurt her," I beseech her. Oh, great Earth, Lark is alive! It gives me a surge of hope that even in the blackest hour there can be a light, however small. But now I don't just have hope, I have one more thing the Center can crush, one more thing they can threaten to take away from me. I have to keep her safe, no matter what the cost. "I'll do anything. I'll let you do anything to my brain that you want."

"You silly, deluded child. Do you still think you have a choice? Do you really think you can resist me for long? You have a resilient brain, it is true. But our methods are getting better all the time. You'll be Yarrow again before long, with no memory of Rowan. Or you'll be someone else. Do you know what I think I'll do with your friend Pearl? Haughty Pearl? I think I'll make her an outer circle gutter rat. Poor, dirty, desperate. A girl who's spent her life in rags, who lives in fear of everyone stronger than her. A victim. Yes, that would suit her.

"And Lark" she goes on viciously. "What shall I make of her? So many possibilities. How nice it will be to crush that vibrant, independent mind. Turn that rebel into a good little follower. Maybe she can work for me! Maybe you both can; mindless little bots who do exactly what they're told. Maybe if you're good, I'll even flip the switch that lets her love you again. That's all love is, you know. Just a switch in the brain. Just a few chemicals."

"No, I'll never believe it," I insist. "We're more than the electrical connections in our brains! You can't do this to people!"

She shrugs. "I have so far. Who's going to stop me?"

"I will!" I say, childishly, knowing how deluded that sounds. "I'll find a way to make you pay for everything you've done. You're evil!"

She laughs softly, and I've never heard a more frightening sound. "Evil?" she asks gently, as if speaking to a small child. "You and the other second children are the ones draining the life out of Eden. You take our resources and contribute nothing. Little parasites scurrying under the city." She leans close to me and whispers, "You believe you can think for your-selves and pick the rules that suit you? Civilization doesn't work that way. Eden is *my* charge. Keeping humans alive is *my* responsibility. Without me, Eden would fall to selfish rebels like you and your friends who think that society can exist without sacrifice. The individual doesn't matter. When I cleaned up the outer circle slums and erased the memories of poverty and crime from thousands of brains, did any of them complain? No, I took away the desperation and greed and selfishness and cruelty and stupidity that turned those circles into slums in the first place, and made those people safe, clean, productive members of society. I made this place a paradise!"

She steps back, and says as if she believes it, "I'm a kind woman." A smile plays around her lips for a moment before they harden into a tight, deadly line. "But I will kill or torture or test every second child I have if it helps me keep Eden safe and stable!"

She's just like Aaron Al-Baz. Her motives are noble, she believes she's doing the right thing. She doesn't realize that she's destroying humanity to save humans. Compassion, kindness are the things that make us human. Sacrifice yourself for humanity, I want to tell her. Don't sacrifice other people. But it wouldn't do any good.

They start pushing me down the endless corridor again.

"There's no need for all this," I say at last. "I know your secret." She stops dead, and the orderlies skitter to a halt a second later. I've touched a nerve. "I know all about the living world outside Eden."

One of the orderlies laughs, then stifles the sound. He's not supposed to have an opinion. The Chief looks relieved. "A living world? You mean that fairy tale you've been telling people about life outside of Eden? A forest, with flowers and birds and deer? Oh yes, Lark told me that, too."

"I saw it! When I escaped from the Center and the earthquake disrupted the EcoPan's illusions and . . ."

She shakes her head dismissively. "A brain glitch. A dream."

"Did you give it to me?" I demand.

"No, but . . ." A fleeting look of confusion crosses her face, then it smooths into serene certainty again. "Are you really that deluded? That's just one more reason why people like you have to be controlled. If you spread that kind of nonsense throughout Eden, some people would be bound to believe it, and there would be civil unrest."

I can tell from her reaction that she really doesn't know there's a living world outside of Eden. I'd thought it was a Center conspiracy to keep the secret from the citizens of Eden for some reason. If that's not the case, then what an amazing difference it would make to prove it to them! The Chief would change. Everyone would change! This need she thinks she has to control the residents of Eden would vanish. There are no limited supplies. There's the whole world! People could have two children without penalty. Three children! As many as they wanted! The world would be ours.

And then, thinking that, I shudder.

The world was ours once. Look what we did with it.

Someone is keeping the secret of the living world from us. If not her, then who?

They take me to another surgical room. "You know the drill. Of course, you were programmed to have no memory of it afterward. Because of course our techniques are *most* unpleasant. But I presume when you got your memory back, that reappeared as well?" I nod. "Oh, good!" she says with spiteful glee. "The anticipation of torment is often even worse than actually going through it. After the trouble you've given me, Rowan, I'm glad you'll be getting the full experience.

You know, I think I'll do the first part myself." She orders the others out of the room. "I might decide to do something unconventional. Always better if there are no witnesses."

She's the one who authorizes these terrible things to be done. What vindictive horror must she be planning for me if she doesn't want her underlings to see?

She picks up a wire, flexible along its length but rigid at the end, and with tortuous slowness brings it closer and closer to my eye.

26

"THERE YOU ARE," she snaps, jerking her hand away from my eye as someone comes through the door. "How unprofessional to be late for surgery."

"I've never missed one of this subject's surgeries," says a male voice. "I wouldn't miss this one for the world."

I gasp. It's my father.

For just a second, I'm home again. I forget all the terrible things he's done, and only remember the sixteen years when he was one of the three people I knew. Even before I knew the truth about him, we had an uncomfortable relationship. And yet, he symbolizes Mom, and Ash, and home. For an instant I feel secure, safe.

Then I remember how he tried to kill me in the womb. How he caused Ash's lung problems in the same botched prenatal assassination. How he turned in his own son just to protect himself. How he helped this evil woman operate on his own daughter.

"Get prepped quickly," my fake mother tells my real father. "She's getting agitated, and I'd rather not have to sedate her. She needs to appreciate this experience fully—without anesthesia."

My father's eyes flick over me. Does he even care that his

daughter is strapped down, about to be tortured, changed, erased?

"How could you do it to me?" I demand. He seems to wither, then collect himself. "You actually helped this horrible woman play with my brain, erase who I was? You're a travesty of a father! I swear if I have one neuron of my memory left when this is over, I will hunt both of you down and kill you!" I scream at them.

The Chief sets down the surgical wire and turns to me. "When this is over, believe me, there won't be a single neuron in your brain that isn't under my direct control."

My father is coming up behind her. He has one of the heavy surgical trays in his hands. To my astonishment, he swings it back, and smashes it across the back of her head. Then with supreme satisfaction I witness that horrid woman crash to the ground.

Satisfaction . . . and bafflement.

Wait, did he get her out of the way so he can kill me? Finish the job he started when I was still in the womb? I tense, ready for anything . . .

Except what happens. He flicks the switch that makes my shackles retract. I'm free.

"I've sent the guards away, and cut the surveillance," he says as he kneels at the Chief's side and injects something into her neck. Her staring glassy eyes flutter and close. "I have a set of surgical scrubs and mask ready for you to disguise yourself. With a little luck you should be able to get out of here and—"

"Why are you doing this?" I ask, rubbing my raw wrists as I sit up. He starts to say something, but I know it is just going to be pathetic so I don't even let him begin. "You think by saving me you can make up for the hell you put Ash and me through? You make me sick. You betrayed your children.

It's your fault that Ash was captured, and now he's probably dead. And it's . . ." My voice catches in a sob. "It's your fault Mom died. You could have protected your family. Instead, you sacrificed us all so you could get ahead."

"It's not like that, Rowan. I never thought . . ."

"I don't want to hear it," I snap at him. "You're letting me go now? This means nothing! I'll probably be captured within ten minutes. I won't let you clear your conscience this easily. You helped the Chief take away everything I am!"

"You have to understand, I had to do the surgery on you. I'm one of the few people qualified, and your chances of survival were much better if I was assisting. And I thought . . . at least some life is better than no life. You could be a first child, a citizen at last. I thought if you didn't remember who you used to be, you'd be happy. I could erase everything that happened to Ash and your mom. Erase every unhappy moment our family has ever had." He swallows hard. "I thought you were the lucky one. You got to forget. I have to remember what I did every day of my life. You have to get dressed, and hurry," he continues. "I cleared a window for you, got all the guards called to different sectors, but you don't have long."

I just sit on the surgical bench and fold my arms across my chest. "I'm not going."

"What do you mean? Why not? That's crazy!"

"This isn't just about me," I tell him. "You, and people like you, people you work with and for, are responsible for ruining the lives of dozens of second children. Not just me. They've captured *kids*. Little children, who are going to be strapped down like I just was and tormented."

"It's not like that," my father insists. "They're just going to take away their memories of being second children. Then they'll integrate them back into society. The kids will be given to families. Couples who can't have children of their own. No one is going to be tortured, I promise."

"Well, isn't that a pretty little lie." I sneer at him. "Do you honestly believe that? You know what they did to me."

"They gave you a new life," he says earnestly. "A better life than I could. They gave you a chance."

"They took away everything I am!" I scream at him. "They took away *me*!" Does he really not realize the enormity of what they did? "And I'm not going to run away and let them do that to other people. You want to set me free? You want to redeem yourself? Then find a way to help me free Lark and all of the second children!"

"But that's not possible," he says, scrunching up his eyes in consternation. Did he really think it would be so easy to win absolution? To feel like a good person again? "There are more than a hundred second children in the cells, and this is a highly secure facility. Every aspect of it is controlled by the EcoPan." He gives a nervous chuckle. "The only hope you'd have to free everyone is to bring down the EcoPan!"

He says it like it is the most ridiculous notion in the world, but it makes me think. I remember when the Earth heaved, toppling the bean trees and hewing a huge crack in the ground that stretched from the perimeter of Eden toward the center. When the ground shook, suddenly every illusion was shattered. The ovens that artificially heated the man-made desert surrounding Eden failed, and the air went from 150 degrees to a balmy fall day. It had to have been because the EcoPan, the vast computer system that controls all of Eden, went down for a while.

Everything is hooked into the EcoPan: all of the energy and food systems, the water and air filters. The lenses . . .

The Center, the security systems. The earthquake shut that all down for a while. Not for long. And maybe not completely. I remember how the guards who captured me after I found the living forest didn't seem to see it. Maybe the lenses keep working, or maybe the subtle programming, the manipulation of their brains that keeps people in Eden from seeing the obvious, keeps them from remembering wars and poverty, persists even when the EcoPan is down.

But the structures and systems. The mechanics and real-time programs all failed. Surely the Center security systems would be included.

"If I could shut down the EcoPan for a while, could you get the second children out?"

He stammers and protests. "That's crazy," he says.

"But if I could," I insist. "Could you help them?"

"Alone? I could get some of them out. Maybe. Rowan, what are you thinking about?"

"The earthquake . . . ," I begin.

"Earthquake?" He scrunches his eyebrows in confusion. Of course, he's controlled like the rest. He can't remember the earthquake.

Suddenly, a portion of my hate for him dissolves. I hated Pearl so much toward the end, until I realized that she, too, was a victim of this ghastly city's manipulation. Every citizen of this place, except for the second children, has been controlled to at least some degree. Influenced, swayed . . . Is *anyone* their true self?

And if they're not, how can I truly hate anyone for the choices they made? My father betrayed his family, did horrible things. But were the choices truly his? Was he made to believe certain things, trust that certain "facts" were true? Surely those beliefs, forced on him, influenced his actions. Could he have resisted? I did . . . but not always, and I had help. I had Lark and Lachlan, devoted to returning me to my true self. My father didn't have anyone to tell him that Eden is a prison and our lives are mostly lies.

And so, to my utter surprise, I forgive him.

I feel a sudden lightness in my chest. A weight off my back. I look down at the Chief, still unconscious on the floor. Maybe she's a victim, too.

Who is the villain, then?

Aaron Al-Baz? Yes, he was, but not anymore. He did unforgivable things, but he created another entity to carry on his work.

To take it a step further.

The EcoPanopticon.

We're all victims of the EcoPan.

"Dad," I say gently, and I see tears well in his flat brown eyes when he hears me use that word. "I think I can bring down EcoPan for a little while. If I do, will you do whatever you can to free the second children?"

I can tell he wants to. He wants my forgiveness. He wants to make up for the bad things he's done. But he's not sure.

"You tried to kill me, Dad," I whisper. "You aimed a focused sound beam at me in the womb to save yourself the trouble of having twins, an illegal second child."

He's crying now. I might forgive him, but I still need him.

"Ash might still be alive. He's really a second child, you know. I was born first. Yes, I know everything. Mom told me. You have to help the second children. They're the only ones who can save Ash, if he's alive. And you owe it to us, Dad. You owe it to all of the second children, to make up for the child you tried to destroy."

"I'll do it," he sobs. "I know people here. They owe me favors. And . . . and outer circle people. I swear, I'll do whatever I can!" He falls to his knees by the surgical table. "Just please forgive me, Rowan. Please. Your mother forgave me."

I stiffen and jerk my hand away. "No, she didn't. She hated you for what you did. She just stayed with you for our sake. For me, and for Ash." His face drains to chalk white. I know he loved Mom so much. "You have to make up for that now, so her spirit can forgive you." She'd never forgive him, I think, but I have to say whatever it takes to convince him.

"I'll get them all out safely, I promise!" he says. "You take down the EcoPan, and I swear I'll do it."

I nod. "Then get me out of here, and get ready to act. I don't know how long it will take. But if it can be done, the EcoPan is going down tonight."

I bend over the Chief's unconscious body and take my necklace from her pocket. When I slip it back over my head, I feel almost whole again.

27

MY FATHER'S WORD is good . . . so far. I make it out in my surgical scrubs disguise and a fake ID he gave me, looking like any one of the dozens of staff running around the place on busy errands. Busy taking away people's lives to create a utopia that's also a prison. Before I escape, I walk down that long corridor, surreptitiously checking each cell. I can't linger too long. It would look suspicious. But I confirm that neither Lachlan nor Ash is there. Neither is Flint. I see Iris. And Adder, her snake tattoos the most vibrant thing about her as she sits dead-eyed in a corner.

And there is Lark. I allow myself to slow as I pass her cell. She has a vague smile on her face, but her eyes are just as empty as the others'. If my father does manage to rescue them when I bring down the EcoPan, will they even go? Or will they just mill in the hall like automatons, waiting for direction, for someone to send them a neural signal that tells them what to do, who to be?

I let my fingers trace along the window into Lark's cell as I pass. A caress she cannot feel. "I'll get you out of here," I whisper. "I promise." She gives me no sign.

I meet no resistance as I leave the Center. My father gave me a very specific path to follow. At every checkpoint, the guards seem to be conveniently elsewhere. Then I'm in the city at dusk, in the vividly gorgeous inner circles just as the nightlife is about to get under way. In the apartments and houses people are getting ready in their evening finery. Delicious smells are emanating from the best restaurants as they prepare to welcome patrons. Already, bass beats are coming from the clubs.

Life is going on just as it always does here in Eden. I want to scream at them that they are all deluded fools. I see a happy couple walking arm in arm, leaning into each other to share some giggly joke. *Don't you know your brain is not your own? You're being told what to think! How do you know your love is real, and not a command of the EcoPan, an implant from Chief Ellena?*

I pass the Rain Forest Club, where I first met Lark. The sound of tropical birds flits from the door, and I glimpse synthetic trees in gaudy colors never found in nature, electric vines that pulse with unnatural hues. *Why are you settling for this artificial world when there's a real one just a few miles away? Why are you so content with your prison?*

But of course I say nothing. I'm on a mission. Screaming at people does no good. Then I'd just be a madwoman. They'll need proof. I saw the real forest, and I still scarcely believe it. There's still some kind of programming in my brain that is making me fight reality, to believe what is easiest to believe. But I am stronger than my programming. Maybe other people can be, too.

If they have role models. If I can rescue the second children before they, too, get lens implants or are irreparably damaged.

I pass through the circles, heading outward. It's too far to walk, so eventually I hop on an autoloop, and get out one station past my destination to throw off anyone who might be following. No one seems to be. I don't even encounter any securitybots. Even the little cleanbots seem to be keeping out of my way. Once I round a corner and one of the mobile little domes skitters almost under my feet. If machines could do a double take! This one looks mechanically surprised, backs up hurriedly, and then zooms away. Did my father manage that, too? How?

I'm worried there will be guards at the slide entrance, but it is completely clear. I remember being told they were blasting through the cave walls in the confusing labyrinth. I'm willing to bet Pearl's tracker showed them where she was, but not how to get there. Without a clue how to find the well-hidden entrance, they probably went through the sewer system, getting as close to her beacon as they could through the infrastructure, and then clumsily blasting their way ever closer.

I slide down, into the labyrinth. I've been through here a few times, and I think I know the way, but it is so confusing! I think, like Pearl, I might be doomed to wander down here forever until I come upon one of the Greenshirts' blast holes. They took a direct route. So I just follow their trail of de-struction . . . and the scent of smoke . . . and eventually come out at the upper portion of the crystal cavern.

Oh, great Earth! How could they have done it? How could the Greenshirts have torched that grand and beautiful queen of trees?

For the majestic camphor tree is hardly more than a charred stump.

All of the branches have been burned through. A few of the heavier ones cracked and fell as they burned, and lie shat-tered all around the cavern floor. Most were just incinerated. The trunk is black, and jagged at the top where the crown shattered in the scorching heat.

Slowly, I walk down each level of stairs. Many of them have been damaged in the fighting, and from subsequent small explosions. Three levels from the bottom, the stairs have collapsed, and I have to let myself down level by level, holding on to the edge and dropping down to the next landing.

I'm so disappointed in humanity. Where else can the blame be laid? Even if the EcoPan is at the heart of all this, who created the EcoPan? A human.

Despondent, almost hopeless, I wonder if we deserve to survive. Even in this small pocket that remains. Maybe this is Aaron Al-Baz's final punishment for mankind's stupidity. Keeping us locked in a prison, while machines and doctors try to turn us into something worthwhile. Never realizing that even goodness is wrong when it is forced on someone.

I try not to look at the tree. It is too horrible.

I try not to think that I'll be joining it soon.

I go to the place that Rainbow showed me. The boom room.

I'm lucky. The entrance is almost covered by rubble, shattered chunks of the cave wall, stalactites, and equipment. A jagged rock the size of a boulder leans tipsily against the entrance, making the passage so narrow I can barely squeeze through. The rock shudders when I brush it, and I hold my breath. If I'm not careful, I'll be trapped inside, or worse, crushed before I can activate the self-destruct sequence.

I don't understand the mechanics of the explosive system. Luckily, I don't have to. What is mysterious about a big red button?

Well, the timing for one thing. When I press it, is the explosion instant? No, there must be a time delay. The second children must have planned to use this as a last resort, if they were discovered and had to cover all trace of their existence. It would have been a last-ditch move of absolute desperation.

They wouldn't have destroyed their home, their tree, except as a final resort.

But now the tree is gone. The second children are gone. If my guess is right, triggering this massive underground explosion under the very heart of Eden will simulate an earthquake closely enough that it will shut down the EcoPan for a while. The second children will have a chance to escape. Maybe, if it stays down long enough, a few people will have a chance to see through the illusions of their prison walls. Maybe it will be a start. Maybe it will be enough.

With the tree already dead, there's really nothing to lose.

Except, of course, my life.

I don't let myself even think about it. It's not a noble sacrifice—it's a necessity. I have to save them. I slam my fist on the red button, squeezing my eyes shut just in case the explosion is instantaneous. What funny animals we are! I'll be obliterated in an instant, turned into particles, and I still think closing my eyes against the inevitable will somehow preserve me.

But there is no obliteration. Instead, a countdown appears on the display below the button. Fifteen minutes.

Plenty of time for a fast volunteer to dash back up the stairs, through the labyrinth, out the alternate exit to the surface. He'd still be close enough to be shaken by the massive blast. Knocked down, maybe concussed. The sound of the blast might deafen him. Buildings would topple, maybe on top of him. The ground might split, swallowing him up. But he'd have a chance to get to safety. He'd have hope.

But as I look at the crumbled stairs I realize there's no way I can get back up to the top in time. Oh, I can climb the walls, probably. I can see a few handholds and footholds already. But not enough. The walls are mostly smooth. I'd have to make a few forays before I found a workable route. Even then, I might need equipment. It might not even be possible. It certainly couldn't be done in fifteen minutes.

I run to the place Rainbow was starting to show me when we were captured—the exit at ground level. But there is nothing but rubble there. Another blast crumbled the cavern wall, and there's no getting around or through the hunks of rock that block that passageway. Even if I could, that route is sure to be as labyrinthine as the overhead one, twisting through an impossibly serpentine course. I'd never find my way out before the blast. I'd be obliterated.

I go back to the boom room. There's a cancellation switch, of course. There would have to be, in case of mistakes. The timer ticks down. A bit more than nine minutes remain.

I can terminate the self-destruct sequence, and look for a route out. But it might take me a day to find one through the confusing passages. Or I might get lost and never find my way back to reactivate the self-destruct. I might take a few hours to figure out a way to climb the almost sheer walls of the cavern until I reach the remaining stairs. But what will happen in those few hours? Someone could discover that the Chief is missing, find her unconscious body. My father's plan could be compromised.

They might start cutting into the innocent, beautiful brains of Rainbow and Lark and the others . . .

Every moment I wait is another moment something terrible, irreversible, can happen.

My hand hovers over the self-destruct cancellation switch. Then I let it fall to my side. Carefully, I slither out through the crack and once on the other side I lean my weight against the big piece of rock. It tilts, then crashes against the wall, almost covering the doorway entirely. Even a child couldn't fit through the space that remains. The explosion can no longer be stopped.

I walk back to the charred remains of the tree, and make a nook for myself among the blackened roots. Soot covers everything. I touch the trunk with my palm, and my hand comes away covered in the gritty black powder. I clap my hands together, and the soot explodes in a little poof.

I smile, and then chuckle at the fact that I'm smiling. Yes, we humans are strange creatures.

I'm about to die, and I feel happier than I have in a very long time.

No, "happy" isn't the right word, of course. I don't want to die. Part of me is frightened, of the pain, about what happens after death. Part of me is sad to be leaving this world, and with it any possibility of friendship or love or any of the good things that seem to remain despite the most grueling hardships.

But I feel at peace.

I'm making this choice. I'm controlling my life. This decision is all mine, not the result of an outside jolt to my brain or an implanted thought. This is me, Rowan, choosing to die so that my friends might have a chance to live a normal life. It might not work, but it's the best I can do. I'm giving all I have to give.

I lay my hands on the burned roots, and I feel something unexpectedly soft and pliant. I look down, and to my amazement there, sprouting from the charred remains of the tree, is a tiny shoot. Just a little arrow of tender green, the incipient leaves still folded over themselves.

Life! Life from death!

I remember Lachlan told me that this camphor tree was a graft taken from a tree that was destroyed in an atomic blast. Everything else was killed, and the tree reduced to a burned, irradiated stump. But it retained a trace of life deep inside.

Not long after the blast, it sprouted new growth. In time, the tree recovered, sending beautiful, strong new life around the dead tree. The roots survived.

We humans have deep roots, I think. Some of us will resist the mind control. Someone will escape the prison. It won't be me, but that seems to matter less and less as the minutes tick by.

I close my eyes and think of the forest. But instead of just the flowers and birds, I picture my friends there, too. I can see Lark running through the meadow, flowers in her streaming lilac hair as she dances and laughs, her bare feet crushing the sweetest smell from the herbs that surround her. I see Ash sitting in the shade of a forest tree, a tree with companions all around it, unlike the lonely camphor. I see Lachlan gathering fruit and nuts, real food, for a feast.

Maybe that dreamworld is possible. Maybe my actions here today can make it so.

I have to live with that hope.

I have to die with that hope.

At first, I think it is part of my near-death imaginings, that in my final moments my brain is giving me daydreams real enough to comfort me before I perish. Because there is Ash, walking toward me. He's covered in soot, and has a burn mark on his forearm, singed spots on his cheeks, but he's giving me a look of incredulous joy. Only when he speaks my name, and I hear the quaver in his voice, do I fully realize he's real, and not a vision.

"I thought you were dead," he says. "I saw you captured. How did you . . ."

But the look of panic on my face stalls him. I jump up and take him by the shoulders. I want to hug him for being alive, and shake him for being here, now, of all times. How much longer do we have? Oh great Earth! How can this be happening? I was at peace with sacrificing myself. But not Ash! Never Ash! I'm supposed to protect him.

While he stammers out questions, I drag him across the cavern. Maybe if he gets on the far side, in one of the rooms. Maybe there's a chance.

He digs in his heels, slowing me down as I try to pull him. "Rowan, what's wrong?"

"Self-destruct," I gasp. "Explosion, any second!" There's no time for more words. Oh, Ash, why? I didn't mind dying if a part of me lived on in you.

He still won't come with me, and I pull him step by agonizingly slow step farther away from the explosives. "Hurry! There's no time! I set the self-destruct to make an earthquake that I hope will sabotage the EcoPan and all of Eden's systems, so the others can escape from the Center. You weren't supposed to be here!"

Maybe because he's been through so much, seen everyone he loved stunned and dragged away, seen the last tree on Earth burned, he seems numbly accepting. He plants his feet, rooted to the earth. "It's okay, Rowan," he says, taking me in his arms. "If the others are safe, I don't mind what happens to me. We're together, Rowan. Like we've been since before we were born." He presses his cheek against mine. "Nothing else matters as long as we're together."

I want to fight, to force him into safety. But then everything seems to happen at once—the flash of a thousand silver beings, and the flash of the explosion, all at the same time. There's no sound, not at first, but I'm hit by heat and a stiff wind, and then almost at the same instant we're covered by a swarm of some kind of bots I've never seen before. In a fraction of a second their parts separate, then tangle together to form first a wall, then a ball around us. It smooths on the inside into a perfect silver sphere. I see our faces, so alike, on the reflective surface.

I see you, Rowan, a voice says. *I've always seen you. Well done.*

Then, finally, the sound follows the flash and I hear the explosion.

Then nothing . . .

28

AT FIRST THE voice is in my head. Then it is everywhere. Then I am everywhere.

I know that sounds crazy. Maybe I blew up. Is this what death feels like? My molecules scattered, becoming one with the universe.

Rowan, the voice says, low and soothing. *Rowan*. Again and again, like a chant.

Like the voice is trying to remind me who I am.

I feel free and disjointed, perplexed but not afraid. Then that vast universal feeling seems to coalesce and I'm standing in a room. No, a sphere, like the one that I now recall surrounded me at the moment of the blast. Only this one is huge, a silver globe as big as the crystal cavern.

I am alone, and not alone. I can feel a presence all around me, but all I can see is the dull silver sheen of the inside of the sphere, each surface holding a faint reflection of myself.

"Where am I?" I ask. And in my head, I wonder, where is Ash?

With me, the voice replies. *As you always were. As everyone always is. But you in particular, Rowan.*

The voice doesn't seem to be coming from any speakers,

or even from within the room. It is in my head, but as clear as if I'm actually hearing it. Am I imagining it?

No, the voice assures me. *I am real, and this place is real.*

I gasp and back up, but there is nowhere to retreat, nowhere to hide. It can hear my thoughts?

Of course I can, it says.

I look around suspiciously. "What are you?" I ask aloud.

Can't you guess?

Of course. What has a connection to almost every human inside of Eden? What is already inside of people's minds?

"You're the EcoPanopticon," I say.

Very good! I hear amusement in its voice.

"Then I want some answers!" I demand.

I will tell you everything, Rowan. You've earned the truth. Truth is a precious gift . . . and a heavy burden. It is not for everyone.

I sit cross-legged in the center of the sphere as the EcoPan tells me a story:

When Aaron Al-Baz, genius inventor, genocidal madman, destroyed humanity with the intention of ultimately saving both it and the planet, he created a program to help him achieve his goals. He made an artificial intelligence of vast capacity with the ability to co-opt any other computer system. Anything connected to a network, anything with a chip in it could be accessed by the EcoPan. It took over factories and created a limitless army of bots to do its bidding. With humanity crumbling under a plague Aaron Al-Baz created, the EcoPan made a paradise for the remaining few. A paradise . . . and a testing ground.

Its programming was intensely complex, but its protocol was simple—protect the environment, and save the human species.

Even the great Aaron Al-Baz didn't know exactly how to

*accomplish this. So he left it to this sentient synthetic system
to decide.*

I was learning, the EcoPan tells me. *Every day, every
generation, I learned more about humans.*

"You controlled them!" I say bitterly. "You twisted them
into creatures you could control!"

The EcoPan laughs. *Control a human? Your species is
virtually ungovernable. Whimsical, emotional, unpredict-
able. There is no amount of neurological intervention that can
completely control a human. No, I have had the lens implants
from the beginning, but they don't control anyone.*

"They do!" I insist. "The citizens don't see the illusions
and the lies that keep them from realizing the world outside
Eden is still alive. They're made to forget entire wars! They've
been convinced Eden has only existed for two hundred years,
when it has been in place for more than a thousand! And now
they are being brainwashed into being docile, unquestioning
citizens, without personalities of their own!"

Yes, the EcoPan admits, a bit sadly I think. *But that is not
my doing.*

The EcoPan tells me that it allows humans to be almost
entirely self-governing. *I have studied your history, your
wars, your kings and queens and presidents and dictators,
and I cannot begin to decide which system is the best way to
preserve humanity. No matter what you choose, there always
seems to be great suffering.*

"You could have made Eden a paradise!" I cry. "Why
are there slums? Why is there crime? Why are there rich and
poor?"

*Those are decisions you humans made. You are given
everything—resources, safety—and still you segregate your-
selves in one way or another. Still the strong dominate the
weak. Still you make laws that keep some people down while*

raising others up to giddy heights. You make systems that reward cruelty and greed.

It has happened so many times, the EcoPan tells me. *Usually money was the divider. Once, in the beginning, the hue of people's skin marked them as members of either the elite or the lower classes. At one time the women of Eden formed a powerful coalition that kept men subjugated.*

Each system collapsed, and when it did, I altered the citizens' memories so they would have a chance to start over without the burden of history. That is the extent of my interference. That, and keeping them from knowing that the planet is healed and healthy.

The rest, it tells me, *is entirely the work of humans. They have used the EcoPan technology to change people's brains. They have co-opted the EcoPan's programming to reprogram people.*

"And you let them?" I ask, aghast.

It is not my place to alter humanity. It is only my place to keep it alive.

"But people die because of these laws and policies. My mother was gunned down in the street because of the second child laws. You could have stopped that!"

That is true. I could have. But I would not interfere with the test.

I freeze. "What do you mean, test?"

All of Eden is a test, Rowan. I choose the people who are worthy to be one with the Earth. I watch every action, I analyze every choice each citizen of Eden makes. Through the lenses, through the bots, through every com and vid and datablock on Eden I watch. And pick those fortunate few I deem worthy.

The EcoPan has been watching me, too. For the first sixteen years it picked up things about me from the home computer system—what I watched, what I said. And it analyzed the brains of the people who knew me—my parents and Ash. It became curious. Only later when I got the implants could it fully connect with me.

It liked what it found.

Your passion, your dedication, your fierce and loving heart made a deep impression on me. You honor the Earth, and you value life, but you are willing to take another human's life for the greater good. You make decisions like I might, Rowan. You have balance.

But it wasn't until the final moment that the EcoPan made its decision.

When you chose to save the other second children, even though you yourself would die, it proved to me that you are the kind of human who will protect the planet. If you are free, you will not be the kind of power-hungry person who crushes the world to stay on top. You understand sacrifice, and patience, and suffering. You have lost everything, and persevered. Now you will gain everything.

I think I understand, but I can't believe it. "What do you mean?" I ask.

You are free, Rowan. You will join the other chosen few out in the world. There is a city of the select—the true elites of Eden. You will live there, among the trees and birds, eating fruit plucked from the trees, in a state of perpetual peace and harmony. You will exist as humans were meant to—as part of the Earth. Not masters, but equals.

My heart is thumping wildly. I can't believe it. After all my struggles and challenges, after all the fear and sorrow and loss, can it be that I'm finally getting what I've yearned for ever since I was trapped behind the high stone walls at my parents' house?

Freedom.

"No," I say blankly. "I won't go. I can't."

Why not?

"There are others who deserve it as much as me. More than me. Bikking hell, everyone deserves it! Even my father. Even Chief Ellena. What gives you the right to make decisions for all of us? You're a machine!" I pound on the nearest wall of the sphere. It makes a hollow clang.

You forget, I can see inside your thoughts, Rowan. I can feel your yearning to be back in the forest.

"No! It doesn't matter what I want! I won't go without the others. The second children at least! Let them have a taste of the safety and freedom they deserve! You can't make me go!"

Do you see, Rowan? Your reaction now is the very reason why you deserve to be free. Even now you would give up your fondest wish to help your friends. Even if you cannot help them, you won't take your heart's desire without them to share it with you. You are a good person. A good human. You are humanity's hope.

"Please!" I beg. "Just send me back. Let me try to break the second children free from the Center."

That's no longer your concern, Rowan. Your new life awaits.

"Please," I say. "Let me bring just one of them with me."

Very well. The air around me seems to shift, and suddenly Ash is beside me. I grab his hand. Can it be possible? Can we really be leaving Eden together?

One of you will go into the world, one of you will stay in Eden.

I swallow hard. Nature, freedom, the wide world have been calling me all my life. I had to live behind walls, and now I have a chance to be truly free at last. If I stay in Eden, I'll be hunted, tortured, killed. The Chief has such a vendetta against me that to hurt me, she'll destroy everyone I love.

And yet, what is freedom without my twin, the other half of me?

"Ash," I say even as my brother opens his mouth to speak. "Ash goes free. I go back to Eden."

I hear a gentle hissing sound, and an odorless gas fills the sphere. My eyelids grow heavy, and I sit down. In my mind I see the forest slipping away from me, and it hurts, so terribly, a deep ache of body and spirit. But there is no other choice. I can't have happiness at anyone's expense. EcoPan is sending me to sleep. I know when I wake up, I'll be in the rubble of the Underground.

My eyes close slowly and heavily. Just before the world goes black I hear the EcoPan's voice. *When you chose your brother, it convinced me to choose you.*

It feels like my eyes open on the next blink.

I'm lying in darkness, alone, in something rough and soft at the same time. Grass? Stars twinkle overhead, brighter than any I've seen before. I hear a rising and falling drone. Crickets! I heard a recording of them in an Egg in school. I sit up and look around. It is darker on the horizon. Trees! I can see the outline of their canopies just visible against the night sky. The wind rustles their branches.

Then I see lights in the distance, moving, flickering. Fireflies? No, they're getting bigger. Five lights, coming closer. Torches held aloft by five figures. They surround me, and I stand up, ready for attack. I can't see beyond the bright dancing torchlight.

Then I hear a voice. "Rowan?" a woman says breathlessly. "Can it be?" Then she shouts to the others, "It's her! At last!"

She hands the torch to someone, and as the figure comes to me with open arms I can finally see her face. The dearest face. . . . My mother. My real mother. Her eyes are welling with tears as she takes me in her arms. Behind her, a forest of real trees rustles in the gentle wind, and I hear an owl's haunting cry.

"My darling girl," she says, and for a moment I feel whole again.

But without my brother, my world will always be broken. As I hug my mother tightly, tears streaming down my face, I make a silent vow. I will do whatever it takes to save Ash, to save *everyone*. I will destroy Eden.

ACKNOWLEDGMENTS

FIRST AND FOREMOST, to my YouTube family, you are more than just my viewers, you are my friends. I don't know where I would be without your constant love and support. I am forever indebted to you, thank you for your dedication throughout the years. I can't wait to continue creating for you all.

To my incredible team of managers, agents, and creatives, I'm so thankful to have your guidance and friendship accompany me through my career.

To Judith, Lisa, Rakesh, and the entire team at Keywords Press and Simon & Schuster, thank you for believing in me and being such amazing people to work with, I'm honored to have this opportunity.

To Laura, thank you for helping bring "Eden" to life, you inspire me.

To the many authors that have animated my imagination along the way, thank you for lending your talent in helping ignite creativity throughout my childhood and giving me the passion to create my own worlds and stories as an adult.

To Whitney, thank you for never letting me feel like my ideas are too big and for always cheering me on.

To all my readers, I hope this adventure brings you as much happiness as I experienced creating it.

And most importantly, to Daniel, you are my partner and my rock. You have always been there for me, especially throughout this long journey of second-guessing myself. Thank you for all that you do, for bringing me to find the right answers within myself, and making me feel confident in my work. I love you always.

ABOUT THE AUTHOR

JOEY GRACEFFA is a leading digital creator, actor, and producer, best known for his scripted and vlog work with YouTube. His memoir, *In Real Life: My Journey to a Pixelated World*, was published in 2015 and became an instant *New York Times* bestseller. Joey ranked third on *Variety's* 2015 #Famechangers list and has been featured in publications such as *People, Forbes, Entertainment Weekly*, and the *Hollywood Reporter*. In 2013, between his daily vlogs and gameplay videos, he produced and starred in his own Kickstarter-funded supernatural series, *Storytellers*, for which he won a Streamy Award. In 2016, he debuted *Escape the Night*, a "sur-reality" competition series for YouTube, which is now in its second season. Joey's other interests include working on his proprietary accessories/home décor line called Crystal Wolf and supporting various nonprofit organizations for literacy, children's health and wellness, and animal welfare. For more information, please visit ChildrenofEdenBook.com.